WITHDRAWN

A Cow Hunter's Lament and Other Stories

A Cow Hunter's Lament and Other Stories

A WESTERN COLLECTION

LARRY D. SWEAZY

THORNDIKE PRESS
A part of Gale, a Cengage Company

Copyright © 2023 by Larry D. Sweazy.
Thorndike Press, a part of Gale, a Cengage Company.

ALL RIGHTS RESERVED
This novel is a work of fiction. Names, characters, places, and incidents are either the product of the author's imagination, or, if real, used fictitiously.
The publisher bears no responsibility for the quality of information provided through author or third-party Web sites and does not have any control over, nor assume any responsibility for, information contained in these sites. Providing these sites should not be construed as an endorsement or approval by the publisher of these organizations or of the positions they may take on various issues.
Thorndike Press® Large Print Hardcover Western.
The text of this Large Print edition is unabridged.
Other aspects of the book may vary from the original edition.
Set in 16 pt. Plantin.

LIBRARY OF CONGRESS CIP DATA ON FILE.
CATALOGUING IN PUBLICATION FOR THIS BOOK
IS AVAILABLE FROM THE LIBRARY OF CONGRESS.

ISBN-13: 978-1-4328-9786-4 (hardcover alk. paper)

Published in 2024 by arrangement with Cherry Weiner Literary Agency

Print Number: 1   Print Year: 2024
Printed in Mexico

CONTENTS

INTRODUCTION 7

A Cow Hunter's Lament 13
Rattlesnakes and Skunks 54
By Way of Angel Mountain 75
The Treasure Box 91
Silent Hill. 112
Lost Mountain Pass 141
The Longest Night 170
The Harrows 201
The Prairie Fire 237
The Buffalo Trace 264
Shadow of the Crow 356

INTRODUCTION

Many years ago, on the first morning of my first writers' conference, trepidation was, no doubt, writ large on my face. My wife and I knew no one there. No one, that is, until a friendly fellow beckoned us over to share a breakfast table with him and his wife.

As you may have guessed, that fellow was, and still is, Larry D. Sweazy. I can happily confirm that Rose and Larry have been dear friends from that day to the present. This valued friendship affords me certain insider knowledge as to the sort of man we're dealing with here.

Let's see . . . he is tall, he is a keen naturalist, and he is also unfailingly kind. Oh, one more thing . . . okay, two more things: He is a good laugher and he is a good listener. For these reasons and numerous others, Larry is someone I turn to for advice, conversation, comradeship, and commiseration, and I always come away better for the experience. I suspect you will feel the same when you've read the wonderful selection of stories in this volume, stories that truly need no formal introduction.

As with their creator, these stories introduce themselves, with, among much else, witty dialogue, clever plotting, and characters who will not be forgotten, all hallmarks of an author who knows how to entertain and enlighten his readers.

This collection of Sweazy's shorter frontier fictions all but shouts howdy. His friendly, arm-around-the-shoulder style ushers you into a toasty cabin on a night colder than the devil's heart. Then you find yourself seated before a snapping fire, handed a warming drink, and, before you know it, you're off to Texas. Or Florida. Or Oklahoma. Or Indiana. . . .

Trust me — anywhere a Sweazy story takes you is a worthwhile outing. Don't worry, you'll make it back. But you won't be the same person you were when you set forth. You'll have met all manner of fascinating folk, and with them you'll have had bold, surprising, sometimes unsettling, but always fulfilling, experiences. After all, isn't that why we read?

It's no mystery that many novelists (of

which Sweazy is a well-regarded one) also write short stories, though not all of them are good at it. But Larry D. Sweazy, as the Brits say, is a dab hand at each. In fact, Sweazy has won awards for both, and because the parts help inform the whole, it is important to note he is also a teacher, a poet, an essayist, and a memoirist.

Other writers read Larry D. Sweazy's work and say, "I wish I had written that." I know so, because I have muttered that phrase a number of times over the years, and several times more while enjoying this very collection. All well and good, you say, but what makes short stories so tricky to write well, and what makes Sweazy so good at writing them?

First things first: A short story, by definition, has to do both more and less than a novel. Precisely because it is short and yet also a story, it is able to explore a solitary, trembling moment, an incident of import that in a novel might otherwise be lost. It must also be artful and tight, poetic and exact, lean and focused, and concise enough to convey a full experience, yet without the extravagance, padding, and sprawl so often employed — and enjoyed — in novels. Each line, each word of a well-crafted short story must ring like a struck bell to the reader.

Larry Sweazy's stories toll with delightful clarity.

In this robust collection, Sweazy defines and makes sense of the mythic and historic American frontier, a large, unruly, ragged-fringed locale in our imaginations and on our maps. His West is peopled with the young and old, women and men, boys and girls, the good, the bad, and the in-between. These hard-bitten lawmen, wronged gamblers, curious youths, war widows, and haggard outlaws share pages with robbed stagecoaches, thundering hooves, and rattlesnakes aplenty. All exciting, and all eclipsed only by the quality of the work in which they exist.

And though there are moments of brute violence, a sad but frequent byproduct of frontier life, they are treated by the author with care and reverence for the lives therein, forever affected. These textured, thoughtful stories run deep, and dare to reveal humanity at its most vulnerable — hearts breaking, hearts broken, hearts mending, hearts seemingly beyond hope. And yet, I'll dare to say that the bedrock sentiment of these stories is the perennial, unstoppable hopefulness of the human heart.

Another powerful, vital theme threading throughout is the author's abiding passion for what so many in our frenzied, modern lives refer to as the "natural world," a place and idea from which most humans today somehow feel the need to separate ourselves. Yet Sweazy understands there is no distinction, that we are one small part of the whole, and he invites us to slow down, breathe deep, and take a close, cautious look around.

He reminds us that the true beauty of the world rests not only within but without, in the simple loveliness of a spring flower, as in "The Harrows," when the war-wearied narrator recognizes that the pretty spring blossoms themselves "signal their death." And yet they endure, ever hopeful, to bloom again the next year.

And so do Sweazy's characters endure, not unlike flowers themselves, wracked by life's winds, droughty conditions, trampled, cut, scorned, gnawed away, yet somehow they remain standing, bent, to be sure, but not broken, driven as they are by hopefulness and blind faith in a sun-bright future.

In Sweazy's hands, even the morally stunted, trigger-happy Bonnie and Clyde ("Shadow of the Crow") are human, capable of the grief of loss and the fleeting splendor of love: "Their hands became a tangle of knowledgeable moves, each one to the delight of the other, and they made love with the same force and enthusiasm as the day they had met."

I could go on citing examples exemplifying Sweazy's ability to write page-turning, pulse-quickening prose peppered with plot twists and subtle poetic turns, but then you would be reading this and not enjoying the feast you came for.

Speak of the devil, there's Larry now, beckoning you on over. So share his table, dig in, and enjoy the company, be they hero, villain, pit viper, skunk, or a little something in between. One thing is for certain — you won't forget any of them any time soon.

And if you are new to the writing of Larry D. Sweazy, I envy you the coming experience. Then again, as the world now has this fine collection in print and in hand, I can tuck in all over again myself. And so I shall, in admiration, in enjoyment, and in friendship.

Matthew P. Mayo
Autumn 2021

A Cow Hunter's Lament

Fort Lauderdale, Florida, June 1928
William Lindel stood flat-footed at the window, wondering if he should leave or stay. Staying meant riding out the storm that was heading straight for him. Leaving would put him out in the world untethered, without solid ground under his feet. "I'm too old for this," he said aloud, to no one. He was alone in the house. Had been for a long time.

The curtain fluttered, caressing William's wrinkled, unshaven face, obscuring the view in lifts and falls. There was no escaping the sound of crashing waves against the nearby ocean shore, the graying of the clouds, or the certainty of the sea's torment rolling toward the doorstep of the small beach cottage he had called home for more years than he could count. A creaky sign hung outside the door on rusty chains, swinging back and forth in the wind, banging against the solid clapboard wall. The letters were too faded to read in the dim light, painted by his father's father in a more joyful time, the scroll proper, but the words, the announcement of ownership, the victory flag stabbed atop a mountain, was invisible, other than being tattooed on William's heart. He could see the sign, new as a dawn morning in his memory, plain, simple, and proud, like all of the Lindels. It read: THE HIDEAWAY. *Where did he run to now?*

Thunder joined the rising violence of the waves with a distant bass drum that promised to grow louder. Lightning danced a mile out at sea, jabbing at rough water, testing it for a place to land, to live or die. The storm had been born a thousand miles away and was searching with all of its might for a place to thrive on the destruction from its touch. Some storms never come ashore. Never leave a person when they make landfall. They force a man into hiding and demand that he judge the changing light, and the taste of electricity in the air with wariness, fear, and dread of what is to come. William knew more about hurricanes, and personal storms, than he cared to admit, had lived through more of them than he could count. Luck and good sense had kept him alive. He wondered how many more storms he could endure and survive. *Is this it? The last one?*

Hurricanes were not uncommon in this part of the world, but the severity of them was hard to gauge. William hadn't seen a hovering kite — a hawklike bird that gathered in trees, past the breakwaters, that would venture south if the storm was going to be bad — all morning. Even the anoles, happy little lizards too tame for their own good, had gone into hiding, sheltering under the bark of the closest palm tree or disappearing into the darkness of the pier foundation under the cottage. But even more than nature's warnings, it was the achy feeling in William's seventy-year-old bones that usually urged him to take to higher ground, fleeing inland with a mix of uncertainty and fear to escape the wrath of Neptune.

There was something about *this* storm, the depth of the humidity, the intensity of the waves, and the absence of the reliable birds and animal life, that made its impending presence stronger and angrier, all the while closing in faster than he had expected it to. The last storm that had come in on him like this had graced him with a waterspout and spawned wayward tornadoes when it made landfall. He almost didn't make it out of that one alive. He could feel the storm's pain and desire, was captivated by its force and smell of seaweed, palm, and the sand of seven islands combined into a duster made of mud and silt. Living hadn't meant so much to him that day. He'd lost another love, was weighed down by another broken heart. He dared the gods to take him. The sun shone on his face with a laugh.

William made the decision right then and there to flee again based on the tremble inside his rib cage, the hollowness in his stomach, and the swirling gray clouds that came together over the sea in a worrisome way; he knew that he had to leave the cottage whether he wanted to or not. He'd given up tempting the elements.

He headed for his bedroom to start packing with the certainty and purpose of a refugee — but was stopped before he reached the first trunk.

An unexpected knock pounded at the door.

He wasn't expecting anyone. He was never expecting anyone.

After a quick glance to the door, then back through the fluttering curtains to the darkening sky, William stood silent, trying to decide whether to feign his presence or not. Hide from the tax collector or an ex-wife unseen and unheard; he'd had the experience of pretense, of faked nonexistence, with both.

Another knock came. This time it was louder, more urgent.

"Hello?" a man's voice called out. "Is anyone home? It's getting a little scary out here. Hello?"

William headed toward the door, reluctant. He owed no one anything these days, and what few friends he had were either dead or lived sensibly inland. The idea of company was a foreign concept to him. His ex-wives, all three of them, had left his carcass for dead, his bleached bones and thin pockets picked clean. Money had created its own storms, departures, and falsehoods for him.

He yanked open the door and found himself staring at a man at least forty years his junior. "Billy Lindel?" the man said. His thin brown hair was parted down the middle of his head, and he had to look up to William, who towered almost a foot over him. William was as tall as a swamp reed and just as skinny. The man before him was short and squat, a hesitant wrestler with soft arms and pale white skin that promised to burn like a red snapper if the sun hit it for longer than a minute. He wore thick round spectacles that made him look fish-eyed to boot, and his store-bought suit coat looked new, shiny black like it had never seen any kind of weather or wear at all. Fresh and afraid. Not what William had been expecting.

"Nobody's called me Billy since I was a boy. Who are you and what the hell do you want?" William looked closer at the man, if he could have been called that. The interloper looked more like a high school student, unable to grow anything but peach fuzz above his lip. His magnified eyes held a full dose of intimidation and the fear of a youngster afraid to set the first foot forward for anything unknown. He would have to be pushed off a cliff to save himself instead of leaping on his own. William knew the feeling. It warmed him a bit.

Beyond the stranger, the waves roiled into a salty stew, about a foot tall. White caps crested ten feet out from the beach, then roared forward in a gala celebration, reaching as far onto the sandy beach as they could. Palm trees swayed in the wind, prepared to bend when the wind took a notion to throw a fit and huff as hard as it could from the other side of the world. Lightning walked closer to shore on spider legs made of fire.

"Can't you see there's a storm coming?"

William said.

The man looked over his shoulder. "I can see that, but I'm on a deadline. I have to get this story, or else I'm cooked." He stuck out a hand to introduce himself that hadn't seen a hard day's work since it had excited the womb. "I'm Randall Clavett. I'm a reporter with the *Miami Herald.*"

"I figured you might be a newspaper man by the look of you. Either that, or a salesman of some kind. Too bad you're not selling lightning rods. I could use a few. They sent a cub who didn't know any better. If I had known you were coming, I would have loaded my shotgun and peppered your ass before you knew what hit you." William stared at the pad of paper in the man's other hand for a long second, then stood back and slammed the door, not bothering to shake Clavett's extended hand. Thunder inside, thunder outside. It was hard to tell the two apart. That warmth he had felt for the boy disappeared at the first mention of the *Miami Herald.* "Go away," he hollered as he stalked away from the door. "Leave me alone. Didn't they tell you that I hate reporters?"

Clavett knocked on the door again. "If I could just have a minute of your time. I just have a couple of questions to ask you, and then I'll leave you alone."

"I said go away," William shouted over the growing chorus of the wind, waves, and rain that had started to ping on the tin roof of the cottage. It sounded like someone was unloading pea gravel on top of the house one rock at a time. A crescendo load was going to bust loose any second.

"I'm sorry I called you Billy. It was what my grandmother called you when she told me stories about you," Clavett yelled.

William was halfway to the bedroom. Clavett's words stopped him with an unexpected force that he couldn't explain. *Billy. He hated being called Billy. He wasn't a boy no more.* He turned around and stomped back to the door. When he opened it, Clavett was still there, soaking wet, his pen and pad of paper huddled under the unbuttoned opening of his thin coat. He protected the pad of paper like it was made of diamonds.

"Who's your grandmother?" William asked.

"Elmira Clavett. But Hassett was her maiden name. Elmira Hassett. That's how you'll know her."

"Christ, boy, why didn't you say you were a Hassett. Get in here before you catch your death." William reached out and pulled

Randall Clavett inside the cottage.

Water dripped off of Clavett onto the slate floor; he looked like a befuddled cat caught in an unexpected rainstorm, a little shocked that he was standing under William Lindel's roof. Fortunes change at the drop of water; and in the middle of a forsaken storm if luck and honesty are on your side.

William searched Clavett's face for some familiarity. It had been a long time since he had seen Elmira Hassett. He thought about her every day. Fifty-eight years' worth of days to be exact. There was no forgetting Elmira Hassett. She and her father and a whole lot of trouble was why reporters had continued to show up at his door, year after year. Everybody wanted to know his side of the story, especially now, since he was in the twilight of his life. There weren't many, if anyone, who was there, that remembered what really happened. William knew, though. Everybody knew that little Billy Lindel had been right in the middle of what everybody called the Lindel-Bartlot Range War.

"I was getting ready to pack out of here," William said. "I got a bad feeling about this storm."

"I won't take up too much of your time."

"Don't you have a home to go to?"

"I let a room in Miami."

"Why are you up here instead of up north where your family hails from?"

"I'm no cow hunter."

William smirked at the term *cow hunter*. They called themselves cowboys out west and in the moving pictures, but they were cow hunters in Florida. Something he knew a little about. "I can see that. So, they sent you off to school to better yourself."

"I always wanted to be writer. I like books better than horses."

"That's too bad."

"I don't think so. You should see me on a horse."

"I can imagine it now that you point it out." William hesitated, looked to the toes of his boots, then back to Clavett. "I was sorry to hear about your grandmother. I couldn't bring myself to go back home. Not even to attend her funeral."

"People looked for you, wondered where you were."

"I'm sure they did." William paused, cocked an ear toward the door, then turned his attention back to Clavett. On closer inspection, he could see a hint of Elmira in the boy. Brown thin hair, sapphire eyes that looked even bluer magnified. His thick body suggested he liked to eat a little more than most people. Elmira hadn't been a pretty girl, but she had been a sweet girl. She wouldn't have killed a spider to save her soul. He'd seen her trap more than one of the eight-legged monsters and release them outside, on the rare occasion that he was inside the Hassett house. "I suppose you've got questions about what happened back then, with your grandmother, my family, and them Bartlots."

"I do," Clavett said. "Grandmother wouldn't never tell me everything. Just about that day, you know. The fire and what happened after, when you and your father showed up."

"I know. I was there." William's mouth went dry and his ears started to hum like they always did when his heart beat a little too fast. "I'll tell you what. You can ask me whatever you want on one condition."

"What's that?"

"That you don't allow one word of what I tell you to be printed in the newspaper."

"I don't know if I can do that. I've got to eat. My job is on the line. Turns out I might not be a good newspaper writer, neither. I'm too slow, like to think things through, make them perfect as I can. My editor says I don't have the time to be no Pulitzer."

"There's plenty of newspapers in this

state. In this country for that matter. If you're a good writer, a good storyteller, you won't go hungry."

"You're sure about that?"

"Doesn't matter if I'm sure or not. Are you?"

"That's the deal, then? No story for the *Miami Herald*? And you'll answer my questions?"

"That's the deal. No story for any newspaper. I'll tell what I know because you got a right to know what happened to your kin. It's not the same now. Nothing stays the same, but those old swamps know some secrets. I guess if I don't tell them, then they'll stay there in the dark amongst the snakes, alligators, and other things that slither in shallow waters. You sure you want to know everything?"

Lightning lit up the inside of the house, and a few seconds later thunder rumbled in from the sea. The curtains stretched out straight as an ironing board, staying that way for longer than they should have been able to. The waves looked like a giant mouth opening up to swallow whatever was in its way.

"Yes," Randall Clavett said, "I want to know what happened to my grandmother that day. I think you know why."

"I have a good idea." William Lindel looked away from Clavett as a reluctant memory leapt into his mind's eye: Elmira screaming, her face bloodied, doing her best to stay alive. That memory, and the memories that came after, were a storm he'd never been able to outrun. It always came back for him, always crashed at his door in the middle of the day when he was trying to be normal and happy, but never could be because the darkness of that day, and his flat-footed reluctance to move one way or the other.

Allendale, Florida, January 1870
Twelve-year-old Billy Lindel saddled his beloved chestnut gelding, Ben, with a little more enthusiasm than usual. After months of pestering his father, Morgan Lindel, to ride on the next roundup, Billy had finally got his way. "You'll ride with Simmey," His father had said with a tap of his pipe to the side of the ashtray on his desk one evening after dinner.

Billy leapt at the chance to ride even if it meant riding with the toughest man of the crew. Simmey had never shown Billy any preference one way or the other. He was stoic as a hawk sitting atop a tree after eating a mouse. Men like Simmey seemed to only have patience with babies, horses, and dogs, and sometimes not them.

Billy couldn't sleep that night or the night before the roundup, knowing that he would bring in a thousand head of cattle. It was his first chance to ride as a cow hunter, something he'd been practicing, hoping for, dreaming of, since he'd first sat in a saddle. He wanted to be just like his pa more than anything. Being the oldest and the only boy of the family, he knew that when the Lazy F Ranch fell to him one day, to love and run, he had to be ready. Now he had to earn his spot with the men who rode closest to his pa.

Simmey Hassett was the best horseman anybody ever saw, and Huck Dayton could smell a sick calf from a mile away. Old Huck, his face always red as a strawberry and just as pitted, knew more about Florida cows than anybody Billy had ever met. He always smelled of peppermint and gun oil. A Texas man had come down to the ranch a few years back trying to tell Huck that horned cows had no place in Florida, couldn't survive on the wet grasses in the swamp and the uneven savannahs instead of the flat, open lands that Texas offered. "You ask a fella in Kansas City if he wants a Texas steak or a Florida steak, he'll probably say he didn't know Florida had cows," the Texas man had said, then guffawed at his own joke even though everybody just stared at him, especially Huck.

By the time the man left to go back where he'd come from, Huck had schooled the befuddled man on the origin of Texas longhorns being related to those original Florida cows that Ponce de León had left behind, and a whole lot more about Cracker Cows that the man didn't care to know but wouldn't soon forget. The Texas man was almost as red in the face as Huck when he hightailed it north. But before he left, the man offered Huck a job as a ranch foreman on ten thousand acres at a ranch south of Dallas for more money than Huck would ever see in his life at one time. Huck declined and swore he'd never leave Florida. Especially for Texas. Huck held an unknown grudge against Texas that was as deep as the ocean and just as wide. Everybody figured it had something to do with the war — but nobody knew for certain, Billy wasn't asking. He gave Huck a wide berth but listened to every word he said about Cracker Cows and everything else related to the ranch. Same with Simmey. What Huck knew about cattle, Simmey knew about horses. He knew how to handle them in scrub, when to let them have their head and cut a calf from its momma, and when not to. His horse was a muscular chestnut gelding, blazed with a diamond on its elegant, perfectly shaped nose, and had the longest, most beautiful legs on a horse that Billy had ever seen. That horse, Pursey McKay's Last Chance, was known to everybody as Chance. Nobody knew who Pursey McKay was, and they didn't ask, either. Simmey had his silences and grudges, too. Chance had gone down on his knees more than once on his own accord, trapping a cow with an upturned lip and a snort that sounded more like a panther snarl than anything that should come from a horse's mouth. Simmey said Chance had the mind of a big cat, the body of a racehorse, and the appetite of a sow in heat, which all combined made him the perfect horse to hunt cows with. Of the three men, his pa, of course, knew everything else about running a ranch in Florida. Where the gators nested. What snakes and spiders were poisonous, and how to encourage men to ride their best and help him turn out a profit year after year. Billy's pa was the smartest man in the world as far as he was concerned. Morgan Lindel cast a long shadow, had his own stories that he wouldn't tell, was honest, quiet, and loyal to a fault. He had brought Huck and Simmey home from the war with him and put them to work because they didn't have anywhere else to go. Billy didn't know what those two men had lost, but he figured it had been everything they ever had, but neither of them seemed sad about it. The Lazy F was their home just like it was his.

Now it was his time to ride. Standing in the barn, Billy cinched the saddle on Ben as tight as he could. He was a tall boy for his age, skinny as a fence post like his pa, but not tall enough to see over the saddle. He didn't have to see anything to know what was going on. Huck, Simmey, and his pa were doing the same thing, preparing for the ride, talking amongst themselves as they went about their chores of leaving. He could hardly contain himself, knowing that he would ride out in the lead, the four of them abreast, pacing down the lane that led away from the barn, the sun at their backs, a day of cow hunting in front of them. Three other crews were already out working other sections of the ranch, punching their finds to the meetup place, Scar's Hill, right square in the middle of the thousand acres of the Lazy F. High ground that never flooded during a hurricane and trailed down into the holding pens where the cows and calves would be sorted and shipped from.

It was as nice a morning as anyone of them could have asked for in the dry season to dip into the woodlands and ferret out the cows — one at a time, if necessary. Crackers usually stayed together in tight-knit herds like most regular cattle were prone to do, but some of them had an independent streak, wandering into swamps for sweet-grasses no matter the danger. Safety in numbers didn't matter to those cows. Billy understood that. It seemed to him that humans were the same. Some men felt safe in a group, while others were more comfortable alone.

Billy was the only one of the four who didn't carry a sidearm. He did have a .22 caliber rifle in the scabbard on Ben's side, and a knife with a six-inch blade, sheathed and hung on his belt. He had been ordered by his pa not use either weapon unless it was necessary. The use of weapons of any kind was always a last resort to Morgan Lindel. There was no need for gunpowder or lead when it came to moving cows.

Being a cow hunter, trailing into the dense woods, cypress swamps, and the lush grasslands of Central Florida, was an age-old occupation, dating back to those original seven Andalusian cattle that everybody now called

Cracker Cows, along with some Spanish horses that had been left to fend for themselves. Those cows multiplied, and the Seminoles in South Florida had taken to domesticating them, rounding them up and surviving off the beef and hides like the Sioux had survived off the buffalo. Seminoles still worked Crackers down in Fakahatchee Strand away from the eyes of the whites, as much as that was possible. The Seminoles were still at war with the invaders.

The scrappy cows that the Lindels ran still looked a lot like the original Andalusians and carried more than a little ancient blood in them. Both males and females had horns — like that Texas man had noted — which was a good thing in a land where there were lots of snakes, alligators, panthers, and a whole load of other animals intent on killing and eating them. Both sexes had attitudes that had led to their long survival. Any man who thought he was dealing with a docile, stupid bovine had never come face-to-face with a mad Cracker Cow defending its calf.

"You ready for this, Boy?" Morgan Lindel said. He was astride his horse, a black-and-gray thoroughbred called Fetch, sitting straight-backed with a felt Stetson comfortably on his head. He wore a Colt Army on his right hip, just like Simmey and Huck; more souvenirs from the war.

Billy's pa always called him Boy. For a long time Billy thought Boy was his name even though he knew better. He smiled at the term of affection. "Yes, I'm ready, Pa." If he were being honest, though, he had a queasy stomach and some fragile nerves bouncing around inside of him. He didn't want to make any mistakes and disappoint his father or make a fool of himself in front of Simmey and Huck. But he couldn't show a lick of fear. His pa might have changed his mind and made him stay at home with his two younger sisters.

Morgan Lindel looked at his son with a question that never came from his mouth, the truth obvious enough to him. Billy was relieved when his pa said, "Go on, then, get on Ben and let's ride."

Billy didn't dillydally. He climbed up onto the six-string saddle, a birthday present his pa had bought for him on a trip to Colorado a year past, settled in, grabbed Ben's reins, and urged the reliable horse on, as his father and Fetch loped out of the barn. Simmey and Huck fell into their respective places, one on each side of their boss. Billy caught up and rode head-to-head with Simmey and

Chance. He was on the outside of Simmey, riding as proud as he could. The departure was just like he had dreamed it would be. The queasiness was gone for now.

The lane curved through a grove of orange trees. Come late March and early April, the trees would be full of white, star-shaped blooms, filling the air with the fragrance of promise, of spring, and rebirth. But now, there was still fruit on the trees for the early harvest, fist-sized globes the color of the sun dangling among evergreen leaves like a hundred planets in a universe all its own. The grove had sustained Billy's family for as long as they had lived on the ranch. The smell of oranges was the smell of home.

Beyond the orange grove, the lane dipped into a slight valley. All four of them crossed a wood bridge that spanned over a thin creek called Lindel's Run. The creek was home to turtles, snakes, frogs, and all of the things little boys liked to take home to keep as their own. But Billy wasn't allowed to cage any animal other than chickens. His pa said, "Wild things were meant to stay wild," and always sent him packing back to the creek to return an errant turtle or a happy little frog to the water.

A trio of white ibises, short white birds with long curved bills, leapt into the air as soon as the first horse's hoof stepped onto the bridge. The constant movement and life in the creek brought all kinds of birds and insects to it. Billy didn't take too much notice of the birds taking flight, was accustomed to their skittish ways. He was focused on staying abreast with Simmey, who, true to character, had not spoken one word to Billy since the ride had started.

The lane stretched out to a clear and wide vista set before them. The only thing to obscure their vision were three shotgun-style houses that sat up in the air on four-foot stilts off the right of the lane. The first house — all of them owned by Billy's father — was where Simmey and his family lived. The Hassetts were a typical family of five. Simmey's wife, Midge, always wore her hair in a bun and an apron that spanned across her wide waist. Most times there was flour dotted on Midge's cheeks. She loved to bake, but her bread tasted like it was made of mud instead of wheat and was as heavy as the rocks the turtles sunned themselves on. Simmey had two sons, Rodge and Pete — both riders in their early twenties and employed on the ranch, out with other crews — and one daughter, the youngest, Elmira. She favored her mother in girth, humor, and brown hair, but was rumored to be a much better cook and baker, though Billy couldn't say that for sure. The one thing he knew and liked about Elmira was that she was as intrigued by the animals, birds and insects that lived at the creek as he was. She cried all day on hog butchering day. Elmira was sitting on the front porch and waved at the quartet of riders as they passed. Billy waved back and caught a whiff of burnt bread in the air. Simmey was going to have his usual supper when he got home from the roundup.

"Midge would have burnt down the house if Elmira wasn't there to remind her that something was amiss in the oven," Simmey said to no one in particular. The three of them, Morgan, Huck, and Billy, nodded, smiled, and kept on riding, heads up, the sun warming their cheeks.

The next house was kept by Huck and Huck alone. His wife, Peg, had died a sudden death a few years back, leaving Huck to fend for himself. They had twin sons who lived up north, one in Chicago, the other in New York City, who wanted nothing to do with farming, ranching, or life in Florida, except for the winter months when the snow in the north was unbearable. They never came around when it was roundup time, though. The other house was empty of tenants. His father was in-between men on the north crew, and everyone supposed that one of Simmey's boys, most likely Rodge, who had a steady girl in town with an eye toward marriage, would eventually move into the house.

Clear of the houses, the land tumbled out in front of the four of them with welcome morning light and nothing to get in their way. The ride out had been the best part of the day, the part that Billy would remember with fondness, though he had always wished he would have listened to that queasy gut and stayed home that day. Fondness always faded to regret for him.

Billy spied the first clump of cows standing outside of a hardwood swamp they called the May Hole because that swamp seemed to be the place where the cows took their calves for their first drink of fresh water after they'd been birthed. Ash, maple, and oak trees thrived in the May Hole, while the cypress swamps that were farther down the trail were deeper, broader, and more dangerous, as far as Billy was concerned. He had never liked the darkness of the cypress swamps. There were rattlesnakes, cottonmouths, and coral snakes to worry about, along with the gators, who had a healthy appetite for Cracker Cows. Insects were thick, but not so much in the dry season as they were in the wet season, which was one of the reasons why his pa rounded up the cattle in January. The other being the market expected the cows, and what the market expected, the market got. Billy had been warned more than once that their livelihood was held in the grips of strangers who set prices and placed demands on them all. That, along with the weather, and men who rustled and stole their cows for their own, made for a precarious life. One that Morgan Lindel had committed to over and over, when times got bad. Billy's pa had no quit in him, and he knew he couldn't have any, either.

"You stay here," Simmey said to Billy, peeling off from the quartet, leaving the three men to sit there and watch Simmey and Chance go to work. Three cows and one calf were standing on the lip of the swamp, and Chance, in all of his chestnut glory, dropped his head and ran straight for the calf, snorting like a wolf longing to take down a sick elk. Simmey had told Billy, when he was training Ben, that he had known that Chance was going to be a good horse from the start, because Simmey had run some dogs through the corral to see how Chance would react, and sure enough, Chance followed after the dogs, was really interested in them, stayed on them with intention, and showed no fear. "He had a lot of cow in him," Simmey had said. All Billy could do now was watch Simmey and Chance work together to separate the calf from the cows. Once they were close, Simmey dropped the reins even more and it seemed to everyone that the horse was driving itself, making all of the decisions, while Simmey was along for the ride, not in charge of the cut at all. Which was pretty much the case. Chance was the true cow hunter. Simmey got to watch it up close and personal and look at the hero that Chance was.

Billy could only smile as the cut was successful, and the calf pushed away from the entrance of the swamp on its own, scurrying and hopping, then coming to a stand in the middle of the open grass before it. It was the first of the calves to be pulled. There would be a hundred more before the day was over, if Morgan Lindel's calculations were right. All Billy could do was hope that he and Ben had the same kind of relationship that Simmey and Chance had someday. He knew he wasn't there yet; he didn't trust himself enough to let the reins go like Simmey did. But cutting wasn't his job. Keeping the herd together and moving them forward was his task. His and Huck's task. His pa and Simmey were the sorters. That kept Billy out of the swamp, away from the dangers lurking in the water and dangling from the trees. It'd take some time before he was allowed to hunt the swamps.

It wasn't long before Billy was in charge of twenty calves, and a quarter of the day had passed by. Simmey pushed five cows out of the swamp and switched places with Huck, taking a break, all the while watching over Billy, Ben, and the growing herd.

Hours seemed to fly by like minutes, and the outlook was promising, everything was working the way it was supposed to, until Billy looked up and saw Rodge Hassett riding straight for them, a frantic look plastered on his pale white face, checking over his shoulder every other gallop of his horse, another chestnut gelding, but not near as perfect and storied as Chance, like he was being chased by something or someone. Billy didn't even know the name of Rodge's horse. But that didn't matter. It was easy to tell that something was wrong.

The sky was clear of clouds, but a storm was heading right toward Billy. He just didn't know how bad of a storm it was.

Nobody knew. The clouds were just starting to show themselves.

Simmey saw Rodge at the same time Billy had. He swung his horse around and headed to meet the oncoming rider. "You keep these calves together, you hear," he ordered, then rode off, leaving a quick cloud of dust behind him.

Billy nodded and cocked his ears toward the swamp. He could hear his pa and Huck working the cows, pushing them forward, rounding up what was left inside the May Hole, but couldn't see them.

The load of calves didn't seem to care about Rodge's panic, but Billy did, especially when he heard him yell, "The Bartlots have stampeded us. They're headin' this way."

The Bartlots. Billy should have figured they'd cause trouble on a day as fine as this one. His pa and Huck, too. They'd had their fair share of problems with the Bartlots over the years. Even the Seminoles had trouble with that bunch. The Bartlots rustled more Crackers than anybody could count from the Indians, and sold them north, all the way up to North Carolina where Clem Bartlot kept more than one of his ranches. Rumor had it that he had a wife in every ranch house, too. They were at least one hundred and fifty miles apart, so the women wouldn't know about each other — but that always puzzled Billy. He was a twelve-year-old boy and he'd heard the rumor, hadn't the women? The larger point, to Billy, was that the Bartlots weren't any good. They were cattle thieves, liars, and a whole lot of other things that he didn't know the names for. Clem Bartlot and his sons were bad people, Confederates still fighting a war that had been over five years, believing their rules and laws were all that mattered, not the Republican laws, like his pa abided by. The Lindels and the Bartlots had been feuding over land, water, and the ownership of the Cracker Cows for as long as Billy could remember in one way or another, but in a distant way, a cow stolen here, a fence cut there to move their own herds, a glare in town across the street, safe with the traffic of daily life in between them. But now, on this day, the trouble between the two families looked to have gotten worse. A whole lot worse. Something had broken, and Billy didn't know what that something was. He never would.

"They stampeded us," Rodge repeated, pushing his horse into a lather right past Simmey, heading up the road that led straight to the ranch house they'd left out of that morning.

It was then that Billy heard the first hoof of thunder, five hundred cows set to worry, afraid, ran forward by a gunshot or a blast of some kind. For what purpose, he didn't know — all he knew was panic and fear filled the air and he had been left standing there guarding the passel of calves that had already been cut from the herd. His body was numb, his mind locked in a debate about what to do. His pa had never had the chance to tell him what to do in a stampede. He was a statue dedicated to fear. Billy couldn't feel anything, but could hear his heart beating fast and furious, like he was in the middle of running a footrace.

"Run!" Simmey shouted.

It would be Simmey who told him what to do, to stir Billy out of his reluctance to flee, to leave his pa and Huck in the May Hole. He looked into the darkness of the swamp and saw the dim movement of cows, and a silhouette of Huck on his horse, but that was all.

Simmey laid into Chance, spurring the horse forward, but he couldn't run full out looking back like he was, eyeing Billy, watching over his charge. "Run!" he yelled again.

The ground under Ben's hooves shook

and vibrated upward to the saddle, and it finally registered in Billy's brain what was happening: If he sat there, he would die. He urged Ben on just as Chance and Simmey spun around to come back for him.

The first Cracker Cow, deranged, running full out, slobber and foam bubbling out of its mouth, as the first brown-and-white steer appeared, twisting his horned head back and forth, fighting off an invisible swarm of hornets. After that one came another and another. Small trees fell to the ground. Tall trees quaked like they were about to be uprooted. Some cows jumped into the darkness of the swamp, while others curved around it, not wanting anything to do with the unknown dangers inside it. Dust rose to the sky, clouded the sun like the worst storms. Somewhere in the distance, from behind the cows or to the opposite side of them, a gunshot rang out, urging the cows to run faster, to be more afraid. Panic tasted like rusted barbed wire on Billy's tongue.

He pushed Ben to run as fast as the horse could, but it, being fully aware of the state of the world around it, needed little encouragement. It was all Billy could do to hang on.

Simmey and Chance were still facing the oncoming cows.

Billy was heading toward them. Chasing after Rodge.

Running for his life.

Sweat ran down his face. His heart was pumping so fast that Billy feared it would burst wide open. His fingers were numb. He couldn't feel the reins between them. Ben was running on his own, his head down, nostrils flared like the best cutting horses did when they were on a cow.

Pain twisted across Simmey's face as he grabbed at his chest. His torso rocked backwards like he had been hit by something or ran into a tree branch. But there were no trees near him. Blood spurted from his fingers and Billy figured out that the gunshot and the blood were the cause and result. Simmey had been shot. He stayed erect in his saddle as Billy ran to him, the cows closing on in his heels.

Simmey's face was pasty, and a look of disbelief was stuck on his face. "Go, Boy, go now. Ride back and warn the others." He meant his family, the women, Midge, Elmira, and the rest. "Don't stop for nothing."

Billy almost couldn't hear the words for his own heartbeat and the oncoming cows.

Another gunshot crackled from somewhere nearby, off to the right of them. Billy winced expected to feel lead break through his skin, but none did. Simmey hadn't been shot, either.

"Go, now," Simmey ordered.

"What about you?"

"I'll be fine." Simmey nodded toward the swamp.

Billy glanced behind him to see his pa and Huck riding out of the darkness, cutting and dancing between the manic cows, heading toward them.

"Go now," There was a weakness in Simmey's voice that Billy had never heard before, and that set him off. He didn't want to leave any of them, but he knew he had to.

Billy kneed Ben and they tore out like lightning had struck two inches behind them. They ran as fast as they could. Billy's head was down next to Ben's neck. He didn't look behind him, kept his eyes forward.

It wasn't long before he saw Rodge's horse running riderless along the edge of the trail. More panic. Searching until he saw Rodge, lying face first on the ground, with a circle of blood between his shoulder blades. He'd been shot in the back.

Billy kept running, kept pushing Ben to go as fast as he could, urging the horse forward. He had never been so afraid in his life. His mouth was dry, and his eyes were wet with tears. He hated those Bartlots. They were throwing a hard punch, trying to steal all of their cows at once.

As he rounded another bend in the trail, Billy saw the first spiral of black smoke reaching into the air. He hoped Midge had set the house on fire baking bread.

Billy slowed Ben and looked behind him. The way was clear. He'd outran the cows and managed not to get shot. But he was too late. The Bartlots had already got to the ranch. He pushed forward then, unsure of what he would find, but there was no going back. Simmey had told him not to stop for anything.

He ran full speed up the lane to the three houses. The empty one, the one meant for Rodge was ablaze, flames reaching outside of the windows, glass broken, door kicked in, the fire breathing like it was alive.

Two horses, no men in the saddles, stood in the middle of the road, waiting, not concerned with anything, not afraid of the fire.

A man, no mistaking that he was a Bartlot boy, black hair, muscles of bull, forehead as wide as a grown man's palm, busted out of Simmey's house, dragging Elmira with him.

She was screaming. Her face was bloodied, like she'd been punched in the nose. They hadn't noticed Billy sitting on Ben thirty yards away.

He had a second to decide what to do.

He grabbed his .22 rifle out of the scabbard, and aimed it at the Bartlot's head, his finger tight on the trigger. His skin was as cold as a Chicago January. The sound of his heartbeat faded away. He was focused on the bead.

The Bartlot boy stopped. Looked at Billy, made eye contact with him, laughed, then kept on going, kept on pulling Elmira until they were out of sight, gone between the two houses. The shot was lost. Billy froze. He was a twelve-year-old boy. He couldn't bring himself to kill a man.

Fort Lauderdale, Florida, June 1928
"That was the last I saw of your grandmother," William said to Randall Clavett, "until the trial. She was just a whisp of herself then. We all were, from what had happened to us, to our families, to our land, and our dreams. They took things from us that we would never get back."

The cottage was buttoned up. The windows secure. Shades and shutters closed as tight as they could be. The doors were blocked with bath towels and rugs rolled up and pushed against the threshold to stop the flow of water coming in; a bandage that wouldn't work if the surf was high and the storm was as angry as William thought it would be. Rain hammered the roof. A thousand ballpeen hammers beating away at the tin. A shutter clanged in the kitchen. They sat in the front room, chairs facing each other, oblivious as they to the storm raging outside the cottage.

"I've read the trial transcripts," Clavett said. "There was nothing in there about you being there, about you seeing a Bartlot carry her off."

"I never told anyone. Until now. Pa knew, of course, he was there."

"But dead men can't tell stories."

"Something like that."

"I'm sorry. It must have been hard for you to see him die."

William nodded. "It wasn't the worst part of that day. What happened to Elmira was worse. You know what happened to her. You read the files."

Clavett nodded. "Clem Bartlot shot your father in cold blood. Rode up and opened fire. The blaze had been their mistake, though. The town came running. My grandmother had been raped. I know that. You don't have to dance around that anymore."

William took a deep breath. "They found Elmira behind the house, crumbled and delirious."

"Which one was it? Which Bartlot boy? I got a right to know, don't I?"

"I suppose you do. That's why I agreed to answer your questions." William settled back in his chair and listened to all of the wind, thunder, and rain dance around the cottage. Sitting before him was a young man willing to risk everything to know the truth. Ride out a hurricane. Track him down. Spend hours in a law library reading transcripts to find out what really had happened that day. "This is about more than the story that you want to write for the newspaper, isn't it?"

"It's about the truth. I've got a right to know that. The people of Orange County got a right to know."

"It was a long time ago."

"It's history. My history."

"He's dead. The Bartlot that done it. You know that, don't you? There's no justice to be served."

"You never told anyone his name."

"I wasn't sure which one of the boys it was. Clem Bartlot had five sons, all a year apart. They looked a lot alike. I didn't know his name then."

"But you do, now."

"Yes, I told you he's dead."

Clavett stood up, his face was as red as Huck's face ever got. He paced between the chair and the door, looking to the ceiling, to the windows, but never directly at William until he stopped in the middle of the room, his eyes glazed with tears that wouldn't fall. "You could have killed him."

William sighed, then looked Randall Clavett in the eye, and said, "I was a boy. I never had the stomach for killing anything. I loved the lives of the animals that lived around our house. I hated hunting unless it was cow hunting, but that was taken from me, too. I couldn't bring myself to pull the trigger and kill a man."

"You could have saved her."

"But if I had killed him, you wouldn't be here. Think about that. I never have until now, until I looked in your eyes when you walked into my house. What other lives would I have taken if I would have killed that man? I know that what he did was the worst thing a man can do to a woman, what one human being can do to another human being. Your grandmother was never right after that day. But you're here, aren't you? You got to live. You have a life."

"My father. He was never right, either. He

drank himself to an early grave."

"And you? What about you? Will you?"

"No," Clavett said. "I don't have a taste for the stuff. All I ever wanted was to know what happened and why. That's all. I figured I had a right to it, a right to know who I was, where I come from. Everybody else knows. Why can't I?" He was deflated, shoulders sagging. His clothes looked three times too big for him. The tear finally escaped his eye. "You had a father. I didn't. But look at the truth of it? I know why my grandmother couldn't tell me anything. She couldn't look me in the eye, either. She bristled when we hugged. How is that fair?"

William could only sit there and stare at him, see the hint of Elmira and Simmey, all of the Hassett blood mixed together with Bartlot blood swirl around and make the man that Randall Clavett was and would be. He stood up and walked over to Clavett and took each of his shoulders into his hands and looked him square in the eye. "All of my life, I've regretted not taking that shot when I had the chance. I froze time and time again when it came time to make a big decision, whether to come or to go, to love or to let go, and now, seeing you, I have to rethink how I've spent my entire life. I think I've been regretting the wrong thing this whole time."

Randall Clavett was staring at his toes, still nodding. "So, the truth does set you free."

"Maybe it does. Maybe that's the story about this old range war that everyone still wants to know. The entire truth has never been told. I think you should go write it."

"Everything?"

"Everything. I've changed my mind. You tell the story just the way I told to you. That might just put an end to all of the questions, and the storm that's been raging inside of us all of our lives." William let go of Clavett and cocked his ear to the roof. "The storm's let up. If I was you, I'd make a run for it while you've still got a chance."

"What about you?"

William smiled wider than he had in a long time. "I think I'll ride this one out. Then after it's over with, I might just head up north and pay my respects to some old friends in the cemetery. It's been a long time since I was home."

Author's Note

I stumbled across the Barber-Mizell Range War (1870) while researching cattle rustling in Florida. I was fascinated with the idea that Florida was as much a cattle state as Texas in the cowboy years, and I wanted to write a story about cowboy life in the Wild East instead of the Wild West. While there are some similarities to the Barber-Mizell Range War and this story, my story is entirely a product of my imagination, not historical fiction, and should not be confused as, or compared to, the actual history or real events that took place. Any research mistakes are my own.

Rattlesnakes and Skunks

Josiah Wolfe sat atop his Appaloosa stallion and watched a rooter skunk push through a dry creek searching for anything that moved or anything that held the slightest hint of green. The skunk, black with a broad white stripe down its back, with a nose that looked like it ought to be on a hog, didn't see the four-foot-long diamondback rattlesnake sunning itself on the bright side of a big boulder a few yards ahead of it.

Wolfe rubbed the butt of his gun, a .45 single-action Peacemaker, and then thought better of interfering. He'd wait it out, see what happened next, though his betting side told him not to count out the skunk.

He gently edged the stallion back up the trail so he'd be down wind when all hell broke loose.

The snake wrangled its tail and set its alarm in motion, but that didn't seem to deter the hognose. In the flash of an eye the skunk recoiled, and without warning jumped straight at the snake capturing it with a determined set of iron jaws just behind the eyes. The snake didn't have time to spit or smell the foul stink that escaped from the skunk's defensive gland. Its head was smashed flatter than a johnnycake. The rattle quickly subsided, a tiny echo in the wind, like the last bell ringing on a funeral coach, and the snake succumbed without the chance of a fair fight.

Wolfe had little use for snakes or skunks, and even less for their human counterparts. If it wasn't for one such critter, Charlie Langdon, he'd be home right now, readying the hard ground for planting even though the dry winter winds had yet to stop blowing.

Not that winter was much of a worry in East Texas, not like in the Dakotas, but the wind still blew cold from the north at times, and the leaves still fell off the trees. Once in a blue moon, snowflakes fell from the sky on Christmas. But spring was coming . . . the smell of renewal was in the air, and honestly, Josiah Wolfe wished more than anything that he was back home to welcome it instead of on the trail to bring a killer to justice.

Wolfe watched the skunk drag the snake

off, probably to a den nearby loaded with babies, hungry mouths and eyes that had yet to see the light of day.

The quick fight amazed him and brought a sting of melancholy to the forefront of his mind he wasn't expecting. He shouldn't have been surprised though, he'd been carrying a wagonload of dread on his shoulders for a quite some time now.

He'd been on and off the trail since the day he had joined up with the Texas Rangers and become a lawman outside the confines of Seerville, the town where he'd been born and raised.

Like his father before him, Josiah had worn the marshal's badge. Life was fine until the town up and died, when the railroad curved and went through Tyler instead of Seerville. There wasn't much left to marshal after that, after nearly everyone moved on or was foreclosed on. But Josiah had the deed to the family homestead and pulling up stakes was something he wouldn't consider — not with all his kin buried on the back forty.

He wasn't much of a farmer, and his land wasn't real hospitable to much of anything of use since most of it was floodplain and swamp, but he made do with what he had.

When the opportunity to become a Ranger

came his way, he leapt at the chance.

He had ridden on a posse with Captain Hiram Fikes in the previous year, and when Fikes heard that Seerville no longer needed a marshal, he sent word to Josiah that he would be a welcome addition to the company of Rangers who covered East Texas.

Luckily the Rangers could live just about anywhere they chose — as long they didn't mind being away from home long stretches at a time.

Josiah didn't mind traveling, not at first anyway. Life was pretty much an adventure when he'd started out with the Rangers. He was nearly twenty-five, had a pretty wife, Lily, he'd been in love with all his life, and three fine-looking daughters. The money he made as a Ranger wasn't much, but it helped keep a couple of cows in the barn, and between that and his hunting skills, there was always meat on the table.

Rangering took him away months at a time, but when he returned it was always to a hero's welcome. Seasons passed, and they all got lulled into a comfortable rhythm — until a year and a half ago when the influenza struck.

First the fevers took Fiona, the youngest. After weeks of battling high fevers, the poor little thing slipped away in her mother's arms. And then, like a wild boar rampaging carelessly through the small pine house, the sickness took Claire and Mavis only days apart.

For the first time in years, Josiah and Lily were left alone, their emotions and hope all but drained out of them. They pretty much wanted to die too — but they held on, fought off the flu with tonics and sheer determination for one simple reason: Lily was pregnant, and the baby was nearly due to birth.

Wolfe shook his head . . . tried to force the thought of Lily from his mind as he brought the horse back up to pace, leaving the stink of the skunk behind him.

There was no escaping the loneliness on the trail. Even the birds were silent. Somewhere in the distance he heard a growl and a yelp, and figured it was the skunk celebrating the snake kill with its brood.

The ridge Wolfe had been riding on flattened out, and he spotted puddles of water up ahead in the dry creek. It had been a good while since he'd watered the Appaloosa. He glanced up at the sun, and figured he'd be in San Antonio by nightfall even with a stop.

It didn't take long to venture down to the water. Vultures soared overhead, and he could hear the first frogs of spring croaking for a mate. The grasses were still brown, but Josiah knew it wouldn't be long before the bluebonnets, red buckeye, and paintbrush would burst into bloom, coloring the dull landscape in all the colors of the rainbow.

Lily loved spring.

The Appaloosa took to the water as if it had been trudging through a desert for days. Wolfe hadn't ridden the horse hard, but he had kept a steady, headlong gait, stopping only to relieve himself and watch the skunk do away with the snake.

With the sun beaming down from a cloudless sky, the air was beginning to warm. Josiah Wolfe propped himself against a boulder the size of a good bull, and closed his eyes, with only the thought of resting, of trying to focus his thoughts away from death and hope, of journeys with bad ends, and the loss of adventure. It was as if he were snake bit himself.

The midwife, a short, rotund Mexican woman who went by the name of Ofelia, stood over Lily's lifeless body and shook her head. "She is dead, señor."

There was no blood, no struggle. Lily did not have the strength to bear a child. She had battled for days between the labor of childbirth, and the onset of influenza. She lay flat on the bed, her belly protruding, beads of sweat still on her forehead. A bowl of steaming hot water sat next to the bed, and the room was filled with an odd sour odor.

Josiah could barely breathe. He staggered to the bed, past Ofelia's helper, a scrawny young thing with saucer-shaped brown eyes rimmed with tears that the midwife referred to as niña, girl, and never by name.

Lily's skin was still warm to the touch. He closed her dull eyes and kissed her forehead without fear of contracting the sickness. Life was too painful. He was willing to die that very moment himself, willing to join his wife and daughters in the land of Heaven, even though he was not much of a believer. Not now. Redemption and resurrection seemed to be nothing more than a folktale. The sickness had showed no mercy, a devil that could not be fought. Where was God's hand in all of this, Josiah had wondered more than once, especially after the preacher man from Tyler had refused to come to the house out of fear for his own health and well-being.

Josiah Wolfe had never felt so empty or so angry in his entire life. It seemed that death was everywhere he looked. He ran out of the house yelling, screaming, venting his rage into the darkness of the night. A coyote answered back.

He fell to the ground in a bundle of tears and spit, and began to pound the ground. He didn't know how long he was there, how long it was that someone had a hand on his shoulder.

"The baby lives, señor, but we do not have much time." Ofelia stood over him, staring down with the eyes of a sad mother. "I cannot reach the feet."

Josiah caught his breath, filled his lungs, but he could not speak. Everything seemed hopeless.

"I will need a butchering knife to save the baby," Ofelia said. "Can you get it for me?"

Wolfe opened his eyes and tried to think of something else, tried to force away the image of Lily lying dead on their marriage bed.

He mounted the horse and headed toward San Antonio. Even the thought of Charlie Langdon dangling from the end of a rope couldn't bring him out of the funk he'd let return to a boil.

Charlie was a lowdown scoundrel if ever there was one. For a time, Charlie had been a deputy in Seerville, but Josiah caught on pretty quick that Charlie was the kind of man that liked to walk on both sides of the law. Charlie made things up as he went, twisted the law so it suited whatever con he was knee-deep in at the time. And that's what got Charlie in trouble. After Wolfe fired him, Charlie went on a cheating and robbing spree that claimed four innocent lives over the next few years — and then Charlie disappeared.

Some said he went to South Texas and was hiding out in the canyons, while others just hoped he was dead. Neither was right. Charlie changed his name and got another badge pinned on his chest. But skunks can't change their stripes any more than a rattlesnake can sneak up quiet on a man, and before long, Charlie was walking on both sides of the law again. It was his bad luck to come up against the Texas Rangers — most notably, Captain Hiram Fikes.

Charlie Langdon was in custody, and it was Wolfe's charge to take him back to Tyler for sentencing for the four previous killings. The circuit court judge was laid up with a broken leg, and the citizens of Tyler were beating the drum to see Charlie hang. But that wasn't Josiah's concern. He figured justice had already been served since Charlie was behind bars, under the watchful eye of Captain Fikes.

His concern was returning home as soon as possible, so the thought of Charlie Langdon hanging did not lighten Wolfe's mood. It wouldn't have bothered him to see Charlie sit in jail and rot for a few months, but that wasn't his call. Duty was one of the few things left in the world he had to hold onto.

The rest of the ride was uneventful. It was dusk when he rode into San Antonio. The liveliness of the town shocked his system. City life always did.

After Lily's death, he stayed as close to home as possible, riding with the Rangers only when he had to. The silence of his land, of Seerville, which was now nothing more than a ghost town, host to only a few Mexican squatters, including Ofelia, was less than comforting. He had never been one for the pleasantries of society — manners and conversation were Lily's gift — so he did not miss being around people on a daily basis. But he did mind the loneliness more than he thought he would.

Oddly, the noise of the streets, of wagons and horses coming to and fro, piano music banging out of the saloons, *were* a tad bit comforting to Wolfe. His dull mood did not lighten, but for the first time in a long while, he began to think about the pleasure of a bath and shave.

He found a livery near the jail, and stabled his horse. Most people paid him no mind. Wolfe was just another face in the crowd since most Rangers didn't wear a badge. The organization was more akin to a brotherhood, and though it wasn't a secret society, it felt like it at times. Most Rangers were well known, operated on the legend of their name like Hiram Fikes, but Josiah hadn't been with the organization long enough for people to recognize him. At a little past thirty, he was still green behind the ears, more tepid and reclusive since Lily's death, and less interested in creating a legend bearing his name.

Captain Fikes wasn't hard to find. He was playing poker in the Silver Dollar Saloon, two doors down from the jail.

"Pull up a chair, Wolfe." Fikes was a beanpole of a man with a head full of solid white hair. His skin was leathery and wrinkled, and from a distance he looked like a stiff wind could blow him away. More than a few brash and arrogant outlaws had underestimated the captain and found themselves six feet under without the chance to beg for forgiveness. The captain was one of the best single-shot aims Josiah Wolfe had ever met.

"Just checking in, Captain. I'll take my leave if you don't mind. I'd like to get the trail dust off my neck."

Fikes nodded and puffed heavily on the cigar that dangled from the corner of his mouth. The other three men at the table looked impatient. It was the captain's turn to deal, and by the size of the chip stacks, it looked as if he was cleaning out some deep pockets.

The music and laughter seemed foreign to Josiah. He tried not to stare at the painted women standing next to the piano, at the picture of a naked woman over the bar. It had been a long time since he been in a room with women, even the lowly kind, and it stirred a deep longing inside him that almost made him blush. Ofelia was nearly the only woman he came into contact with these days . . . and not once had Josiah let his mind wander to the fence of desire since the day he buried Lily next to his three girls.

"We'll be riding out first thing in the morning." Fikes shuffled the cards like a professional dealer, a smile growing on his face as he turned his attention back to the game. "I know you might be wondering why I had you ride all this way, other than Charlie Langdon has a history with you."

"I was, sir, but I'm glad to fulfill the

request."

Fikes flopped out five cards to each man and then stared up at Josiah, the smile gone from his face. "It's time for you to decide if you want to keep Rangering. Time to realize there's people that still count on you, Wolfe."

"I understand, Captain."

"I hope you do. There's trouble brewing up your way, and I'm gonna need every man I can count to keep a spark from turning into a wildfire."

Wolfe wasn't sure what the captain was speaking of, if it had anything to do with Charlie Langdon or not — his guess was that it did. But he did understand the tone, the underlying meaning: Captain Hiram Wilkes wasn't sure he could trust him in his current state of mind. Josiah couldn't blame the man. You had to trust the man you picked to cover your back. He knew right then that the request to ride Charlie Langdon back to Tyler was a show of faith — and Josiah's last chance to prove himself worthy of being a Texas Ranger.

"I don't mean to be anything else other than a Ranger, Captain."

"Good, that's what I was hoping to hear."

There was blood everywhere. The niña

could not take the sight of Ofelia cutting open Lily's belly — she had run from the foul-smelling room in a panic when she saw the midwife's intent. Josiah could barely stand the sight himself. He stood hunkered in the corner, his eyes glazed with tears, his stomach in tatters.

Candles flickered on the table next to the bed, and Ofelia muttered under her breath as she slit Lily's pure white skin. It took Josiah a minute to realize that the woman was praying. "Perdone mí, Dios. . . ." Forgive me, God. . . .

After making a long cut down the center of the stomach, Ofelia motioned for Josiah to come to her. "I will need your help, señor."

Josiah's knees and hands were trembling. He could not look at Lily's lifeless face, or bring himself to speak. The words *I can't* were stuck in his throat.

"Pronto, señor."

Ofelia shook her head with frustration. The knife tumbled to the floor. Josiah had never seen so much blood in his life. He wanted to scream at the Mexican woman and make her stop — but he knew she was doing the right thing.

Slowly, Josiah made his way to the side of the bed.

Ofelia took his hands gently into hers and guided them to Lily's belly. "I am sorry, señor, this must be done to save your baby. You must pull back the skin with all your strength."

Josiah took a deep breath, fought back the bile that was rising from the depths of his body.

In a swift motion, Ofelia thrust her hands deep inside Lilly, tussled and turned her arms, and just as quickly, pulled a lifeless baby up and out of the body. She placed the baby, all covered in blood and dark blue as a stormy summer sky, on the bed, and cut the cord.

Josiah staggered back as Ofelia swatted the baby on the behind. Nothing happened. It looked dead. She swatted again. And again nothing. Finally, she blew into the baby's mucus covered mouth, and smacked the baby on the back, just between the shoulder blades. The baby coughed and heaved and began to cry.

"You have a son, señor. You have a son."

Josiah Wolfe had never paid money to be with a woman and he wasn't going to start now — even though he had faced that temptation in the saloon. It was another surprise to his heart and soul. He almost ran out of the saloon like a scared little boy.

After a quick meal of ham hocks, beans, and cornbread, he gave two bits for a bath, got a shave for another bit, and found the nearest hotel.

He almost felt like a new man, except he was forced to wear the same clothes he had worn on the trail to San Antonio.

As he lay on the soft bed, Captain Fikes's words echoed in his head, and the doubt in the old Ranger's tone was like a screaming rooster, finally waking him up after a long sleep.

It had been nearly a year since Lily had died. His son, Lyle, had grown like a weed. He wasn't very learned when it came to child rearing, and Josiah had relied heavily on Ofelia.

The old Mexican woman was more than happy to help, more than happy to take what bit of food and money he could offer her. There was more to her aid than just money, and Josiah knew it. Ofelia felt as responsible for Lyle as he did, and for that he found some gladness, some comfort.

He had not let his mind wander, though, to finding another wife. At least, not until now. Just the thought of forsaking his love for Lily seemed like blasphemy, a mark on her grave. Guilt had held him prisoner, and he knew it. For whatever reason, he had survived the influenza, and now he had a son to raise, all the while being sworn to uphold the law as a Texas Ranger.

He owed a lot to Captain Fikes for being so thoughtful, for having the foresight to pull him away from the tiny pine cabin and get him on the trail again.

Charlie Langdon struggled atop the saddle as they rounded a struggling creek and started to make their way up a hill.

Langdon was a tall fella with broad shoulders and pure black hair. A thin scar ran down the right side of his face . . . a white mark that was new to Josiah. Charlie always had looked angry, his teeth forever clenched, but trail dirty, and with the scar, he looked a lot meaner. Josiah couldn't imagine why Charlie had turned bad or what his life had been like on the run. Nor did he care. He was anxious to return home.

Captain Fikes was in the lead, and Josiah was bringing up the rear. It had been nearly a day since they had left San Antonio. They were being shadowed by two other rangers, Dobbs and Burke, a quarter mile on each side just in case Charlie tried to escape or his gang had set up an ambush.

Captain Fikes had filled Josiah in on the

troubles brewing in Tyler. It seemed that the circuit court judge had not simply broken his leg — his leg had been broken by a man with a club, waiting for the judge as he made his way home one evening. Fikes figured it was one of the Folsum gang, whom Charlie was riding with when he had been captured.

The Folsum gang was a mean bunch of horse thieves, bank and train robbers, that were gathering force and numbers, taking in every guttersnipe they could find. Fikes expected a showdown before they marched Charlie up to the gallows. Evidently there was a value to Charlie's cheating ways that the Folsums thought was worth fighting for.

"I need to relieve myself," Charlie said, looking over his shoulder.

Josiah brought the Appaloosa to a halt and whistled at the captain. "He needs a break, Captain."

Fikes nodded, scanned the horizon and rising ridge, and circled back. "Looks clear. Bring him down."

Charlie's feet were shackled with a long chain that let him stride the horse, and his hands were bound. Not a comfortable way to ride, but penance came in many forms as far as Josiah was concerned.

Once on the ground, Charlie was inches

from Josiah's face, and the outlaw sucked a good bit of air deep in his chest and spit in his face. "I never did like you, Wolfe. I'll be glad to see the day when you meet your maker."

Before Josiah could react, he heard a round slide into the chamber of the captain's rifle. "One more move like that, Langdon, and I'll save the hangman the trouble of making a trip to Tyler."

Charlie spit again, only this time on the ground, a few inches from Fikes's feet.

Josiah had recoiled, clenching his fists. "Go do your business, you no-good son of a bitch, so we can get on with this."

The captain dismounted and stood shoulder to shoulder with Josiah. "Man ain't worth the lead, Wolfe, or I would have shot him right now and been done with it."

Josiah had been staring at the ground, trying to regain his composure, trying to force his anger back in the right place. When he looked up, Charlie Langdon was a good fifty paces away. A glimmer in the sunlight caught his attention, and then he saw a quick bit of movement on top of a rock a few inches from where Charlie had stopped to unbutton his trousers. Charlie was eye-to-eye with a rattlesnake and was totally unaware of the snake's presence.

Before he could say what came to his mind, Josiah heard the rattlesnake give warning, and then strike. It caught Charlie in the throat, right at the jugular.

Charlie screamed, tried to pull the snake off him, but its fangs were embedded too deep. The outlaw fell to his knees wrestling with the snake, while he pleaded with the Rangers to help.

They both just stood there and watched.

Ofelia was sitting on the porch singing to Lyle when Josiah Wolfe returned home. He took the boy out of the old Mexican woman's arm and hugged him with joy.

For a brief second, Josiah could barely breathe, he was so happy to be home, to hold his son. But as he put the boy back in Ofelia's arms, he knew he had much more to do.

Rangering would continue to take him away, and beyond the boy, there was nothing more that he loved than being a Texas Ranger. But he could not continue to rely on Ofelia forever, she was getting old and tired. Her duty to Lily had been served. It was time to relieve her of the burdens Wolfe had placed on her.

"I think I might go to that social they're having in Tyler on Sunday, Ofelia. What do you think about that?"

Ofelia kissed Lyle on top of the head, and looked up at Josiah with a smile. "I think the ride to San Antonio did you some good, señor. It is past time."

"I think you're right, Ofelia. I need to keep riding."

"Sí, señor."

Lyle squealed and reached up to his father, and Ofelia and Josiah laughed together for the first time in a long, long time.

By Way of Angel Mountain

The snow was nearly two feet deep. Any sign of the trail had long since disappeared, covered under the thick white blanket, along with any sign of travelers, good or bad, that had the poor sense to venture out on such an ugly day.

Wind, strong, furious, and determined, cut down from the north, a gift from Montana, out of the Bitterroots, with a song on its frigid, cold edge — a song that was more warning than anything else: I will sing you to death, I will sing you to death, your skin will freeze along with your heart, if you're not smart.

Ice crystals pummeled and stung Deputy U.S. Marshal Cal Wallace's bearded face as he rode face-first into the growing winter storm. Wallace didn't listen to the wind, didn't care to hear a song — or a warning. He was determined to end a long chase, bring a hard criminal pursuit to a final end.

All he heard was his own voice, urging on his mount, following his gut, constantly pushing the ice from the brim of his hat and his eyebrows. He knew he was close, knew he had to keep going no matter what.

"Get on, let's go. Get on, let's go, fella."

The horse, a hearty solid black stallion bred from stock that had been in his family for thirty years, responded the best it could. Nostrils flared, sweat pushing off the animal's hard muscles, not quite melting the snow and ice that landed on every inch of its coat. The stallion trudged through the snow loyally, giving Wallace everything it could muster with as steady a gait as was possible, considering the miserable circumstances and lack of open trail.

Wallace never named the horse. Didn't believe in such a thing. The horse was a means to an end, not a friend or a pet. If there was need for affection or a harsh command, Wallace called the horse "fella," and nothing else. He urged the stallion on relentlessly, pushing the animal as hard as he pushed himself.

Any thought of quitting, of finding shelter, was quickly absolved, tossed out of his mind, just like the image of comfortable horse pastures of summer from which the stallion had come, and the family Wallace had left behind to become a marshal. Both were frequent visions Wallace held for comfort, or to spur on his continuing anger, to remind himself of what had been lost to him. What was gone. Gone forever. Now was not the time for reminiscing, though, and he knew it. The focus on his prey was his top priority. One mistake, and Cal Wallace would be a dead man with no worries or fear at all.

He had been on Ben "Bad Eye" Matson's warrant for three years, nine months, and seven days, almost catching him twice.

Both men wore the scars from those encounters. A bullet wound for Matson, three inches above his heart. A knife wound for Wallace, solidly in his left shoulder.

Infection had set in the long cut and almost killed the marshal. If he didn't have the constitution and stubbornness of an ox, the chase would have already ended, and Matson would most likely be a free man. The outlaw would be left to spread his savage terror on more unsuspecting communities of the fine, hardworking men, women, and children of the Kansas District and beyond.

He was way beyond Kansas now. The chase had brought him far north, into Wyoming, Yellowstone country, unknown territory for the deputy.

Even through the blinding, blowing snow, Wallace could plainly see heavy drops of blood two feet in front of him, and the blur of uncertain movement. Shadows and snow, maybe the silhouette of a man, maybe not. Maybe just wind. Or a grizzly — if it was spring — a large creature of some kind. But it was blood for certain.

Wallace was sure that he had hit Bad Eye Matson with a decent but faraway shot, before the snow began to dump from the angry sky, and the cold-blooded killer had disappeared, wounded, into the thick ponderosas.

Wallace's Winchester was loaded and ready to fire, his finger nearly frozen to the trigger. All he needed was a sure target.

There would be no missing this time around.

Towering trees on both sides of the way forward continued to guide Wallace along what was normally a throughway, a foot path large enough for a single-file team of horses. Most likely used for sneaking into Montana.

He was sure Matson knew the lay of the land, knew the area when there wasn't snow on the ground. No man was lucky enough to find a trail in the snow like Matson had, without knowing it was there beforehand.

The weather continued to grow worse, but Wallace gave no thought to stopping, not as long as he could see the blood, or the shadowy, uncertain movement ahead. He pushed the stallion harder, and finally, the steed groaned and shook at the bit, complaining that it was already giving everything that it had to give.

Compassion was not a luxury afforded to the horse as far as Wallace was concerned, so he kneed the stallion harder, and prepared himself to lean back and take a swat at the stallion's rump. But the horse stopped suddenly, drawing Wallace's attention back to the trail, startling him, and raising his anger and frustration to a further degree.

Wallace's eyes were nearly iced up, and he immediately smelled the reason for the horse's abruptness before he saw it.

The black stallion reared back with a loud whinnying scream, as a huge mountain lion rushed into clear view, pushing through the heavy curtain of swirling snow and ice, angry, teeth barred, promoting the smell of death and hunger into a terrifying reality as it lunged forward, directly toward the unsuspecting Cal Wallace.

If he was going to die, he expected it to come from a gunshot, fast and quick, Matson hidden behind a tree or a rock. Not from a snarling beast that was interested only in dinner, not revenge, retribution, or the matter of right or wrong.

Wallace didn't have time to raise his Winchester.

The big cat jumped up at him and swatted at the rifle with its giant paw, knocking the weapon clean out of the marshal's grasp. It roared, exposing a cavernous mouth full of sharp, hungry teeth. A second swat quickly followed from the other paw, sending Wallace spiraling off the saddle, the force against his head from the blow so strong and sudden, it was just a matter of fortune that the mountain lion didn't decapitate the man.

The last thing Wallace heard before he blacked out was the distinct report of a gunshot, echoing through the mountains like the thunder of a coming storm — or the final end one, he wasn't sure which.

Cal Wallace wasn't sure whether he was dead or alive as he struggled to open his eyes.

"You're a lucky man, there, Deputy Wallace."

Wallace knew the voice, the timbre of it, anyway. The concerned tone of Bad Eye

Matson's voice confused him, though.

Upon opening his eyes, the deputy saw a fire, smelled meat cooking. His stomach rumbled to life upon the realization that he was actually alive enough to be hungry.

He was cold, but not chilled or frigid. He was covered with several layers of bear skin. Flames flickered off a stone ceiling, and shadows darted all around him. It only took Wallace a minute to realize he was inside a cave, the opening only a few feet to his right. The sky was clear, full of pin-prick silver stars, and a rising, full moon shined down on a snow-covered valley of ponderosa pines.

The recognition of pain followed next. His head felt like he had rammed it straight into the stone wall of the cave. But he knew that wasn't what happened. He'd been pummeled by a mountain lion, a winter-starved cougar set on making him a meal.

Wallace felt a wound on the side of his face, a cat scratch that wasn't too deep, but deep enough to leave a scar — if it healed.

Matson came in to clear view, leaning over Wallace with his pockmarked and hairless face, marred even more by the milky white pupil in his right eye that had given him his name.

"Here, take dis drink of water. Dinner'll

be ready soon," Matson said, offering Wallace a tin cup, filled to the rim with fresh water.

The deputy obliged, taking the water hungrily, glad for the moisture to overcome his dry mouth. He had no idea how long he had been out of consciousness, or in the cave.

"Whoa, whoa, there. Plenty more where dat come from."

Wallace took a breath. Water dribbled down his chin. "Why didn't you kill me."

Bad Eye Matson laughed, ran his hand through his thinning mop of black hair, then looked away from Wallace. "I've done a lot of bad things in my life, Deputy Wallace, but killin' a man on the day of da Lord's birth? Well, even I ain't dat much of a heathen. Killin' a cougar, on the utter hand? Any time I got a shot at one, I'm takin' it."

"Christmas, you say?"

Matson nodded. "At least till midnight, yes, sir. Christmas as plain as day. Only comes once a year."

Wallace forced a smile. Until that very moment, he had no earthly idea what day it was, more less that it was a holiday. All he could think about from one minute to the next was capturing Ben "Bad Eye" Matson, bringing him to justice, or killing him, whichever one came first. Since Wallace had no wife and no children himself, or much religion, for that matter, Christmas was, mostly, just another day.

His senses and strength were returning quickly. Wallace tried to sit up, and immediately discovered that his feet were bound with a heavy rope. His face ached, the wound sore, but Matson, or so Wallace assumed, had put a salve of some kind on it to keep the bleeding at bay, and hopefully, infection. It smelled like mint.

"You're not going anywhere anytime soon, there, Deputy Wallace. Now, I'll peel this bear skin away from you so's you can sit up and join me in some supper, but don't be thinkin' of takin' advantage of my hospitality and makin' any trouble. You're in no shape to wrestle with me, and I'm in no mood to fuss with you any more than I already have. You understand?"

"Where are my guns?"

Matson laughed again. It was an annoying laugh. Matson heehawed like a mule, showing a mouth full of rotted, yellow teeth. "Safe as safe can be. No worry there, lawman. What you need a gun for? Aren't you hungry? Wouldn't you like to rest, just one minute? Have a nice supper instead of worryin' over your duty and the fate of my neck?"

"No, not really. Not with the likes of you about."

"Me? The man who saved your life? Dat's a bit ungrateful, ain't it, Deputy?"

"Perhaps."

Matson stood over Wallace. "I can be gone, now, or we can have a nice Christmas meal. You think about that while I tend to those horses out there."

"My horse," Wallace said. "He's all right?"

"Got a claw down his neck, same as you. But I got the bleedin' stopped, packed it against infection. You'll see, dat horse'll be fine as a newborn once it heals over. Just like you."

Before Wallace could ask Matson again why he was helping him, the outlaw was gone, vanished from the cave like he was never there.

A breeze blew over Wallace, wrapping around the fire, changing the direction of smoke as it went — blowing it right in his face, burning his eyes and throat. He coughed, tried to move out of the way, but found he didn't have the strength — or the will to hardly move an inch. Being bound and incapacitated was something that Cal Wallace was completely unaccustomed to.

It wasn't long before Matson returned, whistling, a smile hung on his face like he had just heard the funniest joke of his life. "You ready for dat meal now, there, Deputy?"

Wallace nodded.

Matson scurried around the fire, filling a blue enamel plate with a thick chunk of meat, a couple of boiled potatoes, and a hearty helping of fresh carrots. He sat the plate down next to Wallace.

"You eat now, no funny bouts of movement. I'll shoot you if I have to, but I'd be obliged to do dat and wait until after midnight."

"I haven't the strength to flee."

Matson continued to smile. "Coffee with your meal, den?"

"Yes." Wallace shoveled food into his mouth, chewing one bite as fast as he could chew the next bite. The meat tasted odd at first, like none other that he'd ever eaten, but it was cooked perfectly and he couldn't resist its flavor. He didn't pay much attention to Matson. Wallace was lost in his own act of celebration of food, of being alive.

Out of his periphery, though, Wallace watched Matson sit and pick at his food, like he wasn't hungry, but didn't pay any close attention to the outlaw until his own plate and coffee cup were empty.

"You cook a fine meal, Matson," Wallace said, wiping his mouth, savoring the remaining flavors that still took residence on his tongue.

"Benjamin. My name is Benjamin."

"As you like."

"I am not the man you think I am, Deputy. This dime novel outlaw, called Bad Eye Matson. Bah, on dat."

"You've never killed a man, then?"

"I never said dat."

"Then you are the outlaw I am obligated to arrest."

The smile faded slowly from Matson's face. "I never kilt a man who didn't draw on me first."

"Save it for the judge."

Matson took a deep breath, stood up, walked to the entrance of the cave, and stared out at the full moon. "Time is running out. Would you like to enjoy a whiskey with me, Deputy?"

"I'm not a drinking man."

Matson turned around, and faced Wallace. "Humor me, Deputy Wallace. Let me believe for a minute, there, dat we are fine friends on this grand holiday. A long way from our family, we are. Time, miles, and deeds separate us all — but we are together sharing a meal. That in itself is a miracle, right there."

There was a look of melancholy on Matson's face that Wallace mistook at first for loneliness. It was something they both shared, and Wallace felt the weight of Matson's words on his own heart, and understood them to be true.

"Well, it is Christmas, after all, and you did save my life."

"Dat I did. It was no lucky shot, neither." Matson hurried to the other side of the cave and produced a whiskey bottle out of a satchel that was laying against a large boulder. "Here you go," he said, offering the bottle to Wallace.

The deputy took a tepid sip, let the whiskey burn its way down, then handed the bottle back to Matson.

They traded back-and-forth more times than Wallace could count, until finally, the comfort of the meal and the natural effect of the whiskey took over, and Cal Wallace drifted off to an easy sleep. The image of Benjamin Matson flickering away like a long, lost memory.

Bright light beaded into the entrance of the cave and eventually woke Wallace. He stirred slowly, his entire body aching, his face sore, but not stinging with infection. Without realizing it, Wallace sat up and stretched his arms out wide — waking like a toddler, freeing himself of the vacant dreamland he had just arrived from.

Only then did he discover that his feet were unbound, and the weight of the bear skin was light.

He was no longer captive, had been set free some time during the night.

The fire was smoldering, but the coffeepot still sat close. Wallace could smell the freshness of the coffee as he wiped away the sleep from his eyes, and gingerly pulled himself up.

There was no sign of Matson. But even more curious was the sight of Wallace's Winchester propped against the opposite wall, along with his fully dressed gun belt laying on the floor of the cave next to the rifle. They almost looked arranged, like gifts.

"Matson? Benjamin? Are you there?"

Only the echo of his own voice answered him. There was no sign of Ben "Bad Eye" Matson, or his gear. He was gone.

To make sure, Wallace grabbed up his rifle, then stumbled to the opening of the cave that looked out over the valley.

There was no sign of any living creature, other than the black stallion tied to a dead ponderosa, the wound on its neck visible and tended to.

Matson's horse was nowhere to be seen, nor was there any sign that the man had left, no tracks, nothing.

"I'll be damned," Wallace said aloud.

Slowly, he gathered himself and packed to leave. It took longer than normal since Wallace was not nearly himself, but he was alive, capable, if he moved slow and carefully, just like his horse.

Once mounted, Deputy U.S. Marshal Cal Wallace eased down the side of the mountain he had found himself on, sure that there was only one way in and one way out. It must have been an outlaw's den, known by certain men, and left stocked by a regular gang. That was the only explanation he could think of for Matson's hospitality, the fine meal he had shared the night before.

Once down on the trail, Wallace had a choice to make. Return the way he'd come, or head north into Montana, in hopes of finding a sign of Matson's presence to latch on to and continue on after the outlaw. Serve the warrant. See the man tried and hung, if it came to that.

Home was a long way off the way he'd come, and for a reason he couldn't very well describe or say out loud, Cal Wallace longed to see the flatlands of Kansas one more time in his life.

Maybe Christmas was still in the air — or maybe it was just time to call an end to the chase, and let the fates wrestle with Benjamin Matson about what was right and wrong.

Somewhere in the distance, a mountain lion screamed . . . the rage bouncing off the side of the mountain like thunder.

"Come on, fella," Wallace said, looking over his shoulder, gently patting the black stallion on the neck, "let's go home."

The Treasure Box

The prison doors slammed shut, and Charley Boles stumbled out into the dim light of freedom for the first time in four years.

A cool, steady breeze blew in off of San Francisco Bay, casting the ground beyond the tall brick wall in a cloud of deep, unwelcoming shadows. Charley stood within inches of San Quentin prison paralyzed like a rabbit, unsure of which way to dart after it had suddenly found itself out in the open under the eyes of a hungry predator, or in Charley's case, *predators*. A crowd had gathered to witness his departure. His freedom had been announced in the newspapers. It was not as festive an occasion as a hanging, but his departure, and the opportunity to see his face in the flesh, had drawn a fair amount of curiosity seekers.

Somewhere in the distance a steamship horn blew for the first time of the day, calling for boarding or departure, Charley wasn't sure which. Nor did he care much about ship schedules. He'd planned on traveling by foot, like usual. Ships made him sick. Horses scared him. Walking calmed him.

Charley hadn't expected the crowd. He figured any fame he might have garnered had dissipated like bay mist in the afternoon by now. He'd really hoped to just get on with it, walk away and leave the prison and his former life behind him, forever.

There was no way he was ever going to return to the terrors held inside those cold, clammy walls. Never. It was a solemn oath he'd sworn to himself every day, every minute he'd been behind bars, from the first second he'd been incarcerated. There was nothing he liked about prison. Nothing. And now that he was free, had survived the nightmare with his physical being mostly intact, he would do whatever he had to do to honor that oath.

Charley was fifty-nine now, but he felt like a very old seventy-nine. His bones ached. His hair had grayed completely from his once boyish black, and his skin was as pale as a flake of Red Devil lye. When he walked, he stooped over a bit, his narrow head forward, his eyes turned up so he could see where he was going. He was frail from the inside out, like a strong wind could knock him over and break him in half just for the fun of it. His health had set him free early. His sentence for armed robbery had been six years, but the warden and the state had taken mercy on him, sure that he wouldn't live to see his freedom if he served his full sentence. For the most part, Charley was in agreement with the powers that be. He smelled his death with each heavy breath.

The only remnant of his past, of his outlaw moniker, that he held onto now was the black duster and black bowler hat he wore. Beyond the two bits in his pocket, and a small satchel, his clothes were the sole possessions of this life. Quite a turn of events for a man who had robbed twenty-eight Wells Fargo stagecoaches in a matter of eight years.

The crowd stared at Charley, most of them disbelieving that he was the man they'd waited to see in the chilly, early morning drizzle. Most had paid a nickel. Others were newspaper reporters. But no one said a word. They just stood with their eyes wide open and mouths agape, confused or angry, Charley wasn't sure which.

The newspapers and dime novels had made him a mean rascal, a hero to some and the bane to others, before he'd ever set one foot in prison. Most surely Wells Fargo itself. Their stagecoaches and treasure boxes had been his focus, the only target he'd sought out during his career as a robber and thief.

Realizing the situation and his circumstance, Charley chuckled. Low at first, then out loud, like a madman — which was extremely out of character for him. He was a demure man, polite to a fault in most cases. And it wasn't as if Charley was a coldhearted killer. Hardly. He'd never even fired the shotgun he carried during the robberies, much less cause a man harm. Mostly, he used trickery. His first holdup was nothing more than convincing the driver and shotgun messenger that they were surrounded by armed bandits — when in truth, the bandits were nothing more than well-placed sticks in the scrub, set to resemble rifles. Violence and blood were not his cause. He hadn't been called "the gentleman bandit" for nothing.

The crowd murmured, stepped back, and turned their heads away from Charley. They parted slowly, expectantly, not out of fear or revulsion, as a long shadow and the sound of heavy horse's hooves gave the onlookers cause to part.

Charley blinked to clear his vision. His

eyes were unaccustomed to the outside light. Even the shadows seemed harsh and bright to him.

The chuckle died in his throat as a tall, well-muscled horse pushed through the crowd, a familiar rider saddled comfortably atop it.

"Thought I'd come to see you out, Charley," the rider said.

The man sat stiff and erect in the saddle and looked to be nearly the same age as Charley, but of much better health and stature. There was not a speck of dust to be seen on the rider's clothing, all gray with the exception of a heavily starched white shirt and shiny black riding boots with worn heels. There was no badge on his chest, but he carried himself like a lawman, a man on a mission with given power, whether from the state or some other entity. It was, of course, a well-earned posture, as the pearl-handled, silver-plated Colt on his hip suggested.

"I didn't expect to see you again, Hume," Charley said. "I figured you would be after some angry soul who had done your fine company wrong." His voice cracked and his fingers tingled. If there had been a rock nearby worth throwing, Charley would have thought about heaving it toward Hume's head, witnesses or not, but there wasn't a pebble to be found that could offer any serious injury to the man. He wouldn't do such a thing anyway — but he sure would think about it. The last four years were a misery of troubles worth a healthy dose of revenge.

James B. Hume was a Wells Fargo detective. He was the detective who had captured Charley after tracking down a simple, bloody handkerchief to a laundry. A bloody handkerchief that Charley had left behind, at a robbery, after being shot in the left hand. The wound still ached to this day. It was his only injury from his escapades, as he liked to think about the robberies. Funny he'd be the only one to get hurt, and caught because of it.

Hume had sat in wait for Charley after visiting almost a hundred laundries in San Francisco, trying to find the area he lived in. If it hadn't of been for the loss of that piece of cloth with those numbers on it, Charley was sure Hume would not have caught him when he did. Not then. Maybe the next time, or the next. Hume was a hard, dogged man, and he'd set his sights on Charley's capture as his one true calling in life. Obviously, four years hadn't dulled Hume's focus.

Hume nodded, but didn't smile. He

looked Charley hard in the eye. "That's what I'm doing here, sir. I've come after you. Our business is far from over."

"My debt is paid." Charley had not moved from the shadow, from next to the San Quentin wall, but Hume had rode his horse up so close to him that they were nearly touching nose-to-nose. The horse smelled of fresh soap, and its chestnut coat shined in the late morning light.

"You were convicted for one robbery, not twenty-eight," Hume said. His eyes were hard, gray as his overcoat, glazed over with the hollow emotion of a gunfighter, thoughtless to the life of his opponent. In another circumstance, Hume might have gunned Charley down right then and there, regardless of the law or moral outrage against it.

"There is no solid proof that I was involved in any of those robberies."

"As far as the local court of law is concerned, you are correct."

"Then I am a free man. I am not an illiterate, sir. I know my legal rights."

Hume nodded reluctantly. "Know this, Charley Boles. I will follow you to the ends of the earth. I will haunt your life every minute of every day, until you take your last breath, until I have succeeded in recovering what is duly owed to Wells Fargo. I will ensure that you never take another coin from the stagecoach line again. Is that clear?" He said it loud, and over his shoulder, so the whole crowd could hear his declaration.

"I returned that money. All I had," Charley protested. "I have made restitution for my actions, sir. I am a free man from this day forward, and I have the papers to prove it." He tapped his chest.

"You are not a free man, Charley Boles. And you never will be. Wells Fargo never forgets."

Charley nodded. He believed Hume. He surely did. Every word that the detective said. But Hume didn't know what Charley did. His life of crime was over. He'd had enough.

"I will commit no more crimes, sir. Of that, you can be assured and go to your grave with. I am reformed."

Hume scoffed with disbelief but said nothing. Perhaps he held his tongue for fear of what might come out in front of the crowd, which was peppered with newspaper reporters. Or maybe, he believed Charley. It was hard to tell. Regardless, Hume withdrew a small parchment, tied with a fancy knot, from his breast pocket, and tossed it down to Charley. "A wanted poster as a reminder of what lies ahead if you so much as sit on the bench in front of a Wells Fargo office."

Charley caught the parchment and quickly stuffed it in his own pocket, next to his walking papers.

A reporter pushed up alongside Hume's chestnut gelding. The crowd didn't hold back then, and they all rushed forward, ignoring Hume, or dismissing him now that he'd had his say.

"Tell us the true story, sir!" another reporter demanded. "Tell us of your escapades. Readers all over the country want to know of your intentions, your stories."

Charley cowered back against the wall, his eyes never leaving Hume's, who was backing up now, carefully, to avoid hurting anyone in the crowd.

The steamship horn blew again, and the drizzle grew heavier, into a slow, steady rain. Water dripped off Charley's bowler, and he longed to get moving, but found the crowd impassible. And there was a part of him, something held deep inside that he thought had died — enduring four years of impalpable food, vicious men without hope or manners at all — that enjoyed the attention. With his family long abandoned and long suffering, unaware of his health situation that had allowed for his freedom, as far as he knew, he'd expected to face this day alone, without celebration or a crowd of any kind.

"Tell us then, will you be trying your hand at more poetry?" the reporter demanded.

Charley smiled. To rouse and taunt Hume, he'd left some of his poetry behind at the holdups, but that poetry could never be traced back to him. At least not officially.

The one that everyone knew, the one that had been printed in the newspaper upon his capture, went like this:

> I've labored long and hard for bread,
> For honor, and for riches,
> But on my corns long you've tread,
> You fine-haired sons of bitches.*

Charley smiled at the thought of the poem. There was a pen stuffed inside the breast pocket of his coat. It was the only weapon he carried, now that he considered it. One that had caused him more grief than it was worth at times. He'd always fancied himself a writer. A famous writer. He wanted nothing but a life of finery, of wealth and stature, gleaned from words he put on the page. He'd tried, tried real hard, to sell

*The poem included in this story is attributed to Black Bart, but the author is not known for certain.

his stories and poetry when he was a young man, just off the boat from England, but he'd only met with failure. Abject failure. He couldn't raise a halfpenny for anything he wrote no matter how persistent he was with New York editors.

Charley had been so demoralized and so desperate for wealth and success that eventually he'd chosen robbing stagecoaches instead of continuing on with the pursuit of his dream of ever being a writer.

"Young man," Charley replied to the man inquiring about his further poetry endeavors, "didn't you just hear me say I'll commit no more crimes?"

It was a long journey to Visalia. Hardly a sprawling city like San Francisco, Visalia was a small town built largely by the gold rush, and serviced, thankfully, by the Butterfield Overland Stagecoach instead of the Wells Fargo line.

No one challenged Charley, or was any the wiser about his identity, on the stagecoach.

The sky had cleared, and more than a day had passed since Charley had had a decent meal. He made his way quickly to the Palace Hotel after departing the Butterfield, checked in under one of his many aliases,

C. E. Bolton, washed his face in the cheapest room he could let, then went down to the restaurant and quickly found a table.

The table was stuffed in a corner, in the shadow of a heavily draped window, so he could not be spotted, or if he was, not identified as the once-famous outlaw he knew himself to be. He wanted to eat in peace, and get on with whatever was next. After all of the desire he'd once had for fame, Charley Boles wanted nothing more than to be left alone.

The restaurant was dim and barely populated, leaving the cavernous room nearly quiet as a forgotten tomb. The walls and ceiling were covered with dark walnut. Oil sconces on the walls flickered lazily. The smell of the coal oil was overcome by the smells emanating from the kitchen, causing Charley's mouth to water even before he ordered his meal.

The closest patron was three tables away, an unseen man with his face stuck in a newspaper, obscuring Charley's view.

A waiter appeared at his table, a pimply-faced young man with a flop of black hair that looked like a whole host of rats might live atop his head. "What can I get you, sir?"

Charley stared at the menu, disregarding the price of any of the meals. The two bits in his pocket had multiplied, though Charley was not sure yet if he was comfortable with the cause. The trip to Visalia had been a compromise, an escape, a temptation. "I'll have the bean with crust soup, and the beef with vegetables," he said.

"Roast or boiled?"

"Roast."

"A vegetable?"

"Parsnips."

"Anything else?"

"Gravy," Charley said. "Lots of gravy."

The waiter nodded, then hurried back to the kitchen. Charley looked over to the man reading the paper, but he was gone. The chair was empty, and a half-empty glass of water sat on the table, the only hint that anyone had been there in the first place. He looked around and saw nothing, then shrugged. Again, it was of no matter to him. Just odd. People come and go all of the time. Something he'd have to get used to if he was going to stay in California, or anywhere near a Wells Fargo line. It was a choice he would have to make soon enough.

Time ticked away, and weakness came on Charley pretty quickly from the lack of consistent meals. He was off schedule, off time, off everything since leaving San Quentin, where everything had been done and decided for him. He wondered if he'd ever adjust on his own, or whether he'd just wither away and die.

Sometimes dying seemed the smart thing to do, the only thing to do. But there were still a few things he wanted to accomplish, and see, before he left this world.

"Here is your meal, sir." It was a different waiter. The man was older than the previous rat-haired boy. His thin, recently trimmed hair was speckled with a healthy dose of gray. He wore wireless glasses, exposing curious blue eyes, and he was dressed in a black suit, with a heavily starched shirt and no tie. In a swift, dancer-like move, the man slid a plate in front of Charley and promptly lifted a silver cloche, exposing more food than he was expecting.

There were two large pieces of roasted beef, a double helping of parsnips, all covered in a rich, velvety gravy, along with a bunch of cooked carrots and two oversized sourdough biscuits drenched in melted butter. He held a bowl of crusted bean soup in the other hand and swiftly placed it next to the plate in front of Charley.

The aroma from the meal was sweet and raw, appealing to his deepest, most primal desires. He had to swallow hard to keep from drooling.

"Does this suit you, sir?" the man asked.

"What happened to the boy?" Charley asked, staring at the food, stunned by the amount of it all, by the breathless beauty of each piece of it. A naked woman would have been less welcome before him.

"I thought I should serve you, sir. It's an honor to have you in my establishment."

"You're the owner?"

The man nodded, then smiled broadly. "I am. It is a rare occasion that we get a man of such renown in our presence."

"I beg your pardon?"

"Aren't you . . . ?"

"I'm nobody," Charley said, cutting the man off before he could say his name, standing up abruptly. The chair toppled over behind him. He stared at the plate longingly. "I'm nobody," he repeated. "I regret to say it, but I must leave your fine establishment. I hope you understand."

He didn't wait for the owner to give permission, or comment. Charley pushed by the man, holding his breath as tightly as he could so he wouldn't breath in one more whiff of the fine plate of beef and fixings he was leaving behind.

Without looking back, Charley rushed up to his room, grabbed up what few belongings he could claim, and rushed out of the

Palace Hotel without speaking a word to another human being.

The train whistled early in the morning, and the sway and grind of the brakes woke Charley from a light sleep. He glanced out the window, the ground flat as far as he could see, the sky gray, the color of a mourning suit. His memories of the whistle-stop rose from deep in his mind, offering a metallic taste on his tongue and a slow, melancholy exhale. He'd thought he would never leave California, and never ever return to Hannibal, Missouri.

Charley squared himself in the bench seat, gaining his balance as the train came to a full stop. It would be easy to stay on and keep on going, to stay seated, but there was something he had to see, something he had to know.

Charley made his way slowly off the train. He hated to leave it. He'd found some peace there, once he'd boarded in Nevada. No one recognized him. He was faceless, just another person traveling east, broken by the West, only a few dreams left, but hardly any energy to pursue them. Hope rode toward the Pacific, not away from it.

The air smelled of mud and dead fish, a far cry from the saltiness of the sea that had pervaded his nose and body during his stay in San Quentin. Charley had forgotten how the mighty Mississippi River touched everything in Hannibal, from the air to the soft, silty ground. He was glad he was going away from the river, away from the smell of death and uncertainty.

He was sure of his destination, and it was a short, uneventful journey to the house he sought to find. The trees seemed taller than the last time he was there, nearly doubled in size, but the house itself was small, two stories, with a white picket fence, nicely tended to with nary a weed showing at the foundation. Without double-checking, Charley knew instinctively that this house was where his wife, Mary Elizabeth, called home.

He stopped in the shadows of a great oak, three houses away on the opposite side of the street, swallowing hard, doing his best to remain hidden, hugging the tree tight.

Mary Elizabeth had been his wife for over thirty years, almost forty. She had seen him off to the goldfields of California twice, on an adventure to gain wealth, but which only left him with two dead brothers, empty pockets, and the sense of defeat that would never leave him. Then he was off again, to the War Between the States where he served with the 116th Illinois for three years, returning with all of his limbs but with a memory of horrors and of being wounded in Vicksburg. After recuperating, he was off again, this time to Idaho and Montana, prospecting, desperate for success, finding it eventually, but not fully, as a stagecoach robber in California.

Charley had stopped writing Mary after the first successful robbery in Calaveras County. It had been nearly thirteen years, and he hoped upon hope that she had gotten on with her life, claimed him as dead, her struggles with him over.

In the times that Charley was home, when he'd shared Mary's bed, he managed to father four children. Children who barely knew that they had a father. He knew nothing of them now, what they had grown up to be. But he knew as sure as the sun rose in the East that they probably hated the ground he walked on for abandoning them for his own selfish dreams. Still, he had to see for himself.

Charley stood against the tree for nearly an hour before catching a glimpse of Mary Elizabeth. The sky had remained an unchanging gray, offering neither rain nor the optimism of a blue patch. It was as if the world was in a sorrowful mood, unrelenting in its effort to color the day with sadness.

A buggy stopped in front of the small white house, and a young man with familiar features, well-dressed and neat as the yard, hopped quickly to the ground and ran to the door. In a blink, the man was escorting Mary Elizabeth to the buggy. She was well-dressed, too, right down to the bustle that had long since gone out of favor in California.

Charley strained to see Mary Elizabeth's face, to remember the touch of her skin, the smell of her neck, but he stood back then, pushing away any carnal desires he might still hold. Those days were past. Love and the consistency of affection were never of greater value to him than gold or adventure, and that wasn't going to change now.

The buggy headed up the street, and Charley had to slide around the tree so he would not be seen. The man was one of his sons, David or Robert, he wasn't sure which. Regardless, there was a smile on his face and in his eyes. Mary's, too. She seemed healthy and content, off on a pre-arranged errand it looked, maybe to a lunch or tea, that would not have given any regard to the weather.

He heard Mary Elizabeth laugh as the buggy sped by. The sound of her happiness almost folded him over. His failures hit him like a ton of rocks falling out of the sky. He hadn't expected to find anything else. As a matter of fact, he'd hoped to find that Mary Elizabeth had gotten on with her life, and from the looks of it, she had. Showing his face now would only destroy any work she had done to find a soft place in the world. And no matter his age, or his health, Charley knew that he would grow restless if he stayed in Hannibal. He'd leave Mary Elizabeth again as sure as the sky was blue above those depressing gray clouds.

He'd found what he came for.

It was a quiet trip to New York City. But before leaving Hannibal for good, Charley wired James B. Hume and accepted his final offer: Go east, and Wells Fargo will pay you five thousand dollars for your troubles.

The offer, along with fifty dollars stuffed in the parchment Hume had tossed Charley outside of San Quentin, had gotten him to Visalia, and then on to Hannibal, and now back to his original American home, New York City.

The up-front money was a peace offering, a good-faith down payment on what was to come, if Charley promised to vacate the West, and never rob another Wells Fargo stagecoach again. It was a promise he gladly made.

It didn't take long for the money to show up in Charley's bank account. But, of course, it wasn't in Charley's name. This time he chose C. B. Black. It would be the last time he would ever need to change his name again.

The city welcomed Charley, and he welcomed the pulse of it, embraced it, so much so that he felt a little younger, a little hopeful, more optimistic than he thought he would. He decided not to sit around and wait to die — even though he thought plenty about the day when he would no longer walk on the earth.

So it was that Charley Boles, C. E. Bolton, C. B. Black, and a host of other aliases, most notoriously, Black Bart, found himself on the steps of the *New York Times*, itching to start a new career, a new job, that didn't require adventure or travel, both of which had worn him out, but instead required only the pen that he carried in a small wood box in his coat pocket and a piece of paper.

Charley Boles worked every day for the next twenty-two years as an obituary writer — writing, of course, his own obituary over and over again, more times than he could count.

Silent Hill

I followed the trail, and the wind, into the town. My throat was raw, my nose filled with dust and dirt, and my chest heaved like my lungs were soaked in kerosene. Oddly, as winded as I was, I could not feel my heart beating in my chest.

I had no map, and after wandering for days, I was certain that I was lost. The town, no name posted on its perimeter, offered hope, a reprieve, a place to rest.

As is my custom when arriving in a new town, I headed straight for the saloon.

The barkeep waited for my two bits to appear out of my pocket before he offered to pour my whiskey. I obliged, though reluctantly. Lady Luck left my side a hundred miles ago, leaving my coffer, as well as my body, in a meager, unhealthy state.

"You look like you need more than a dose of whiskey." A half-full glass slid toward me after the last of my coins disappeared into the barkeep's massive hand. "If you're lookin' for a game, the players that matter won't be in until the sun sets."

The pomade had long since washed out of my hair, and my linen vest was covered with the same dust that filled my nose, but I imagine a barkeep knows a down-on-his-luck gambler when he sees one.

"Could be," I said. "But I was hoping you could help me find a woman."

I coughed, then fought it back so I would not alarm the few patrons in the back of the bar. My malady had yet to fully show itself, but I could feel it growing, eating away at my insides like a maggot gnawing on the flesh of a winterkill elk.

The barkeep's eyes narrowed. His stomach was as big as a side of beef, his arms looked like hammers, and his apron was worn and tattered at the hems. Just like the saloon, the barkeep looked like he had seen better days.

"This ain't a cat house, stranger." He grabbed a broom.

"No, no. You misunderstand." I reached into my pocket, not breaking eye contact with the barkeep. "My name's Eddie. Edward, really. Edward Blackstone. Most folks call me Blackjack Eddie."

Before I could pull out the neatly folded

placard from my breast pocket, the barkeep took a hard swing at my head with the broom and sent me sprawling to the floor.

The placard flew from my hand and skittered across the floor.

I have only two items in my possession that remain of the life I once lived, the placard and a small locket I wear around my neck. They both are more valuable to me than a bag full of gold.

The locket and placard are dear to me, for they are the only love I have known since my boyhood and the long, two-thousand-mile train ride west. Without them, a long-ago promise will remain unfulfilled, and I will be truly alone in this world . . . and, perhaps, the next.

My father arrived home every day promptly at 4:30 in the afternoon. He would usually have a fresh cut of meat in hand for our dinner and the day's newspaper for stories to regale afterward. He always had time for a warm and generous hug for my younger sister, Gillian, and I. Father did not play favorites; his affection was measured just like everything else in his life.

He worked as an accountant in a financial firm, Slade, Crothers, & Lieberman, a block from the new Chemical Bank. Everything was a bustle in New York City then, new construction, new people arriving every day. The city throbbed with vibrations of every sort — language, food, and music.

It was enough to overwhelm the senses, but as a child my environs just fed my taste buds and my ability to appreciate the most delicious aromas. All are just a memory now, evoked only in dreams and nightmares.

My mother taught piano to those who could afford it. Her reputation had followed her from her home country, England, and her wares floated out of our third-story apartment window like sweet cooing doves.

Every afternoon, our parlor was filled with the comings and goings of well-heeled girls, prim and proper, and a few reticent boys, as our mother took them through the paces of Bach, Beethoven, and Chopin.

Music was the heart of our home, but to me it was mostly the unstructured noise of tiresome beginners.

We were by no means wealthy, but we did not have to look far to know how lucky we were. My parents had prospered once they arrived in America, unlike so many others, left to the dingy streets of New York to fend for themselves, with few skills and no family.

I have seen coyotes show more manners

than some people fresh off the boat.

I loved the city, loved the warmth of our apartment with the heavy mahogany furniture and thick wool carpets shipped across the ocean, and the wondrous taste of biscuits and cucumber sandwiches set upon silver plates with our afternoon tea.

But Gillian loved the city, and our life, even more than I. She was a prodigy on the piano. My mother's best student. She could play "Chopsticks" and make us all cry — but she was beyond that, even at five.

Each note of Chopin's Piano Concerto no. 2 in F Minor was so full of exuberance and emotion that you thought your eardrums were going to shatter and your heart was going to break.

People would gather on the street below to listen to the sweeping arpeggios and themes from various nocturnes.

Gillian was unaware of her gift, of the attention it brought to her. Her talent was not a surprise to anyone in our household, no more so than my growing skill of calculating large numbers off the top of my head — a game my father and I used to play as we walked the streets on an errand for my mother.

Our life was a dream come true.

Until the fire took it all away.

∎ ∎ ∎ ∎

The barkeep's foot rested heavily on my wrist. "I've seen way too many derringers appear out of nowhere from the likes of you to risk my life over a shot of whiskey."

"I assure you, sir, I have no intention of drawing a weapon." I struggled to pull my hand out from under the man's buffalo-sized boot. My chest burned like it was on fire. Spittle seeped out of the corner of my mouth.

He pressed his boot down harder, eliciting a sharp groan from the depths of my gut. I feared my wrist was going to break, an injury that would surely be my last — for my body has chosen to rebel against itself.

"Liars are a dime a dozen. I have the scars to prove it," the barkeep said.

"Let him go, Moses."

It was a woman's voice, strong and demanding, coming from behind me. The pressure on my wrist immediately ceased as the heavy man stepped away.

I sat up, my eyes scanning the floor for the placard and the physical presence of my rescuer.

My bones were intact, but what pride or hope I had left had almost escaped me entirely.

The woman was two heads shorter than the barkeep, Moses, I presumed, but her bulky frame was similar to his, as were her eyes: narrow and dark as a moonless night, void of pupil or emotion. She was no dancing queen, but she was attractive in an odd sort of way, with flaming red hair, and dressed in a green satin dress that was perfectly fitted. Her frilly hat was made for Sundays and sashaying down the street of a finer city than the one I had found myself in. The brilliance of her colorful appearance was calming, like a rainbow after a fierce storm. She looked oddly out of place, and for a moment, I wasn't sure she was real.

The woman unfolded the placard as I sat up and was staring at me curiously. "Gillian?" she whispered softly.

I nodded. "Yes. You know of her?" I coughed again, deeper this time. I had found the placard posted outside a saloon five years before, my first clue that Gillian was still alive, playing piano professionally like I always knew she would.

She returned the gesture. "Pour the man a drink, Moses. A friend has joined us."

The blow had weakened me, but the woman's acknowledgment of Gillian's presence gave me a boost of energy that I thought was long gone.

I was on my feet without any effort at all.

Moses scurried behind the bar, his head down.

"You'll have to forgive my brother, Mr. Blackstone."

"Edward. Eddie if you prefer."

"Moses and I try to run a clean establishment, Edward. To many we are sinners, but that does not mean we cannot offer entertainment services to those who seek them. Though we do not profit off of the sale of feminine pleasures, we do profit off a fair bottle, an honest game of faro, and the best music to be found anywhere near or far. What remains of our clientele appreciates our efforts, but I fear our days here are numbered. This town is on its last breath, as is our establishment. The Devil has decided to claim our property and dreams. We are all on edge. Leery of strangers."

"I didn't intend to offend anyone," I said.

"Moses is quick to react since his heart was broken by a woman of, how shall I say it? Nightly manners?"

"Gillian?" My own heart sank.

The woman laughed suddenly like I had said something funny. "Oh, no. I'm sorry to imply such a thing." She extended her hand. "My name is Ruth Hathaway, or Miss Ruth, as your sister insisted on calling me on our first meeting. Please sit down, Edward. We have a lot to talk about."

I led Gillian out of the blazing apartment building in the wee hours of the night, smoke roiling around our feet, wet shirts thrown over our heads. We both thought our mother and father were right behind us, for it was they who had roused us out of bed when the fire broke through to our apartment. But we got separated in the trample, in the chorus of screams, in the disorienting pleas for help from the floors above.

They died when a flaming beam fell on them. Their bodies were crushed and burned beyond recognition.

I would like to believe they had left us only to offer someone of less strength and courage aid and rescue. The only identifying remnants of their earthly existence were their wedding rings and the two small gold lockets my mother wore around her neck.

The lockets held pictures of Gillian and I. The picture of Gillian was taken when she was just a girl of five, golden curls flowing over her shoulder onto a fragile lace collar — an expensive portrait that serves as another reminder that our lives were once full, and rich. Gillian's angelic beauty was evident, even then.

I have worn the locket around my neck ever since. And Gillian wears the locket that holds the picture of me, a miniature version of my father in physical appearance and like mind.

Void of any relatives, we were whisked off to the Children's Aid Society shortly after our parents' bones and ashes were laid ceremonially to rest in a pauper's grave.

The fire destroyed everything that they owned, and though my father worked at a financial firm, there was no record of any investments — we had no money. At least that is what we were told, by a man with thinning hair and tobacco breath who stood in representation of Slade, Crothers, & Lieberman, at the end of the funeral.

The Children's Aid Society offered few comforts, and more terror than one child, much less two, should be left to imagine.

The only thing that Gillian and I had to hang onto was each other. We vowed early on, after our shock and grief began to subside, to remain together no matter the cost.

And so we did.

Until that solemn day when we both boarded the Orphan Train, and were shepherded out of our wonderful city on the harbor, full of tall ships, teems of people, wonderful smells of food, and the memories of our parents.

We began our journey west, nervous and afraid, to a land that seemed barren, dry, and populated with people who eyed us with only opportunity and greed.

Moses set a full glass of whiskey on the table in front of me. Miss Ruth sat across from me, her mass so large the chair all but disappeared in a sea of green.

"Tell me of Gillian, please. You are the first person in my travels who has known of her. Is she still here, in this town?" I asked.

Miss Ruth shook her head no. "I'm sorry, Edward, she has been gone from here for nearly two years. Ages, it seems, since someone has touched the piano with such finesse. She was a sweet nectar, her talents were far above the stature of our lowly establishment. Her presence was a blessing, and I was sad to see her go. My pockets have not been as full since, and I don't expect they ever will be again now that we teeter on the edge of loss."

I smiled, ignoring the soulful moan of Miss Ruth's mention of her current calamity. How could I not? "I always knew Gillian would be great, perhaps, even famous.

She would have traveled the world if our parents would not have died when we were children," I said.

"Instead of playing for kings and queens," Miss Ruth said, "she played for the likes of Moses and me. All the while, watching out of the corner of her eye, hoping that you would walk through the door."

"She searched for me, as well?"

"Still does, as far as I know."

I took a drink of the whiskey. My chest had began to boil, and the last thing I wanted to do was break into a coughing fit.

The news of Gillian was an elixir, a salve that soothed any thought of my illness. I wanted to touch the keys on the piano that she touched and feel close to her, feel the warmth of her touch, share the sameness of our blood and memories that have been missing from my life for so long, but I could not move. I was weak, and afraid I would miss a word of Miss Ruth's tale of my long-lost sister.

"She knew of your reputation," Miss Ruth continued. "Knew that you gained a certain amount of fame yourself. But you moved around too frequently for her to catch up with you. She missed you by two days in Dodge City. She searched all sixteen saloons until, finally, someone at the Long Branch told her of your victory in a card game there."

"Blackjack Eddie? She knew of me as a gambler?"

"You look surprised."

"My father would be ashamed that I have used my skills for a deviant cause."

"Surviving is not deviant."

"Ah, but cheating is."

"Gillian told me of your skills, so please be aware that you won't be counting any cards here. My till is thin enough."

"My gaming days are nearly at an end," I said. "My pockets are empty, and I have lost the will to maintain my fame. I promised Gillian that I would come for her, and I hope to fulfill that promise. Do you know where she went?"

"Yes," Miss Ruth said. "I do."

We did not know we were leaving until the day before. It was a Monday bath that warned us. Of course, by then, we had seen many children leave the confines of the Children's Aid Society before us. They vanished like they had never existed, nary a trace of them left behind. Our fear, Gillian's and mine, was that we would be separated; only one of us sent West, while the other remained behind in New York.

Fate spared us the blow of separation, if only temporarily, when we both found a new set of clothes on our beds and our hair tended to like we were to be department store models after our "special" bath.

The next day, we were herded to the train station and pushed on board the Orphan Train under the watchful eye of the placing agent who was to accompany us. The man's name escapes me, but he was flustered and mean, overwhelmed by the forty or so waifs and street urchins put in his charge.

The novelty of the train ride soon fell away. It was miserably hot inside because of the unrelenting summer heat. The seats were thin and uncomfortable, and worse than anything else, the passenger car was filled with the smell of bile from children suffering from the constant sway of the rail car. Gillian was afflicted far worse than I.

We held hands continually.

"Promise me we'll always be together," Gillian said just after we crossed the Mississippi River.

Our parents had been dead for nearly three years. Gillian was ten years old, and just as I was a mirror image of my father, Gillian favored my mother. I could not look into her eyes without wanting to cry.

"I promise."

We had both been cheated, stolen from, and lied to since the day of the fire. I wasn't sure I could keep my promise to her any longer, but I could not bear to see her afraid.

She rested her head against my shoulder, the golden curls straight now and lacking any hint of luster. Even then Gillian looked frail, haunted by fire and the misery of loneliness.

I could only hope the home we were going to would be gentle, our new parents understanding and kind. Anything had to better than the institutional life two thousand miles behind us — at least, that is what I thought at the time.

Sleep came intermittently, and our nerves were on end at every stop. No one knew how long it would take us to arrive in Kansas. Each time the brakes squealed, Gillian clutched my hand with all of the energy she had, afraid that we had arrived at our final destination.

I can still feel the pain of her touch when I squeeze my hands together.

"Gillian told me to tell you that she would go to Silent Hill and wait for you there. If the wait became too long, she would leave word of her whereabouts at the saloon, just like she has done here," Miss Ruth said.

"Silent Hill," I uttered, barely able to speak the name of the town aloud.

"Gillian felt the same way, I'm afraid. But she thought you might look for her there."

"I vowed never to return."

"I tried to persuade her to stay. But she is willful."

"She was good for your business."

"It was more than that," Miss Ruth said, clenching her teeth after the words had left her mouth, forcing the fullness of her face to draw so tightly her lifeless eyes bulged.

"I'm sorry, I didn't mean to offend you, Miss Ruth. My sister and I have been on the stiff for so long cynicism has become a code."

"I cared for your sister. She was like a canary with a broken wing. I have never had any children of my own so love does not come easy for me. Moses has always been my protector, my closest confidant. I felt her emptiness immediately."

I sat back in my chair and studied Miss Ruth. Her emotion was forced, her eyes averted to the door, away from me. For the first time since our conversation began, I felt like she was not telling me everything, that she was hiding something. My gambler's instinct warned me something was wrong — that it was time to stand up from the table before I lost everything I had.

I was uncertain of my location, how far I had wandered before stumbling on Miss Ruth's saloon. "How far is Silent Hill from here?" I asked, as I pushed my chair away to stand up.

"A day's ride, more or less, true north," Miss Ruth said. "Why don't you rest up for the night before leaving? There's a bunk in the storeroom, and a good meal wouldn't hurt you none."

The thought of climbing back in the saddle did not appeal to me, at least not physically. I wasn't sure I had the strength to make the trip. But knowing Gillian was close, that I had caught a whiff of her trail, gladdened my heart, even if I had trepidation about Miss Ruth's intentions.

I relaxed back into the chair, wooed by the thought of food. "In the morning, then."

"Good," Miss Ruth said. "But I have a favor to ask of you before you leave."

"A favor?" I was as far down on my luck as I could go, and I was short of favors — but Miss Ruth had given me something that I had longed for, a thin piece of hope that Gillian still walked this earth. Still, even with the gift, I was distrustful.

The door of the saloon pushed open and

a sudden burst of wind snaked around my ankles. A cold chill, that had no association with fever, ran up the back of my neck. I followed Miss Ruth's gaze to the door.

Upon seeing the fellow striding into the saloon, dressed impeccably, fresh pomade eliciting a confident shine that extended all of the way down to his highly polished boots, I knew the favor Miss Ruth asked.

She aimed to profit off my skills, just as she had Gillian's. I knew the gentleman, and the gentleman knew me.

Mysterious John Harvey and I had a long history.

If my instinct was still intact, something told me there was far more at stake for me than a set of clean sheets and a piece of well-cooked meat.

Rain had just stopped falling when the train came to its final stop.

There were twelve of us boys and only one girl, Gillian, remaining on the train. The rest of our group of orphans from the Children's Aid Society had already set upon their new lives at various stops across the state of Kansas. I could only hope that their journey, like ours, would lead to a happy end.

A creaking sign, waving in the persistent,

cold wind informed us that we had arrived in Silent Hill, Kansas.

The placing agent led us single file down the main street of town.

Silent Hill looked nothing like New York City, like anything Gillian and I were accustomed to. Muddy streets. Single-level wood frame buildings that were sparse and weathered. The sky was larger than I could have ever imagined it truly was — gray and moody, full of rolling, bubbling rain clouds that seemed to go on forever.

Even in the middle of the day, there was an eerie quiet, a lack of human activity in the town. The only consistent sound was the whine of the wind. It felt strong enough to topple us over, or go in one ear and all of the way out the other.

"I don't like this place," Gillian said.

I could hardly feel my fingers, she was squeezing my hand so hard.

"It's not so bad," I lied.

A crowd was hovering outside the opera house. They parted silently as we approached.

As we passed, I searched the crowd, hoping to find a kind face, a nod, an acknowledgement, from someone that seemed recognizable. I realize now that I was looking for love, a hint of it anyway. Why would someone agree to adopt an unknown child from two thousand miles away if there was not love in their heart?

I saw only fear and judgement in the eyes of those we passed. Love was a lost memory, never to be truly found again.

I was to be a workhorse, a laborer, a body to tend to as if it were nothing more than an animal that could easily be put down and replaced.

My boyish desire for comfort and understanding was dying as I made the walk up to the stage in that opera house — but I didn't know it, couldn't imagine it, then. I still believed in the goodness of people . . . and myself.

We stood there like cattle, facing a crowd of strangers whose presence promised to change our lives forever.

The placing agent, who looked even angrier and more exhausted than he did when we first left New York City, joined three men and one woman. They spoke in soft tones, and pointed to the crowd. The three men and woman were obviously members of the committee in Silent Hill that had lined up potential families to adopt those of us from hopeless circumstances.

One of the men, dressed in black and no bigger around than a twig, announced,

"The children are now available for inspection."

The placing agent nodded in agreement.

Slowly, the crowd broke apart, and people approached us curiously. Some checked our ears to see if they were clean. One man grabbed my arm and squeezed as hard as he could, trying to determine the size of my muscles.

I jerked my arm away, and though I was tempted to spit at the man, I restrained the urge. I didn't want to make a bad show of myself. I knew my manners, and I hoped my discomfort at being prodded and poked would not overcome them.

The man eventually moved on, though he eyed me like he might have found what he was looking for.

Gillian stood behind me, shivering.

Fear has a metallic taste to it — and the air was filled with gunmetal, iron, and hidden tears. Each time someone touched me, I nearly let go of my bladder.

A woman dressed in widow weeds stopped in front of me. The placing agent was two steps behind her.

"Well," the woman said. "Aren't you a fine-looking little fellow."

I could hardly believe my ears.

The woman sounded just like my mother,

her accent proper English. Not only did the woman look formal, fully in mourning, but there was a softness in her eyes that made my heart melt. I could almost taste a cucumber sandwich.

Gillian peered out from behind me.

"And you must be the girl I've heard so much of," the woman said, a smile appearing on her face like a ray of sunshine peeking from behind a dark cloud. "I understand you play the piano beautifully. Is that true?"

"Yes, ma'am," Gillian whispered.

"Oh, that is lovely. Just lovely. I have a piano in my parlor. Would you like to come and see it?" The woman extended her hand, a gold band still on her finger.

"Yes." Gillian had not touched a piano since the night before our parents died. She took the widow's hand and looked over her shoulder at me. "What about Edward?"

It was then that I noticed the man who squeezed my arm, standing behind the placing agent. The taste of cucumber sandwiches washed out of my mouth, replaced by iron and gunmetal.

"I'm sorry. I only have room for one."

Gillian's screams sounded like the wind on the worst Kansas day. Her eyes were filled with terror and tears as she disappeared from my view for the last time, fighting to escape the widow's grasp.

The placing agent, and the man who would become my adopted father and tormenter, restrained me as I fought futilely to reach Gillian. It was the end of everything I knew — and the start of an even more miserable existence.

"I'll come for you, I promise!" I screamed after Gillian. "I'll come for you."

But I couldn't. I was a prisoner on a farm in Silent Hill, fed gruel and beat with a belt when I didn't do what I supposed to do, or sassed back at Wilmer Beatty, the meanest man in the world. Even though I quit believing in God, I prayed every night that Gillian's life was better than mine.

I escaped when I was seventeen, and not being privileged to the location of the widow's home, I've been searching for Gillian ever since.

Mysterious John Harvey sat down at the table, opposite me. "I heard you were dead," he said.

"Funny. I heard the same thing about you."

Harvey motioned for Moses to come over to the table. Miss Ruth was now standing at the bar, watching us both with trepidation, the exact details of her favor interrupted by

Mysterious John Harvey's entrance.

"A whiskey for me and my friend."

"I've had enough," I said.

"A game then? If I remember right, the last time we met you walked away from the table before I had the chance to empty your pockets."

"My pockets are empty now." Our last meeting was a hundred miles ago, when Lady Luck and my body turned on me the final time, and I was too weak to keep count of the cards. I wandered for days, in and out of consciousness, in and out of towns, where I heard Mysterious John Harvey was shot, just outside of Dodge City when he was caught cheating, an ace up his sleeve.

Moses set a whiskey in front of Harvey. "No," he said to me, "they're not. He's playing for the house, Mr. Harvey."

A laugh escaped Mysterious John Harvey's tight mouth. "You have very little left to lose, Ruth. I will own this place if Blackjack Eddie's luck is as miserable as it looks. Are you sure you're willing to risk everything on a stranger?"

"He's no stranger," Miss Ruth said.

"Very well. Eddie?"

I stared at Harvey, knowing full well he would do anything to win. I had to wonder if I was up to the challenge, even if it was prideful. I turned my attention to Miss Ruth. "So if Mysterious John wins, your establishment is his? What is my prize?"

Before Miss Ruth could answer, Moses plopped down a deck of cards between Harvey and I. "Your freedom," he said, digging a handful of chips out of his apron.

I must have had an astonished look on my face, because Harvey burst out laughing. "Looks like a high stakes game. Stud poker?"

"I'm sorry, Edward. I should have told you. Gillian took the last of our prospects with her. You're our only hope. You have to stay to repay her debt."

I took a deep breath, not fully comprehending the situation, other than I knew I had to play. And I had to win to repay whatever my sister's debt was. "Stud poker it is," I said.

Time seemed to stand still. The light outside did not change, and I would not have noticed if it did. A man in the back walked to the piano and began to play *That Old Gang of Mine.* I had not noticed him before, he seemed to appear out of nowhere.

Our stacks stayed even for several hands, until the luck shifted and Mysterious John Harvey hit a winning streak. I suspected he was cheating. He knew I was counting, but my marks weren't holding, my mind foggy, so I quit the effort.

"Take off your vest, Harvey. I want to see your sleeves."

Miss Ruth and Moses hovered behind me like I was giving birth to a baby. My whiskey glass was never empty.

Harvey did not do as I asked; instead, he glared at me and dealt. "This is a fair game, Eddie."

My first card up was an eight of clubs. The hole card was a queen of hearts. I had no choice but to bet. I was growing weaker by the moment. The next card, dealt up, was an ace of spades. I bet half of my stack. Harvey did the same. He was showing a pair of kings. My chances of winning were slim, and we both knew it.

The next card Harvey dealt me face up was an eight of diamonds. I bet half again, leading Harvey to do the same in kind, raising three times until I had one chip left.

My chest heaved and my vision was beginning to blur.

The last card dealt was an ace of hearts. Harvey was showing a pair of kings, an ace of clubs and a two of diamonds. I did not take my eyes off him. The piano player quit playing. Silence engulfed the room when I threw in my last chip, called and flipped over my cards. Aces and eights.

"The dead man's hand," Harvey whispered.

"Take off your vest, Harvey," I repeated, as I slid my hand under the table and grappled for the derringer in my boot.

This time Mysterious John Harvey obliged. An ace of spades spilled onto the table out of his sleeve. I smelled a familiar aroma, iron — fear, I thought, until I saw the bullet hole and bloodstain on Harvey's shirt, just underneath his heart. He smiled at me and nodded, acknowledging what I had feared since I had begun to play. My weapon would do me no good against a dead man.

I realized then that tuberculosis had somehow captured me, soaked my lungs one last time. I just couldn't place when — somewhere in my wandering, along the dusty trail, before I stumbled into Miss Ruth's saloon. Dead, even though I didn't know it.

Harvey turned his card over. All in all he had a pair of kings, an ace of clubs, a two of diamonds, and a two of spades. My guess was he was going to slip in the ace of spades until he saw mine. He'd done it before.

"What is the name of this town?" I asked, trying to stand.

"Purgatory," Miss Ruth said. "You're in Purgatory."

There was piano music in the wind as I entered Silent Hill. The opera house looked like it had received a new coat of paint, the streets were clean, free of mud, and the sky was crystal clear. Sapphire blue. The color of Gillian's eyes. I never imagined Silent Hill would look like Heaven, if there was such a thing.

I felt revived, free of pain, once I left Miss Ruth and Moses in Purgatory. Mysterious John Harvey was left to pay off his debt — I'm not sure what his penance was. Mine had been playing a fair game, winning without cheating.

I could not contain myself when I walked into the saloon. Gillian was sitting at the piano, playing Chopin. She turned and looked at me, blonde curls falling over her shoulder, a glow about her I could only remember seeing when she was a child, and rushed to me, her embrace warm and happy. Tears flowed down her cheeks.

"I've been waiting for you," she said happily.

"I know. I'm sorry it took me so long."

We stood looking at each other for what seemed eternity. Death had taken her, too, somehow, somewhere. She obviously had a debt to repay — it was the only way to explain her presence in Purgatory. I was burgeoning with questions about her life.

After a moment, Gillian grabbed my hand. "Come, we must go."

It was then that I heard the train whistle, felt the thunder of the locomotive pulling into town.

"Where are we going?" I asked.

"Home," Gillian said with a smile. "Back to our city. Together. Forever."

Lost Mountain Pass

Three pairs of boots pointed straight down. A long second of silence followed, the crowd waiting, uncertain, until the ropes quit swinging. Murmurs grew then, almost in unison, like an amen at the end of a long prayer. The entire town stood still, nervous to leave, eyes shaded toward the three dead men, making sure the twitching and breathing was finally done and over with.

It had been a picture-perfect day for a hanging in Kosoma. Part celebration, part melodrama that had come to a quick, neck-breaking end. More than anything, the hanging was a cause for the boomtown to grind to a stop and witness the execution of Cleatus Darby and his two younger brothers.

The Darbys were legendary in Kosoma now, or potentially just lost names in a long line of lawless men whose bones would crumble back into dust and become nothing more than the dirt from where they came. Memory or records of their deeds might never be spoken of again unless absolutely necessary. The only ounce of fame the Darbys owned while they walked the earth was for their meanness, for their unrelenting efforts to bring suffering to all of those that got in their way, and some that didn't. Someone new would surely fill their place. Meanness in and around Kosoma was as plentiful as rain in the early spring.

"Looks like my job here is done," Oklahoma Circuit Court Judge Gordon Hadesworth said. He was as tall and thin as a cornstalk, stately with a well-trimmed white goatee, and a suit that, like all of his suits, was shipped to him directly from New York from a company called Brooks Brothers.

"I suppose you'll be wantin' a bite of dinner before we start toward Enid?" The questioner was Hadesworth's protection and escort, Deputy U.S. Marshal Hank Snowden — most often referred to as "Trusty," by judges and outlaws alike.

Hank Snowden had never lost a judge, and more than a few lawless idiots had thought they could outwit him, finding themselves at the smoking end of his Henry rifle or dangling from the gallows, like the three fellas before him — though he had nothing to do with their capture, sentencing, or the quick send-off to meet their maker.

"Between you and me, Trusty, I'd just as soon get out of this stinking town as soon as possible," the judge said, lowering his voice so no one could hear or take offense to his comment.

Kosoma actually meant "place of stinking water" in the Choctaw language. There was a myriad of bubbling, steaming springs fingering off the Kiamichi River, and they were all thick with stinky sulfur. A slight breeze pushed the pungent smell of rotten eggs straight down Main Street of the new town, and then into every nook, cranny, and alleyway, soiling any pleasant aroma it could find. There was nothing to overcome the putrid smell, and no way to escape it. You just got used to it . . . or you didn't.

Not even the smell of opportunity found in fresh-cut lumber, that was so prevalent now that the St. Louis–San Francisco Railroad, more commonly referred to as the Frisco, could vanquish the residue of the springs from the senses or threads of your clothes.

The Frisco had built a new rail line running from the north to the south, straight through the Choctaw Nation, connecting

Fort Smith with Paris, Texas, and Kosoma was perfectly located to capitalize on the new line, smell or no smell.

The railroad followed the Kiamichi River, exploiting the water for steam and power. Living with the stink was a small price to pay when there was more than a pile of money to be made. Kosoma was a classic territory town; a field of nothingness one minute, a bustling center of commerce the next, and there wasn't much of anything, smells or otherwise, that could keep the hopeful, the schemers, and the dreamers away. Especially now that order of law had been enforced judiciously, fairly, and without prejudice. The Darbys were longtimers, some of the first whites to settle the area. They were immune to the smell but not to the new ways of accountability and laws that stifled their unseemly behavior. Murder had been frowned upon long before there was ever a town, but the Darbys didn't understand that.

Hank Snowden figured he hadn't been in town long enough to reach the point of immunity of any of his senses and had no intention of staying any longer than necessary. He was greatly relieved to hear the judge wanted to leave immediately.

"Not one of the nicer smelling places I've

ever been," Hank replied to the judge. He didn't take to his nickname much. He thought referring to himself as Trusty was boastful and dangerous to believe in. Truth be told, he knew he'd just been lucky more than once, regardless of how prepared, or how good a shot he actually was.

The judge smiled and nodded. "Not from the stories I hear tell. There's a line of whorehouses from San Antonio to Abilene that still tell of your exploits."

"You'd think a judge would be immune to hearsay."

"We get bored, Trusty. We like a little rumor and gossip as much as any other man. Besides, you've a reputation to uphold, I'm just contributing to your resume."

"Some of those spots smelled right nice." Hank's face flushed red. There was no question he liked the company of women. One in particular, but she was a hundred miles away, married to another man, his heart still hers, though, any time she came asking, silver braided ring or not. "Ain't nothin' but tales about me anyways, Judge. The past is the past. I'm a reformed man."

"You mean you've found Jesus?"

"Not lately, anyways, not in the places I've been. Course I haven't been lookin' much for Him, neither. I was just an energetic youngun', that's all. Women tend to complicate a man's life, at least this man's life."

"You just keep thinking that, Trusty, and we'll all have plenty to talk about for a long time to come."

Hank laughed uncomfortably. "Let's get your belongin's from the hotel and dust our way out of here before the sun starts to dive west too fast. I'd like to get through Lost Mountain Pass before night settles in."

"Expecting trouble, Trusty?" the judge asked with a raised eyebrow.

"Always, Judge. I'm always expectin' trouble. 'Specially after a hangin' as well-deserved as this one."

Hank cinched the saddle on his horse, a paint gelding that he'd never got around to naming. He called the horse, and it didn't seem to mind. The two of them had traveled a lot of miles together, knew each other pretty well, but Hank wasn't one to hold a high affection for any animal on a long-term basis. There was a job to do, and that was that. Attachments were a danger to the job as far as he was concerned. The escapade with the married woman had taught him that, along with a long string of hard lessons learned before then that he didn't care to revisit any time soon.

"I was hoping I would find you here."

The voice was a female's. It startled Hank. He hadn't heard anyone come up behind him, which at once concerned and scared him, but he didn't show it. Letting your guard down for one second on a day like today could get you killed, and he knew it. Another stroke of luck as far as he was concerned, as he took in the woman standing before him.

"I'm sorry, ma'am, do I know you?"

She shook her head. "No, sir, you do not." She was more a girl than a woman. Lucky to be twenty years old, at that, probably younger. Dressed in a plain white blouse and a long skirt, deep blue, almost black, parts of it matte, other parts shiny, sewed in a tight horizontal pattern, along with traveling boots and a straw bonnet with dangling chin straps. Her face was hard set with a birdlike nose, eyes the color of granite, and dark brunette hair pulled back and swept up under the bonnet — all of which was stacked up on a skinny, flat body. There was nothing about the girl that Hank found attractive. She instantly annoyed him, considering her stealthy skills.

The livery was quiet, not much going on. It was just the two of them as far as Hank knew. A few stalls over, a horse snorted, then took a healthy piss.

"I understand you are on your way to Enid?" the girl said.

"Yes, ma'am, that would be correct."

"I would like to secure passage in your company."

Hank wiped his hands. "I'm sorry, ma'am, I'm a deputy U.S. marshal, not an escort. You'll need to make other arrangements. I don't hire out."

"Are you not Trusty Snowden?"

He flinched at the nickname. "I am. Sure as it's daylight, I am. But most folks call me Hank."

"Most folks call you Trusty, and that is the only reason why I have sought you out. Your reputation as a drinker and a womanizer is overridden by the fact that your gun skills are rumored to be superb, the best in the territory from what I understand. I need protection, Deputy, or I will surely not make it out of Kosoma alive."

"Your life's in danger? How's that?"

The woman stared at Hank like he had just asked the stupidest question in the world. "Fine. This was a waste of my time, just as I suspected it would be," she said, spinning in perfect balance on the heels of her boots, pushing off with the intention of stalking off. "My blood is on your hands,

Deputy. Remember I said that," she added, snarling over her shoulder.

By the time Hank caught up with the girl, she had gone about twenty feet away from him, nearly to the barn's double doors that stood wide open. A slight breeze pushed stinky air through the barn, mixing with the horseshit and piss. He really wanted to get the hell out of Kosoma.

"Wait," Hank said, grabbing the girl's arm, bringing her to a stop. "There's no need to go gettin' all haughty, just tell me what's going on. If you're in trouble, that's another thing entirely."

With a glare that cut through her tear-filled eyes, she said. "It's too late. I might as well succumb to my fate. You are my last chance. I will approach this journey on my own, and take my chances, thank you very much."

Maybe it was the tears in her once rock-hard eyes, the vulnerability now apparent, but her features had softened. There was a beauty to her, a sweet smell, that Hank had failed to see, somehow had overlooked at first glance. She was not the kind of woman he'd consider pursuing, but she wasn't an ugly bird at all.

"Let's start over," Hank said. "What's your name, ma'am?" he asked in his softest, most seductive voice he could muster at the moment.

"Matilda. Matilda Darby." She watched Hank's reaction closely, surely accustomed to a negative response. When his face showed no change, she continued. "Cleatus was my brother. Horace and Rascal, too. And just because I'm of the same blood, people think I'm a killer, thief, and a liar, too. Folks around town think we're all just meaner than snakes, and not fit to walk on this earth. That I'm just like them. I guess I can't blame them. The three boys robbed anyone with a nickel, and when they finally took to killing, they did it like it was fun. Old man Robinson, the one they hanged for, was target practice. They emptied their guns on him long after he was dead. Why should I be surprised, then, that everyone, and probably you, think I'm no better than them?"

Hank let his hand slide away from Matilda's arm. "I'm sorry, I had no idea."

"How could you, you're not from these parts."

"I'll talk to the marshal, see about gettin' you some protection. Maybe it'd be best to just let things settle down a bit before you go makin' a rash decision like leavin' town."

"I have had pig's blood thrown on my

porch. Service refused me at the mercantile. No one will extend me credit or hire out my skills as a milliner. I am nearly broke, sir, left with no kin to fall back on, or any prospects for the future in this town at all, other than the certainty of my death. Just this morning, someone fired a gunshot through my front window. It is only a matter of luck that I was not walking through the front room, or I would be lying in a coffin along with my brothers up on Poor Man's Hill. I fear for my life, Deputy, surely you must understand that."

Hank shifted uncomfortably. "How do I know that this isn't some kind of ploy to exact revenge on the judge for renderin' a well-deserved death sentence on your brothers, ma'am? How do I know you don't have a plot to kill him? I'm sorry to ask, ma'am, but I have to, the judge is my charge. I have taken an oath to die for him, if it comes to that. You sure don't look like a killer to me, but I've seen some sweet ones, let me tell you."

Matilda stared at Hank with her deep gray eyes unflinching. She had wiped away her tears, and it was like they had never existed in the first place. "I would expect that you would think of such a thing. Three things should be reason enough to believe me,

Deputy. One. I have never hurt a fly. Never. You can ask anyone in this town. Two. I am the last of the Darbys in this town. When I am gone, there will be no legacy for anyone to shoulder, and all of my family's debts will be paid in full. The Darbys will be a bad memory, quickly forgotten, and unknown to the greedy hordes that are filling the town in search of their fortunes. Three. I hated my brothers and what they stood for. They deserved to hang. They were cold-blooded killers and earned their punishments, what they got in the end. I have no mind for revenge, no need to set the record straight by bringing any harm to Judge Hadesworth. My only desire is to start a new life as far away from Kosoma as possible. It is that simple, Deputy. That is my story, and there is nothing I can add, other than the guarantee of my word that I mean no one any harm, especially the judge."

Hank took a deep breath and stared up at the rafters. "I'll have to clear it with the judge, you understand."

"No need," Matilda said, "I already have."

They rode toward the end of town, three horses abreast. A few people stopped on the boardwalks and glared. Some even turned their backs, shunning Matilda Darby purposefully, leaving no question to what their intention was. The sighting of such disregard fortified Matilda's story and made it seem true. Hank was relieved more than he was appalled by the sight.

Matilda stared straight ahead, her eyes set on the horizon, not allowing one gaze that fell upon her to dent her attitude or touch her heart. At least that she showed on the outside from what Hank could see.

Hank had his trusted Henry rifle laying across his lap and one hand dangling inches from his six-shooter, a Colt Double Action Army .45. The .45 had an enlarged trigger, making it comfortable for Hank's fat finger. He was a big man, over six foot tall, and fit but not skinny. His father had been a smithy in St. Louis, outfitting trappers and explorers in the early days, and Hank had inherited his father's stout body and ability to build and keep muscle on as needed.

Horse had his ears erect, alert, sensing the tension in the air. One ear was white, the other red, or strawberry roan, depending on who was doing the describing. Hank liked to think Horse's ear was red. Like a sunset falling behind a snow-covered mountain. Strawberry sounded sissified, and there was nothing about Horse that suggested he *was* sissified.

Just as they were about to cross the last street before leaving Kosoma, a wagon passed in front of them, causing all three horses to come to a stop and wait.

The wagon was loaded with the Darby brothers' coffins and was heading toward a cemetery on the opposite end of town, the place Matilda had called Poor Man's Hill. There was no parade of mourners following along. The preacher sat shotgun next to a glum teamster, both of them stiff and on tenterhooks, as if they expected something to happen at any second.

Judge Hadesworth shifted uncomfortably in his saddle. "You sure you don't want to attend the funeral of your brothers, Miss Darby?"

"No, sir. I have no more tears left to shed for those three. Rascal held the greatest amount of promise, and I will miss him the most. But in the end, his deeds were influenced by the other two, competing to be noticed and accepted, so they wouldn't treat him as a dunce or a punching bag. It never happened. Rascal died still trying to impress Cleatus. Whatever awaits them on the other side of this life will be no different, I imagine. If there is such a thing."

"You are not a believer, then?" the judge asked.

Matilda turned her attention away from the coffins, and stared Judge Hadesworth directly in the eye. "Let's just say I have questions. And you, Judge?"

Hank stayed out of the conversation, his eyes darting to the rooftops, and to the shadows of the alleyway that cut alongside a mercantile and an empty storefront with a FOR RENT sign in the front window.

"My father was a Methodist minister," the judge said. "I was raised in the ways of the Lord. But I am not one to proselytize, so you have no need to worry of my pestering you for a conversion or deep conversation based on verses put to memory as a child."

"That is the least of my worries on this journey, Judge," Matilda said.

The wagon moved on, and the way forward cleared. Dust settled to the ground, and a thin, wavering cloud of flies chased after the coffins, drawn by the smell of death and the opportunity that a human body provided. Three dead men were a jackpot of food and a virgin breeding ground. Flies obviously knew a boomtown when they saw it too.

"Your decision is final then, ma'am?" Hank asked.

"Yes, Trusty, it is. The sooner I'm out of this town, the sooner my new life begins."

■ ■ ■ ■

Hank trailed behind, keeping a short distance behind Matilda and the blond sorrel she rode. The sorrel looked a little old, and a little lazy. Hank wondered if it could make the trip all the way to Enid but kept those concerns to himself. And Matilda was not an expert rider. The sorrel had a habit of snatching fresh grass that had sprung up alongside the well-trammeled path, eating at every chance it could find, slowing them down. If the act lasted much longer, Hank knew he would have to say something about it. Safe time on the trail was running out.

Judge Hadesworth was in the lead, pushing them up the trail as it eased away from a fertile valley. There was a clearing about halfway up that Hank had camped in before. He hoped they made it before dark, disappointed that time had run out on them.

They had taken longer to leave than Hank had planned on, helping Matilda finish up packing. She traveled light for a woman. Especially a woman planning on setting up a milliner shop in Enid. But she had explained that most of her materials had been sold or given away with the knowledge that she would be leaving town — or be dead, one or the other. Fleeing was more like it, so Hank supposed her easy load made sense. Still, it troubled him some.

The sun was falling rapidly, and pink fingers stretched out in front of the three riders, fading sunlight reflecting on the underside of long bits of clouds, like arrows pointing them in the right direction.

A breeze had followed them out of Kosoma, but thankfully, the stink of the springs had been left behind. The higher they rode up the trail, the cooler it got, and long before night set in, Hank was sure he'd need his duster. Spring was a trickster, fickle with its weather. Hot days, shivering cold nights. Lucky for all of them that there were no storms on the horizon. At least, none that Hank could see at the moment.

Without Matilda along, as had been originally planned, Hank and the judge would have more than likely rode side by side, when possible, participating in a slow but interesting conversation about the law, politics, and most assuredly, women. And they would have been much farther along, through the Lost Mountain Pass, and safe on the other side in an open stretch of land, skirting Spirit Lake.

The sorrel grabbed another mouthful of grass, forcing Hank to slow for the last time.

"You're gonna have to get that horse of yours under control," he said, after kneeing Horse, and whipping the reins to the right, urging the paint into a slight run up next to Matilda.

"He has a mind of his own, Deputy." Matilda's face was tense with frustration. Her eyes were hard, and cut through Hank like he was a schoolboy about to get his knuckles rapped. "Do we have much farther?" It was more of a demand than a question.

"No, ma'am." Hank let off the reins, slowing Horse, letting him fall back to his position. He was in no mood to offer horse riding lessons to a testy little woman who was short on manners and long on attitude, no matter how fine she talked.

The pink fingers quickly turned gray, and though they were still heading upward on the trail, Hank could see the blackness of night eating into the grayness of twilight. The first star was visible, and the ghost of a crescent moon began to take form, its tips stabbing into a cloudless sky that would bring glory and thrills to coyote and nighttime hunters.

The fire crackled comfortably, and the smell of boiling beans, with a hint of bacon tossed in for flavor, permeated the air throughout the camp.

There hadn't been enough time to hunt a rabbit, or any other eatable varmint before the sun crashed below the horizon, leaving the threesome in the dark and with only a minimum of supplies.

Hank had counted on getting farther, on being able to use his rifle skills to feed them for the remainder of the trip, but that had not happened. He was almost certain that Matilda was slowing them down on purpose, and it was that thought, that inkling of discomfort that kept him in camp, close to the judge. Acquiring trust was more dangerous than naming a horse as far as Hank was concerned.

The ground was flat, and a collection of boulders, some as big as sheds and houses, shielded them on three sides, while the thick torso of the mountain stretched upward, towering over them, dotted with a collection of pine trees that provided shelter and food for a variety of birds, deer, and an occasional mountain lion.

From where they sat, the view looked east out over the valley, out over the Kiamichi River, as it snaked from behind the mountain back out to Kosoma. The town wasn't visible, but there was no question it was there, still within a good hard ride.

"Quite a spot you picked here, Trusty," the judge said. He had not abandoned his jacket and hat. Like Hank thought, the night had grown chilly. But Hadesworth sat comfortably, sucking on the end of his pipe as he arched a safety match to the bowl, offering the smell of tobacco to the pleasantness of the camp as the bowl came alive, glowing like an ember from the fire.

Hank sat next to the judge, square in the middle, between him and Matilda. "Been forced to use it now and again. It's good if the weather kicks up like it's apt to do. Fire reflects off the walls, gives us plenty of light, some warmth which we'll appreciate come the middle of the night. Critters usually stay away."

"We can probably be seen from a mile away," Matilda offered with a scowl.

The Henry rifle was inches from Hank's hand. He tapped the stock. "If anything should be called Trusty, it's this old rifle. Don't you worry none, ma'am. I'll keep watch. This is the best spot we could be in. There's an escape passage between them rocks over there. Takes us right down to the valley floor in a hard minute if it comes to that."

"You seem pretty sure of yourself, Deputy."

Before Hank could say another word, the judge interjected. "You've no idea of this man's skills, Miss Darby. Of all the U.S. deputies that I know and have ridden with, Trusty, here, is the best."

"I'm aware of his reputation, Judge Hadesworth," Matilda said.

Hank stiffened. "Don't believe everything you hear."

A coyote yipped in the distance, not that far from them, off the trail. The call echoed upward, dashing into the night like a warning, a conversation about to begin. But nothing followed.

Hank eyed the judge, and Hadesworth, a veteran of trips under the dark of night, slid his coat to the side, exposing a holstered Peacemaker. A nod from both men followed, and Hank stood, edging into the shadows, stopping at the rim of the open arc of boulders.

The horses were tethered together behind the judge and Matilda, as far back away from the fire as possible, hard to see, but close to the passage Hank spoke of. They were suddenly tense, slightly pulling at the ropes, not yet in a full fledge panic, but working up to it. Even the sorrel showed some spunk, some concern.

Hank looked over his shoulder, and the judge had pulled Matilda back along the rock, huddling together like they were seeking protection from a hard rain, the Peacemaker in full view, cocked and ready to go.

Plans had been previously laid between the judge and Hank if any concern showed itself. Matilda was not part of the plan, but an active participant now.

At the rim the whole valley laid before them, along with the trail that led up to the camp. It was one of the reasons Hank had chosen the spot so long ago. It wasn't perfect, but it was the only offering of comfortable and safe shelter until you were on the other side of the mountain.

The crescent moon offered a little light, but not the brilliance a full moon would have happily provided. Still, Hank was able to see pretty well once his eyes adjusted from the fire. He saw nothing, no movement on the trail, or below. The coyote remained quiet; one yip, that's all. Now Hank was not even so sure it *was* a coyote he'd heard.

He stood still for several minutes, giving whatever it was a chance to show itself, before he relaxed, and sat the Henry rifle back down. Finally, it became obvious to him that he'd overreacted, that it was his tension the horses were reacting to, that he was just being too darned cautious.

The beans smelled good, and his stomach rumbled with a request to be tended to. Hank drew a deep breath, and turned around, ready to call off the alarm.

He found himself facing Matilda with a gun pointed at him, a derringer she'd obviously hidden under her skirt.

Matilda was a step away from the judge, who looked just as surprised as Hank. Before either man could say a word, in the matter of a split second, thunder boomed from above, crackling like a familiar song in Hank's ear, and flashing instantly, an odd poof of orange lightning catching his eye. It wasn't thunder; it was a gunshot.

Hank's fear had come true. Bringing Matilda along had been a huge mistake. His mouth went dry, and as the bullet hit its target, shock and dismay were pushed aside as all of his training and instinct kicked in. He whirled around, firing the Henry rifle up onto the first exposed ledge, into the shadows, at the first sign of movement.

He hit the man with the second shot. The shooter tumbled forward, bouncing down on the rock, his skull crashing hard, breaking in an audible crash. If the bullet didn't kill him, then the fall did. The shooter landed flat on the ground with a thud, and a quick glance told Hank that he had no idea who the man was — but that wasn't his concern, at the moment.

Matilda lay on the ground, face up, staring at the stars, blood oozing out of her shoulder. She hadn't pointed the gun at Hank, she was protecting herself, them.

"She's been hit, Hank," Judge Hadesworth yelled. "She's been hit bad." He was already at the girl's side, putting pressure on the wound, his fingers bloody.

Matilda coughed, and drew in a breath, as Hank reached her. "I knew they'd come after me," she said, her voice weak.

"Who?" Hank asked. The derringer lay a few feet from Matilda, lost when she took the hit. She had been prepared for the attack, but it hadn't done any good. Another second and Hank would have taken her for the shooter, the threat, like he had supposed she was, and just might of shot her instead. He shuddered at the thought.

"Old man Robinson's son. He said his family wouldn't rest until there were no more Darbys walking on this earth. I believed him then and I believe him now. I told you that I had to leave that town, and I meant it."

"He's dead," Hank said. "He can't hurt you now."

Matilda nodded, tried to force a smile, and coughed again.

"You need to get her back to town, Hank," the judge said, his voice booming with authority.

"We do."

"No. I'll only slow you down. I can look out for myself."

"I can't do that, Judge. It's my job to look after you. He might not be the only one. More might be waitin', aimin' to take revenge on you for shelterin' her."

"There's only one son," Matilda struggled to say.

"You can't let her die, Trusty. I'll be fine. Take her into Kosoma, and find a doctor."

Matilda grew pale, and as she attempted to say something else, to put her own two cents into the conversation like they had come to expect of her, the shock and pain of the injury became too much, and she lost consciousness.

"Now, Trusty, before it's too late! Get her to a doctor now!" the judge ordered.

The sun came up in Kosoma, barreling up into the sky like it had been shot from a cannon. Along with daylight coming on strong, the stink seemed stronger, more potent, thicker than Hank recalled from just the day before. But then again, he'd been sitting motionless on a bench outside the doctor's office for more than five hours.

There was no wind, nothing to move along the stink or his worry. Just because Matilda said there was only one Robinson left, set on revenge, didn't make it true. He was as concerned about the judge's welfare as he was Matilda's.

The door finally opened, and the doc walked out, a young man with spectacles, fresh from one of the schools back East. "Looks like she's going to make it, Deputy. But she'll need some care, and a good dose of peace and quiet for a while."

"She hasn't got any family," Hank said. "Can she stay here?"

"I've only got two beds, and it's just me. Maybe for a day, but not for as long as she needs tending to."

Hank sighed. "You're sure?"

The doc nodded. "I'm sorry, but she'll need to be moved out of here."

"All right, I'll see what I can do."

A week later, a knock came at the door. "Telegram!"

Hank stood up from the chair and looked

out to the balcony. The French doors were open and a breeze was blowing in, ruffling the thin curtains, offering a peaceful wave into the hotel room. Matilda sat outside, sunning herself in the late afternoon light, her right arm bound tight to her side, a calm, rested look on her face.

Hank pulled his Colt out of the holster, hugged it to the side of his leg, then opened the door cautiously. Kosoma still posed a threat to Matilda as far as he was concerned, and as soon as she was able to travel, they were going to complete their journey to Enid.

The runner from the telegraph office smiled broadly at Hank; he was just a boy, maybe twelve, wearing knickers and an expectant look on his face. "You Trusty Snowden?"

"I guess I am," Hank said with resignation.

"Telegram for you, then." The boy handed the paper to Hank, who took the paper, and dug into his pocket for a nickel.

The boy groaned as he took the coin, then spun around and disappeared quickly down the stairs.

Hank closed the door, locked it, and opened the telegram. It was from Judge Hadesworth.

ARRIVED IN ENID. RECEIVED NEWS OF MATILDA'S CONDITION. SPOKE TO MARSHAL LANDON. TAKE LEAVE UNTIL YOU ARRIVE BACK IN ENID. BEST WISHES. JUDGE GORDON P. HADESWORTH, ESQ.

Hank walked out to the balcony. "Telegram just came from the judge. He arrived safely and arranged for me to take as much time as I need to get us back to Enid."

Matilda looked up at Hank and smiled. "That's good news."

Hank returned the smile, put a hand comfortably on her opposite shoulder, the one that wasn't bound. "I'm going to my room to get cleaned up for dinner, do you need anything?"

His room was right next door.

"No," Matilda said. "I think I have everything I need." Her face was soft, just like her features now that she'd relaxed and come to peace with the lack of threats — or it may have been Hank's constant presence. He was never far, looking out for her like a mother hen, or a judge put in his charge. It was difficult for him to walk away from her, to leave her room.

In a short time, he'd come to learn that there was little question that Matilda Darby was more woman than girl. He was a little older than her, but it felt good to have someone need him.

Only time would tell whether or not she'd be the one he'd settle down with. She had potential. But until that time, Hank planned on taking it slow and easy — and getting out of Kosoma as soon as possible.

The Longest Night

The flames had died down, leaving only the glowing orange coals to give off any heat. Neither man noticed; they were fast asleep after a long journey. But the wolves noticed. They could smell the meat of a fresh kill, see the white-tailed deer strung up from a gangly cottonwood by its hooves, left, oddly, to bleed out overnight.

The alpha, a stoic gray wolf, his fur dotted with more than a fair share of scars, padded around the perimeter of the makeshift camp as softly as he could. The deer felt like bait left out to draw in the pack. Something wasn't right. The behavior of the humans was unusual — or the alpha assumed they were stupid. Unaware of the way of the world beyond the fire.

The rest of the pack stood in wait, just beyond the shadows, listening for the grunts and growls that would command them into action.

The deer was easy pickings for a pack this size, bound and hung like it was, the hard work of the kill already done for them. There were twelve wolves in all, most of them hungry — but not starving. The pack was glad to see, and feel, the depths of winter, when the hunting was easier. The sick and tired were less of a challenge, less trouble to bring down. Especially the bison, weak, and caught knee-deep in snow. The snow season was more bountiful, but some of the pack still longed for the long days of summer when the sun offered more time to play — and kill.

There was snow on the ground, but not so much that it was difficult to walk. The leaves had turned to gold on the aspens and fallen to the ground, urging the elk to move to higher ground, off the moraine, more than two moons ago. The bison had begun to move, too, albeit slowly, gobbling at what tender roots they could find under the snow. All in the world was right, progressing along the way as it should. Except for the presence of the humans.

While not unheard of, they were rare in this part of the pack's territory, especially this time of year. And these men, they smelled different — odder than any other human any of them had ever encountered.

It was for that reason alone that the alpha himself had gone into the camp first, alone. His curiosity was piqued not only by the bait and their odd behavior, but by the difference of their presence.

One of the men snored deeply. He was tall and meaty with a heavy ring of fat around his waist that made him the more appetizing of the two. The other one was skinny, had thick black hair braided at the back, and his skin was brown as the dirt, unlike the other one who looked like his skin was made of ice and snow. The brown one smelled the worst of the two. He was the killer, the one good with the weapon that glimmered silver in the moonlight. The aroma of death was thick, pungent, like the brown man had rolled in something he had killed, then consumed its soul — he smelled from the inside out. The alpha gave the smaller brown man a wide swath. But the snore stopped him, stopped him dead in his tracks.

The big gray wolf faded into the blackness of the moonless night. Only his yellow eyes were visible to the human eye. The alpha regulated his breathing, did his level best to become invisible from the threat of being seen.

There was no question what the wolf

would do if the man awoke and caught him this close to the camp: he would run. Run as fast as he could back into the middle of the pack, back into the safe haven he had known for so long. Every muscle in the wolf's body was poised to flee. He was tense and ready.

Suddenly, the meaty white man jumped up, his eyes wide open, his nostrils flared. "I know you're out there," he said, his hand grasping at his side for a gun and holster that wasn't there. "I can smell you."

"What's your problem, East?" the skinny brown man grumbled, as he stirred awake.

"We're close. I can feel them, too."

The brown man sat up, and sniffed deeply. "Relax, it's just a pack of hungry wolves." And then in another language, a language born of the earth and understood by the ears of all of the furry warmbloods, the man said, *"Go away brothers — but not too far. We mean you no harm. But if you are desperate and venture to my fire, I will use it to kill you. Otherwise, the slaughter will be yours, but you must come when I call on you if you taste one bite of this bounty."* The words were lyrical, soft and without malice, like they were the truth in its most singular form. A whisper on the wind, a promise of another age, though firmly rooted in the present, and completely understood.

The alpha wolf drew in a deep breath — he had not run. It was like his feet were frozen to the ground, like he had lost all his free will. And he was shocked to hear the words so clearly.

These were not ordinary men.

The words gave proof to the brown man's aroma; he walked in both worlds, held the knowledge of the few and ancient. The brown packs of humans called men like this one a medicine man. But he was more than a healer. He had walked among the dead and had lived to tell of it. The alpha had only encountered one other human in his life that held this power — and smell — and he had barely lived to tell about it.

The alpha wolf backed away, grunted in retreat, his paws suddenly freed, and offered no answer other than the pad of its paws, echoing away from the fire. This was not the time to answer, to make a deal with these humans — with this brown-skinned medicine man.

"I hate it when you do that," Blanchard East said. "You know I don't understand that tongue."

"They will leave us alone now."

"I thought you were on watch."

The Indian glared at the white man. "We

are safe, aren't we?"

"Only because I heard them."

"If that is what you want to believe, then so be it."

The pack parted and let the alpha pass through, then they all turned and followed him into the darkness, resisting the urge to howl and holler, setting off the alarm to the rest of the world of the two men's presence.

It was only when the pack was within the safety of the forest that the alpha stopped, turned, and howled his answer to the Indian. One way or another, they would all feast on this night, before the moon settled behind the mountains, and the sun rose on the snowy plains.

The town looked dead, even on the horizon, from so far away. It was nothing but a collection of shadows, barren of light, of even one flicker of a candle. The buildings were easy to define, mostly two-story affairs, false-fronted stores, banks, and offices, all built to serve a small population. If their senses hadn't told them otherwise, both men would have thought it was a ghost town, lost of all of its earthly inhabitants long ago. But that was not the case. There was a collection of humans in the town. A gathering of citizens, hiding from something, or someone. The fear of darkness was more than apparent, and just one of the signs Blanchard East had been looking for. "They will know we are coming," East said, "if we ride in under darkness."

"They already know we are coming."

"The wolves told them?"

"No," the Indian said, walking away from Blanchard East, without the slightest flinch. "They can smell you. Just because they don't have fur and warm blood doesn't mean they aren't animals. You should know as much by now."

"What about you?"

"I am not new to them." The Indian squared his shoulders and headed straight for the town, leaving Blanchard East with no choice but to follow — or abandon the mission altogether. That wasn't going to happen. There was too much at stake.

"Well, if there's no use hiding, then we can head straight to the saloon," East said, scurrying to catch up with the Indian.

"That, my friend, is the smartest thing you have said in a month."

East sighed heavily. He had grown accustomed to the Indian's snide ways, but that didn't mean he liked it, or took too kindly to the man's sharp tongue. He had little choice but to deal with it, though, and both men knew it. They needed each other, had formed an unlikely partnership in a moment of dire need. Blanchard East owed the Indian a life, and the Indian carried the same debt, though begrudgingly.

They were on the main street of the town almost before they knew it. Up close, like from a distance, the buildings were all dark. There was not an open window to be found; they all were blacked out with drawn curtains. There was no sound to be heard, just the crunch of each man's footfall, echoing off the cold wood of the buildings like they were walking into a deep canyon instead of a forgotten small town.

There was a loneliness to the town that East had felt before. He could almost taste the fear, too. It was all he could do not to turn and run. He knew what was waiting for them.

To their good fortune, a streak of light shimmered slightly from underneath the closed door of the saloon.

The Indian stopped in the middle of the street, looked at the saloon, which had the unlikely name of the Falling Sun Saloon, and turned his attention to the three-story hotel behind him. "They are not here. But they are close."

East felt the stare of something unknown on the back of his neck. His fingers quivered, and he had to steel himself to prevent a quick glance over his shoulder. It was most likely the townspeople staring out from behind closed curtains, curious, and afraid of the two strangers who had just wandered into town.

"I'm thrilled to hear it," East said, rubbing his hands together. "A whiskey will taste right nice, now, won't it?"

"It will. But don't get carried away. You'll need your senses."

"I'll need more than that."

The Indian's lip turned up, threatening a smile, but it faded quickly when the sound of breaking glass erupted from inside the saloon. He glanced over to East, who was already reaching for his sidearm, a Colt Army, and shook his head. "There'll be no need for that."

"Says you."

"Have it your way. We will need more than bullets to win this fight. And it is not our enemy who awaits us inside, only the evil they have left in their wake."

"Fear and hate?"

"Yes."

Blanchard East nodded, exhaled deeply, let his gun hand relax, and followed the

Indian up the steps into the Falling Sun Saloon.

Two men were about to come to blows. Shards of glass littered the floor. The room smelled of whiskey, anger, and piss, like one of the men had let himself go. A bald-headed barkeep sweated profusely behind the bar. All of the color had drained from the man's chubby face, his skin nearly as white as his apron, but he still had the sense to reach for a twelve-gauge scattergun, stowed away for occasions such as this.

The saloon was packed full of men. There wasn't an empty seat in the house. But it was oddly quiet, restrained, as Blanchard East and the Indian pushed in from the outside. A slight gust of wind followed them, curling snow around their feet like ghost snakes scattering to get out of their way.

The men having the fight, both of about the same build, slight and muscular, with hard callused hands that gave away their toil as ranch hands, froze in place. Their arms were suspended in the air, held by an unseen rope, the blows undelivered. The surprise on each man's face was sculpted in disbelief so severe it threatened to be there forever.

"Gentlemen," the Indian said, "The enemy awaits us all in the distance. You are only making their attack easier."

Blanchard East slammed the door closed behind him. Found the peg lock and slid it into place. There was no need to pull either Colt from its holster or show his other weapons hidden about his body, but he swept his duster open so the guns were in plain sight.

The ranch hands' fists fell to their sides, each offering a surprised look on his face. The taller one rubbed his fist like he had just found it for the first time, somehow regained control of it from some unseen force.

The barkeep leveled the scattergun at the Indian. "Who are you, stranger, and what do you want?"

"We are the answer to your prayers."

East stood back and let the Indian do the talking. The Indian was better at talking than he was.

"Ain't no salvation from a dirty Indian," a man from the crowd said. Everyone remained seated, like they were chained in place, but unaware of the fact.

"Insults are a bad foot to get off on," the Indian said. "Allow me a moment of your time."

"You talk funny," the barkeep said.

"I talk clearly so you can understand me, sir. This is not my native tongue."

"Then you have us drunk on magic," another man said from the crowd.

"You are all already under the spell of darkness. You know it is true. I am only here to help. I do not believe in magic, only in the energy of the Great Father."

"There's nothin' that can help us now," the barkeep said. It looked like he wanted to relax, to lower the scattergun, but it remained in place. His eyes, though, drooped in defeat.

"We can help," Blanchard East said, causing the Indian to cast him a harsh glance. He ignored it. "Look here, fellas, I know you ain't got reason to trust us, 'specially with my friend here bein' an Indian and all. I know the troubles you had settlin' this valley. We all do. I don't blame you for your distrust. But hear my friend out, that's all I'm askin'. If you don't like what he has to say, well, we'll just walk away. Disappear the same way we just walked in, unannounced and uninvited. But the trouble you're facin' now ain't nothin' like it was with the Indians. It's worse, and you know it."

The room went even quieter, and the

Indian exhaled deeply. When the last bit of breath escaped his lips, the barkeep's arm relaxed, and the scattergun slipped out of his grip. The gun bounced off the top of the bar, the thud of it jolting every man in the Falling Sun Saloon in their chair, causing them to jump in surprise.

"They have our children," one man said. He stood up. His shoulders sagged, and his suit looked to have been finely tailored at one time but was dusty and worn from daily wear now.

"And most of our women, too," another man said. He looked like a banker with speckle glasses and shiny gold cuff links. His face was as haggard and worried as those of the other men in the room.

There was shuffling of feet, of men reaching for their guns.

"There will be no need for weapons," the Indian said. "They will not work in my presence, anyway. At least your fingers will not work."

"That's a powerful trick," the barkeep said.

"It is no trick," the Indian answered. "No trick at all. Hear me out, like my friend here said. If you do not like what I have to say, the trouble you face is yours. You have already seen my power, felt its restraint.

Everything that you have tried has failed, has it not?"

No man answered, but a few nodded silently in response to the question.

"We have seen this before, but the time of their weakness draws near," the Indian said. "It is their time of celebration. They call it *Longissima Nocte.* The Longest Night. It is the time of darkness, when the sun is farthest from the earth. At midnight, light promises to return quicker to the earth, only in seconds instead of minutes, but still they grow weaker, their time awake, shorter. But the nightmare will not end, not if they have celebrated by feeding on the young and the females are able to breed. They will be too strong to stop. Even for me, and those of my kind."

"It is nearly Christmas. We can sing them away with our faith," a man at the back of the room whispered.

The words drew the Indian's attention to the man. He was dressed in a black cassock and wore a sad, unshaven face. "There is power in what you say, padre, but not enough to stop them all. I will need you at my side if you are willing to fight."

"I am a man of peace."

"There is no such thing at the moment. Once they have feasted, they will take this town as their own. You are already dead men, you just do not know it yet."

"Then we will face salvation together," the papist said.

"If that is what you believe," the Indian said. "Then so be it."

"You will help us?" the barkeep said. "Help us get our families back?"

"Yes," Blanchard East answered, ignoring the Indian, not waiting any longer to have his say and take his place. "For a price."

Seven men rode away from the Falling Sun Saloon in the hour before dawn, when the night was darkest.

A thick bed of clouds hung overhead, covering any sight of the moon or stars, of any dim light that might find its way to the ground. The Indian confidently led the way with Blanchard East and the padre, a man known as Father Michael, equally at each side. The banker, the barkeep, and the two ranch hands followed close behind, as comfortable as they could be in their secondary roles. The rest of the men hadn't taken the time to offer up their names. It didn't matter to East. They were more of a posse, not a gang. There would be time enough for names after they had completed their cause — if any of them lived to tell about it.

Certain death awaited some — if not all — of them.

If what the Indian said was true, there was no need for a surprise attack, less a full-on assault at the moment of their greatest strength but more of a simple ride up to their front door.

It was a foolhardy expedition, and all of the men had been made fully aware of what lay ahead of them. Doing nothing was not an option. Waiting in the town and stockading in their homes, allowing the tension to rise and causing them to fight each other, was no longer an option, either. It was die now or die later. That's what the Indian had said to convince the men that his plan was the only plan that made sense. Of course, a few of them balked at having to pay, particularly the banker, but finally they agreed. Half up front, half on return of the women and children who were held captive.

Any way the townspeople looked at it, death was imminent, set to descend on the town like the citizens were nothing but captured mice, surrounded by a pack of angry, hungry cats. In the end, all the men in the saloon had offered to fight to the death. All of them but Father Michael. He promised to see their souls safely off to

Heaven if they perished and he survived. It was a great assumption, considering what they faced. None of them but East and the Indian knew for sure what awaited them — and neither man was saying. Nightmares were best left unspoken until a man had to look evil square in the face for himself.

It was like the Indian knew where he was, where he was going, like he had been on this specific trail before. But Blanchard East knew it was the man's magic leading him, the presence of their quarry pulling him from deep in his gut. East felt it, too, but it was different for him. Not repulsive, but like a call to home, to something that he was part of, not apart from or desired to destroy. It was a new feeling, and it confused him.

The snow wasn't so deep that it slowed the horses, and they all followed the Indian, riding hard, full out, as if it were a bright summer day. The animals offered no fear or resistance. But that was no surprise — they were under the Indian's spell, too, just like the men in the saloon who had not been able to raise their own hands to protect themselves.

East had seen the Indian perform the same feats before, and there was always a price to be paid, days of weakness and healing needed. He didn't understand and asked no questions. Most of the time, East was glad of his companion's abilities. Sometimes it scared him, made him uncomfortable. But this use of the power was different. It was a no-holds-barred assault, all or nothing. It was worthy of worry if the Indian had enough strength to see them to their destination and face a fight of the magnitude that was more than a promise. Time would tell, though East counted on the Indian, had no choice but to put his full faith in the man. It was the only choice he and the other riders had.

The ground began to get rough and a little slicker. It began to rise on a slope as they made their way out of the valley and into a high wind-and-water-carved limestone pass. The Indian slowed, then brought his horse to a stop, turned around, and faced the men, whose horses had also come to a stop.

"We are close," the Indian said. "If any man does not have a pure heart and does not desire to fight to the death, then this is your last chance to depart, to flee with your life. Though it will not be yours for long. By one hand or another, you will be the first to die after the battle has been lost."

No one said a word, just sat stiffly on their horse's back, staring into the darkness that awaited them.

A healthy flame flickered in the cabin's window, offering a view of what seemed to be an empty room. It was hard to tell, with the shadows of the night so deep and thick.

The silhouette of a tall, lanky man stood on the porch, smoking a neatly rolled cigarette. He didn't wear any fur to warm himself, or a duster to hold the weather at bay, just a long-sleeve black shirt tucked into black pants, high-top riding boots, and a black Stetson to match.

The effect of the cold wind of the night was lost on the man, seemed to be the least of his concerns. He wore a gun belt with a holster pulled tight on each hip, offering two pearl-gripped Colts for all to see. The grips glowed in the dark. They were not the man's only weapons; it was rare for one of his kind to be so heavily armed. It was hard to see the man's face in the shadows, but there was no mistaking his pure white skin, abhorrent to the sun's rays, and the warmth of any light, internal or external. There was barely any difference between his skin and the pearl grips on the gun.

The seven men had arrived at their destination, unbidden and undeterred. There had been no watch, no confrontations, no effort to slow their assault.

The absence of guards made Blanchard East uneasy, like they were riding straight into a trap. Then he remembered the Indian saying to him that "he was new to them, that they would know he was coming." They had the same feeling he did. Like something was returning, instead of danger coming their way.

There was something else welling up from deep inside of East, though. A foreign feeling that burned with rage and hate. It was not directed at the men who held the women and children of the town but at the men he rode with. For the Indian most of all. He wanted to kill the medicine man, rip his head off with his bare hands. And it was only by sheer will, and his dedication to the Indian for all that he had done for him, that Blanchard East was able to hold back and not act on the rage.

He didn't know how long he could hold the rage back.

Sweat dripped down East's forehead, and he suddenly felt like he was on fire, even though it was freezing cold outside, the wind whisking about, flecking snow and ice up from the ground like it was sand, piercing his eyes. He felt no pain, just spiking hate, like he was being stung with a thousand sharp-pointed needles from the inside out and the outside in.

The Indian stopped his horse about twenty feet from the cabin. The man on the porch didn't flinch, just took a deep draw off his cigarette.

"Get a hold of yourself, East," the Indian said with a low growl.

East's breathing was hard, and he felt like he was about to split in two. "How did you know?"

The Indian hesitated, stared directly into East's eyes, which had always been a rarity, then finally said, "I have always known what would happen when you faced your brothers for the first time."

Blanchard East had met the Indian just outside of St. Louis more than a year prior to their journey west together.

It was a cold night, much like this one, only far past the joyful days of Christmas, deep into January when the nights were growing shorter and the cold was so bitter and harsh a man's fingers could fall off without him knowing it.

The weather shouldn't have mattered since East had been riding shotgun on the Butterfield Overland Mail route toward Memphis with the ultimate destination of

Texas, but a cold, hard wind had blown down out of Canada, freezing everything in its path, then dumping a foot of snow in the storm's wake.

It was a perfect combination for a holdup, but East could have never imagined the outcome of such an uncommon winter storm.

There was only one passenger on the stage, an odd man dressed all in black who dared say anything except an offer of money and the desire to load his belongings, and himself, the night before they departed St. Louis. The man had paid an extra ten dollars for the privilege of early boarding. He was silent on the ride and kept the curtains drawn tight as possible. Just looking at the man gave East the shivers — all the way from his head to his toes and back again.

He should have known something was wrong right then and there, but he didn't pay heed to the warning. He and the teamster, a fella named Harvey Link, barreled out of St. Louis, desperate to make Memphis, trying to outrun the fierce cold and snow, to make their deadline. The lone passenger and the mail their only cargo.

The first night came fast, and with it, a wall of snow so thick it was hard to see the closest mule's tail. "We have to stop," Harvey Link had said, his beard nothing but icicles and snowy dandruff. His cheeks were burnt red with frostbite.

East had argued, protesting that they would run late and end up fired, without a job in hard times. But after struggling to drive the team another ten minutes, Link pulled the stagecoach off the trail, down a ravine, next to a river that was in the process of freezing over. "I ain't dyin' for no damn job." They were the last words he ever spoke.

The door to the interior of the Butterfield stagecoach flew open before the back wheels came to a final stop, and the man in black jumped outside in a fury. He was on the top seat before East could really digest what was happening.

East's fingers were so cold, his fur mittens so thick, he could barely grasp the shotgun. It didn't matter. The passenger took hold of Harvey Link's head, and with a quick twist, easily broke the man's neck. It snapped like a twig. The break echoed, and East could hardly believe his eyes. Fear took hold, and he felt helpless as a statue.

The man in black smiled, opened his mouth, then tore into Harvey Link's neck like he was a starving animal. It was the first time Blanchard East had ever seen fangs inside a human mouth. Fangs that looked like they belonged to a wild animal, a wolf or a rabid dog.

Blanchard East pissed his pants and tried to fire the shotgun, but he was too late. Out of the corner of his eye, he saw a shadow rise out of the river, heard a scream and a growl, saw another figure of a man rush toward the stagecoach and the man in black descend down to the ground. A fight ensued, leaving East frozen on the sideline, unable to move, barely able to breathe. Glad for a brief second that he had been rescued.

But his relief only lasted another second. The man in black tore away from the unseen and unknown paladin and jumped directly onto the driver's seat. East could smell his attacker's breath, foul and old, tinged with the thick smell of blood and death. He recoiled, tried to skitter away, but he was too slow. The man bit him.

And then everything went black.

When Blanchard East awoke, the Indian was sitting next to him, a fire raging between the river and the stagecoach, the smell of an odd meat cooking. The snow had stopped falling, and there was no wind to speak of. The weather didn't seem to have an effect on him. Actually, he couldn't feel a thing, which was an odd relief.

Neither of them spoke of the attack, of the man who had disappeared, but East knew he was in the Indian's debt. There was no job with the Butterfield to consider any longer, but a larger mission. There were other men in black in the world, the Indian had told East, and he would not rest until there were no more of them walking the earth.

Tricks of the memory were just one of the Indian's powers. Certain events of that night had been taken from Blanchard East, and they were just coming back to him, pushed over by the flood of rage and the promise of never being alone again.

"I see you have brought us a present, Indian," the man on the porch said.

"It is *Longissima Nocte,* is it not?"

The man's face was still hidden in the dark, but his eyes glowed orange, like hot embers in the bottom of a fire pit. "You know our ways."

"I do, but wish I did not."

"The secret of our existence is known to few."

"I was only lucky enough to survive."

"We feasted on someone you loved, and now you wish to return the favor with revenge?"

"I have an offering." The Indian turned to Blanchard East, showing no emotion, offering no tells to his intentions.

The man laughed. It was a hideous sound, echoing deeply past the seven men and out of the canyon. "He already belongs to us. He just doesn't know it."

"I know it," East said. "I know it now." He felt betrayed, tricked, used, and all of those feelings fueled the rage that was growing inside of him.

The Indian smiled. "I was the only friend you had. I kept you safe in the daylight, so you did not burn. I killed deer and drained their blood for you to sustain yourself. When there was a dead human near, I snuck into the parlor like a thief, and drained them, too. If you remember nothing else of our time together, remember that. I taught you how to survive this life you were given. I kept you alive."

"Beware of the coyote's tricks, brother," the man in black said.

Blanchard East drew in a deep breath. When he released it, nothing came out but a scream — a scream that could, and did, wake the dead, calling all that were like him out of their hiding places.

The clouds parted, and the moon beamed

enough light down onto the ground for Blanchard East to see a well-worn path from the cabin to a limestone wall that rose up behind it. There was a mine entrance twenty yards away. It was where the *Longissima Nocte* gathering was being held, the celebration of the longest night of the year, the feast for which all of the men who wore black hungered.

A transformation was occurring inside Blanchard East's body. His bones were changing. His teeth were changing. He could smell, taste, sense things more clearly than he ever had. It felt like he was breaking free of a spell. His fangs extruded from his teeth; sharp, white knives ready to shred the nearest bit of human flesh.

Torchlight flickered out of the mine entrance, dim at first, then bright, followed by movement like the flap of wings, but in reality, it was the hustle of boots, an army of black-clothed men set on alarm, drawn to a fight, like moths to a flame. The rush of them was like an explosion of bats bursting out of a cave at sunset, pushing out into the world to feed, to wreak havoc on whatever was in their path. There were more men in the army rushing out of the mine than East could have imagined. Seven would be no match. Six, if he joined his newly found brothers.

It was then that he heard the soft voice of the Indian, speaking in the earthly tongue that East didn't understand but had always found comfort in. But it was different now, now that he was free. It was the Indian calling on the wolves, calling on all of the forces of nature that would answer him, to conspire against the darkness of evil that they all faced.

"Come brothers, fight with us one more time," was all Blanchard East was able to digest, before he was forced to make his choice.

The battle was long and bloody. The wolves came in force, matching every soulless man with two of their own. The canines fought valiantly, dying with honor when they lost, but delivering death, too, the bite of their teeth enough to stagger the enemy, until a wooden stake could be driven into its chest. The Indian had packed a cache of the weapons in each man's saddlebag. Knowledge of the war and the required weaponry were his, and only his.

Snakes, scorpions, and locusts were all roused from their nighttime rests to offer aid to the Indian, who in the end faced down the strongest of the men in black, the man who was waiting on the porch.

"I will not beg for mercy," the man said.

"You will not receive it," the Indian answered.

Blanchard East stood at the Indian's side, along with Father Michael, who had found it in himself to kill an evil he could never imagine. A few of the wolves stood behind the three of them, joined in the cause.

"There are more of us than you know," the man said. He was the last man in black standing, at least that they knew of. His hands were at his side, ready to draw his pearl-handled Colts; a last measure of survival for the creature.

"Then we will hunt you all down, one at a time, or in times like this, *Longissima Nocte,* times when you are drunk with arrogance and celebration."

"Then we will meet another night." The man on the porch laughed again, then jumped up into the air as if he were a bird, disappearing into the shadows, leaving no sign of his existence. Before anyone could move, the man was gone, escaped.

"Where'd he go?" Blanchard East said.

"To seek out more of his kind. You will, too. We will find him. Our paths will cross again, I assure you of that. He knew he was about to die."

East understood then. He had been tamed, saved, tricked, to be a finder for the Indian. It was the only power he had that was his own, and even then, he was unaware of it.

Another sound came that redirected East's attention away from the barren sky. It was the sound of whimpers and cries of women and children — all calling out to be rescued and saved. East knew what that felt like.

The Indian said nothing, but looked to the horizon with a worried expression, then turned his attention to Father Michael. "Go free your women and children. Take them home." Without waiting for an answer, he walked over to his horse and pulled out a small bag, then returned to the papist priest and handed it to him. "Make a tea of this and make sure all that you rescue drink it. It will restore their health and ease their memories. No human should walk with the truth of these nightmares living in their hearts and minds."

Father Michael took the bag. "What will become of you?"

The Indian looked to Blanchard East and smiled as much as he could. "I must see my friend to darkness and keep him safe." He turned, then, to the three wolves, to the alpha, who had survived, acquiring more scars, adding another legend to his existence within the pack and beyond, and said, "Thank you, my brother. May we meet in the presence of the Great Father and recount these days with gladness."

The alpha lowered his head, pawed at the ground, then turned and ran down the pass, followed by his two pack mates, yipping all the way, celebrating the victory over darkness.

"You've given our town a great gift by arriving when you did," Father Michael said, "and saving our women and children. We are forever in your debt."

"Perhaps," the Indian said, "your town will look kindly on simple men when they wander onto your streets. A welcoming heart, and the coin that you have already paid us, has settled that debt."

"I will see to it, then, I promise," Father Michael said. "I promise all men will be welcome in our town. Indians and Anglo alike. All men deserve peace and comfort, especially on days like this."

The Harrows

May 1865

1
Eliza's Return

There is a heartening that I can hardly put into words as the land transforms itself from mystery to familiar. My body secretly relaxes and falls into a comfortable rhythm with the rise and fall of a known hill or a recognizable oak tree with its arms wide open, reaching out with a welcoming sigh; *I've been waiting for your return.* Wind off the mountain is an old friend, too. The moment of recognition is framed in perfection all the way down to the ray of light piercing the untested forest canopy. I imagined and hoped for this sight under the darkness of a thousand uncertain nights; in the throes of rage and weakness, at my best moment and at my worst, covered in blood, surrounded by death, fighting for life, searching for a sign of any kind of lightness and joy at all. I am tempted to pinch myself to see if I am awake. *If I am truly home.*

The air, too, is tainted with memories of all of the seasons. With it being late spring, the season of hope and renewal is my most favorite. I can almost conjure an ounce of faith, truly believe that bodies and spirits can actually be restored, wounds of war healed, and the past laid to rest. The springs of my youth were idyllic, perfect in every way, until the shadow of man's hate turned to darkness, and the greed of battle blew everything I loved and cherished to the four corners of this broken nation. My father and brothers marched off long before I did; they took up arms while I was left to mend the wounds of their battles, nursing them and their comrades as was my lot, whether I chose it or nor. I've had the healing touch since I was but a girl. I knew how to set a broken goldfinch's wing before I could explain why it needed done. Seeds I planted sprouted in dirt where nothing else would grow. Stitches in skin I sewed barely left a mark. All of which seemed as natural as breathing to me and my family. I come from a long line of healers; the women in my history have always wrapped the men in their lives with linen and love, set their bones just as easy as we've captured their hearts. Those skills and gifts served my days and fortified my nights. We all longed for the end of the war, for the blood to stop flowing. When it came, I was as surprised as anyone else that any of us were left standing.

The spring beauties are past their prime since they are one of the first flowers to rise up from the ground after a long winter's sleep, but Solomon's seal, fragrant as any perfume I have had the pleasure to smell, hovers along the hillside in clumps that remind me of small villages; white flags surrendering over every house. I have never considered abundant beauty in defeat until now. There are other flowers to be noticed by my beleaguered eyes as I travel forth; three different kinds of trillium, yellow violets, and a striped trout-lily here and there if I look close enough. They all litter the floor of the thick woods along the road, reaching for the sun, aching for warmth and the touch of a bee's wing. And this is where the twain meets, my return home and my fear of it; anxiousness and dread roiled together just under my thinned and burgeoning skin. The land before me looks unscarred, but I know the closer to my destination that I travel, it will not be. I have heard tell in my three years of duty of more than one bloody battle fought on the soil of my family's legacy. I fear there is nothing left of my former life.

I cannot force myself to relax on the buckboard seat. Instead I pull forward to the edge, dressed in my tattered scarlet travel clothes, carpetbag at my feet, pressed against the back of my calves, pining to see around the next bend. Thankfully, my driver, a Mister Paxton Byles, from Greeneville, has remained quiet in our travels. He is as uninterested in my company as I am his. I hold no fervent desire to discuss my departure from Charleston, my previous experiences, or my views held of the occupation that I have so recently departed. He is aware of my destination, of my good name, and the assurance that I can pay a decent fare for my transport. There is no other requirement of our venture. I have never been much for small talk, especially with strangers. The less I know of Mister Byles, the better, and the less he knows about me and the future of my endeavors, the better off he is. His eyes and ears do not appear to be able to bear one more tale of sadness and defeat.

The bed of the lorry holds a load of empty gunny sacks, bundled and stacked waist high. It is a light load, a slight demand on the efforts of the two mules that pull us toward our mutual destinations. His, I was told in Charleston, was the mill at Fortner's Creek, though I had to wonder why, with it being planting season instead of the harvest. I do have to restrain the question, but I find the purpose of the load odd and unknowable. The gunny sacks are made of old burlap, the stenciling faded so deep that I cannot make out any of the words. None of the bags are the same, which seems more of a curiosity, but only because I occupy myself with the thought, fearing what I will encounter up the road.

The sight of the spring beauties and the trillium pain my heart in a way for which I am not prepared. They are too fragile, too untouched; I envy their short life more than my own. I know their season is brief, their days under the sun numbered and in decline. The blooms signal their death, their return to the dirt. In all of their glory, I grieve for the tiny flowers, too, as much as everything else. It is impossible to look away from melancholy and death. My blood is tainted with a gray affliction just as my touch is gifted to heal.

"I'll be getting off right around the bend, Mister Byles," I say.

He doesn't respond right away. His eyes

are fixed forward, burned into the space that separates the mules. "I suppose you will." He glances over to me then, looks me in the eye, then to the bump in my belly that I've tried so hard to conceal. "You best prepare yourself. There's not much left."

"I've heard, but thank you just the same."

Mister Byles looks away then, focuses his attention back on the mules, starts to rein them in and slow their pace. "Don't expect you need any surprises in your condition."

The words pierce my ears like the sting of a hornet. *In your condition.* I am embarrassed, ashamed. There is no hiding the coming of another life no matter how hard I try to deny that it is true.

2
HARROW HOUSE

I stand on the side of the road and bid Mister Byles adieu. My carpetbag sits at my feet, and my pride and worth is lost to the wind. He offered no explanation of his load and had barely said good-bye. I suppose I should get accustomed to such treatment, even though he knows nothing of why I travel alone, or of the origin of my presupposed condition.

There is no one to greet me. I have not sent word of my impending arrival. The lane that leads up to Harrow House looks just as I remember it: Lined with ancient oak trees, their vibrant and healthy arms reaching upward, adorned with moss that looks like dyed sheets, shredded green by wind and time. The ground is carpeted with spring beauties, and the moisture of the new season smells fresh and clean; fragrant with possibility instead of the reality of dread from the past winter. Once upon a time, I wove a crown of flowers and pretended that I was a fairy princess among giants in the very place that I stand. Oak trees acted as ogres and I was adorned with special powers because I was the only girl in my family. I was just a child then, before William Thrombo tried to kiss me under the shelter of deep leaves in a pouring rainstorm, before the reality of my age caught up with me, and I was forced to watch my three brothers walk up this very lane for a waiting company of soldiers. I can still hear them marching off, each foot in unison with the other, each sole falling to the ground echoing the solemn drumbeat of war.

I have to gird myself for more sad news as I walk forward, toward home, toward Harrow House. I do my best to blink away tears that are seeded by the pain of the past and the presence of the future. I cannot see the house. It sits at the crest of a hill, just past a slight lean in the road, overlooking the creek that has ran aside our house and lives since the beginning of time. The sound of running water is a comfort that I have longed for on the loneliest nights of my absence.

I square my shoulders, breathe deep, and force my feet to carry me the rest of the way up the lane. The truth is, I have nowhere else to go. I can only hope that there is someone waiting for me in the place of my birth, that a roof still stands to cover us from the inclement weather and the storms that are sure to come.

No one is truly relieved that the war is over. There is a painful healing to come. Scars to bind and toughen up. It will take years to rebuild what has been destroyed. Anger and rage still salt the wounds of the victors, who will surely gloat with nothing more than their mere presence. We are now a union of one nation once again, though I do not believe that for a minute, and no one else that I know, especially those who served in some capacity of the cause, believes it either. We are shattered and lost, and no amount of peace-talking rhetoric can force all of the broken pieces back together. Only time can do that, and I am not certain that such a thing is possible. I have seen broken things mended with great attempt, and they are never the same again.

I quicken my pace, certain of the knowledge of the house that waits just at the bend. I pray it into existence, have cherished the memory of it since my departure. It is all I can do not to collapse when at last I lay my eyes upon the very place that kept me safe and warm for most all of my life. There is hardly anything I recognize that still stands.

I stop, close my eyes, and do my best to will every nail, every joist, rafter, and shingle back to its original place. When I open my eyes, I see nothing but a ruin: three red brick chimneys jutting into the air, marred by soot and ash, all blurred by the touch of tears. Blackened beams have crashed through the floor, then burned away, leaving piles of dust. Posts that once held up the veranda are weak and coated by the remains of fire. There is no second floor, no roof, no windows. Only the ghost in my mind of what once was. The entire house has been destroyed. There can be no repair. Reconstruction is beyond consideration. That would take more money than I can ever consider stumbling across. I only have a few coins in my purse. I'm not even sure how I am going to eat dinner, much less provide a roof over my head now that I see the truth of what I have been told. My heart sinks into a deep, irretrievable pit. I shiver even though it is a luscious, warm spring day.

I can hardly begin to consider the loss of the contents inside the house, of all the possessions accumulated over a lifetime by my family. All that came before me and after is lost to the touch of a flame. And for what? How much blood and treasury were spent to destroy the dreams of those who wanted nothing to do with a war in the first place? Even the victors must face their own ounce of destruction upon returning from the battlefield. Sadness falls over my entire body like it has been attacked by an incurable sickness.

I can hardly see forward as my vision is blurred so severely by salty tears. The world is warped, foggy, fragile, water-filled, and to be honest, what hope I had stashed away is forsaken; gone in the moment of one long breath. I have lost my home, my center, the place that begged me to return in my dreams and waking moments. *What is there in this world for me now?*

Even filtered through my tears, I see movement, the image of a man coming toward me. He limps, looks familiar, but distant, like the memory of someone I once knew. I wipe my eyes clear, and before me, walking toward me with a look of great surprise, is my middle brother, Titus. Titus Milan Harrow. Two years older than I, and a survivor of war. I cannot believe he is here, before me, alive, crying at the sight of me just as I am him.

But he is not whole, not untouched by the ravages of conflict any more than I am. I can see that right away. The limp is not a limp. It is the walk of a man who only has one leg. He stands with the aid of a crutch carved from a hickory tree. He stops thirty feet from me and clears his eyes, just as I do my own. He can't believe I am alive. He must wonder if I am real in my godforsaken state. He must see in me what everyone else sees: a wisp of what I once was, changed like a dead tree facing north, spindly and gray, no longer reaching for the burn of the sun. Icarus lies at my feet, dead in a heap; the cautionary tale reverberates in my mind with warning and gladness.

3

TITUS'S GARDEN

We have never been a family who greets each other with physical contact, with a warm embrace, but the aftermath of war changes a person's restrictions just as it changes the face of a nation. Titus and I collapse into each other and hold on for fear of falling off the earth. He smells of woodsmoke and sweat. I wonder if he is able to toil at will, or if the joy of work has been taken from him, too. Titus always worked harder than the rest of us. He had to prove himself being the middle son. It was easy to get lost between Clendon's beauty and Emerson's God-given talents. Emerson could mend anything that was broken, including the hearts of half of the girls in the county. Clendon glowed even when he slept, especially when he slept. My brothers have always been like Greek gods to me.

Titus pulls back and looks at me. I can see the wear of pain and loss on his face; his skin is tight over his jaw, and black whiskers struggle to grow. He reminds me of a fallow field in the winter, the stubbles touched lightly by an unexpected snow.

"I feared you were dead, sister," Titus whispers. He holds both of my shoulders with his hands — hands that still bear heavy calluses — but remain tender in their touch.

"And I you."

"You heard of Clendon's brave death at Chancellorsville?"

"Regrettably so," I say. My gaze falls to

the ground as Titus allows both of his hands to fall to his side. One, the right, automatically steadies the crutch as he shifts his weight. I think he feared I would collapse if I did not already know of Clendon's fate. "A letter of Mother's found me in Atlanta, three months past the news. It nearly took my feet from under me."

"You two were very close," he says.

"I love all of my brothers."

Titus stares at me, forces a smile, then looks grimly to the remains of the house. "There's not much left. Mother tried to put the fire out. But that was her undoing. She should have let it burn."

It is my turn to whisper. "She is dead?"

Titus shakes his head. "She only wishes so. She suffers from the burns on her hands and on the skin of half her body. Infections come and go doing their best to force her under the ground, but she resists. She is waiting for Father to walk up the lane. And, you, of course. She missed you the most."

I can hardly stand the thought of being my mother's favorite, but I know what Titus says is true. My mother, Cleda Dawnitide Farrell Harrow, is a headstrong woman, thick with opinions that live on the tip of her quick tongue. It has been said that she and I are just alike. And I suppose we are, which has always presented itself as the friction between us that has lit a thousand flares, as well as provided the grease that complements us in our unified efforts. I smile at the thought of our battles. They would shoo the boys from the kitchen, causing them to return on tepid feet, as if all the carpets in the house were made of brittle and combustible fibers. Mother and I, of course, would be long past the eruption, and most likely be in the middle of consideration for the design of my latest dress or bonnet.

"I am happy that she survives," I say.

Titus looks at me, takes me in just as I took him in. I did not know that he had lost a leg, and he, of course, knows nothing of my condition.

"You surprise me, Eliza," he says.

"And why is that?"

"I thought your heart only belonged to William Thrombo."

It takes all I have not to pepper him with daggers from both eyes. Titus is the last person I wish to discuss my loves and losses with. But he has always been bold that way, saying what no one else would to me — out of earshot of Mother, of course. Along with his work ethic, his boldness was how he competed against his brothers for my attention, even when it brought a rage upon him.

"We will have a lot to talk about once I get settled," I finally say.

"Yes, I suppose we will." Titus turns away from me, and starts to make his way up the lane, one hop and one crutch at a time. "I was about to pick some radishes from the garden when I saw you. Are you coming with me?" he asks, over his shoulder.

It would be just like Titus not to offer to throw my bag over his back. I would have insisted on carrying it myself anyway. But the offer would have been nice. The warmth of our embrace has faded quickly, and it is the first realization that I have arrived, at last, to my one and only home.

4
ALL MY FALLEN LEAVES

Only one shanty stands beyond the remains of Harrow House. The rest of them have burned to the ground. As I look out over the rise, over what once was a wide vista of cotton fields covering everything in sight — flowering, then offering an abundance of fabric to the world; spun, woven, mended, all burned now as fuel for a former rage — I am saddened all over again by the loss of what once was. All that remains is my broken memory. Now, the perennial plants of cotton rise to maturity, offering praise and hope. The fields have grown amuck, unattended for a matter of years. Experienced hands have fled to the North. The shot at Sumter was an alarm bell, awakening the living and dead, offering them the chance to run if they so chose. Father was early in his recognition that the cause would fail. Keeping human labor always troubled his converted Methodist heart, but he had inherited the land, the house, and the sins of his father. War offered him the opportunity to break the chain. The separation from the past cost him his life and the future fortune his heirs may have received. Perhaps there is luck in that. It is too early to tell. My heart breaks at just the thought of it.

"Mother will not leave the shack," Titus says. "She fears the light, and the gaze of judgmental eyes upon her discolored skin."

"It is all she has," I say.

Titus holds a bunch of radishes and bib lettuce. It is our dinner. That, and what remains of an unfortunate rabbit who wandered into Titus's bead before my arrival. Sustenance is no longer an immediate concern, and for that I am glad.

My words cause a look of confusion to cross Titus's weathered face. His nose has always been hooked and his eyes are a little closer together than they should be. Daguerreotypes suggest he favors the Farrells, Mother's side of the family. The resemblance and severity of his permanent expression has always made it easy for Titus to be misunderstood. He looks perpetually angry, enraged at the world for all that has occurred in his short lifetime. It is no wonder that he favors rage, but I wish he would turn that gaze to those who deserve it.

"You know how people are," he says.

My body reacts. My chin drops toward the ground in acknowledgement. But I say nothing. Titus's gaze falls again to pry at the unusual growth in my belly. I offer him no explanation, even though one must come eventually. I cannot keep the condition a secret much longer, but the ground under my feet is soft and unsure. I am yet to fully acknowledge the life that grows under my skin as my own; lest I say it was not of my doing. My body was another landscape in the war to be plundered and pillaged.

"You should tell her I am here," I say. "I don't want to startle her."

"You should prepare yourself."

"One must always be prepared."

"Her words."

"They follow me wherever I go."

"It is your choice, then." Titus lowers his

head, walks to the shack, and deposits the vegetables in a stained wicker basket that stands next to the door. He hesitates before walking inside, allowing me time to pick up my carpetbag and join him.

Mother does not gasp with surprise when she first lays eyes on me. She wavers a bit before looking at me wholly, then says, "Of all my children, I knew it would be you that would return home fully intact. I knew it would be Eliza who would make the venture home to find me burned, withered, and unrecognizable. But you, too, have been touched by the mood of demolition. I see no ring on your finger," she says, wearing the same question as Titus on her wrinkled face. "Is this a joy or a tragedy, dear daughter?"

"Tragedy," I say, offering no more. I do not need to. Mother understands what has happened to me. I pray that I will be saved of sharing the details, but I know I will not be.

"Ah, then all of my leaves have fallen. A cold season lays on us even though the earth celebrates with warmth and birdsong. How sad."

5
A Midnight Scar

There are just the three of us in this life now. The last of the Harrows. Clendon and Emerson are lost to us, their earthly remains buried near Chancellorsville and Shiloh, while Father's body is scattered in the soil of Gettysburg. Each of us bear external and internal injuries from the war. Mother and her burns. Titus with the loss of his leg. And me, with the burden of a child that will soon venture into the world, innocent for only a moment. The world and all of its voices will have their say about the child's prospects, about its heritage, and the place of certainty or uncertainty in the line of Harrows. The poor infant survives on tainted blood and a loveless beginning. What lie must I tell so I may be looked upon as a decent mother? I worry that I will not be able to offer any kind of love to the progeny of the enemy, of a war-mad stranger. Where is the comfort in the results of a nightmare, perpetuated in heat of battle? Can I heal myself? This baby? These thoughts are my own. Titus and Mother have their own difficulties to face.

One day passes to the next and for the most part our lives are isolated and remote. Society has suffered an eclipse; a transition from dark to light, but no one has the money to host balls or cotillions, and I, above all, hold no desire to attend Sunday services or venture into town for provisions and small talk. The desire for normal life to return exists only in the distant gaze of survivors. Titus wears the face of the Farrells and Harrows. Though there is rumor in town of my return, I cannot find it in myself to show my face to familiar eyes. I cannot answer questions that I do not have answers to. Instead, I stay and work the land, planting, weeding, clearing, ensuring that we all will have enough food for the coming winter. Titus has secured a small flock of bantam hens, allowing for a sudden bounty of eggs and the occasional pot of meat on our table. The recollection of low battle rations is never far from my mind. Not only did I witness physical effects of the lack of food, but of the spirit and mind, as well. A man with rickets and no hope is a horrible sight, one that can never be expunged from any decent human being's memory.

 The days have settled into a comfortable rhythm with mornings left to my touch on Mother's skin with the attempt to heal what has burned away. I have nothing but the medicines found in the woods and in my memory. Mud protects open wounds. Stinging nettle nourishes mother's muscles and digestion. The flower called self heal aides in the mending of her skin, though it will always be rippled by the flames. Mother glints in the sunlight when she dares to venture out into it; her glow is one of pain, unlike Clendon's. Along with the bantams, Titus has also been able to secure codeine from town to ease Mother's pain. Beyond these medicines, keeping Mother's dressings clean and changed is all that I can offer her. Attending to her spirits is more of a challenge. She grieves deeply for her husband and sons. As do we all.

There is plenty of fieldwork to attend to as the cotton grows toward the summer harvest. Between his errands to town and tending the chickens and garden, Titus stays busy. He rarely complains, but navigating with one leg frustrates him. He wants to do more. I do what healing I can for him, too, attending to his stump as it continues to heal. He does not talk about his dark day, and has, to my great relief, relinquished expectations of me to talk of mine. Once I offered no explanation and did not moon over some unknown beau, Titus arrived at a silent conclusion about the cause of my condition on his own. He knows the abominable acts men commit in war. He has killed more men than he ever dreamed he would. Sins regardless, but somehow forgiven, at least in the light of day, for those who take up arms for the state. A government's permission to kill overrides God's command not to, but there is punishment, nonetheless. Titus is restless at night. Sometimes he whimpers like a suckling pig in search of its mother.

As the days roll on, the life in me continues to grow. I have yet to decide whether the baby is a boy or a girl. Mother cringes when I call the child an *it,* but I know of nothing else to call it. She fears for the baby's safety now and after it arrives but doesn't say so aloud. It has never occurred to me to inflict pain or distress to the child inside me. I have spent my life healing wounds, first at home, then at war as a nurse in the surgeon's tent, and now, back home again. Harming the unborn seems unconscionable to me, though deep in my own difficult nights, I worry if it is a boy, if it will grow into the same kind of man who conquered my flesh and left a deep wound on my soul. Can I prevent that? I shall try. But I worry of it just the same. I worry, too, if the child is a girl. What do I know of this man who left me with a child to raise on my own? He knows nothing of the result of his loathsome deed. He does not care what happens to the seed he has sown. Has the government forgiven him this act of war, too? Is that what I am to tell this child of mine? That the father is forgiven? I know they will call her a bastard. Will they berate a dear daughter even though she had nothing to do with how she came into this world? I suppose they will. I will do what I must to prevent that, too.

I hide among the poppies when the post arrives, and do my best, like Mother, to keep myself unseen, but it is impossible, especially once Titus employs the services of Mira Smoot, the local midwife. I objected, of course, certain that I could attend to the birth on my own, but Titus insisted on telling Mira Smoot of my predicament. She arrives once weekly astride a swayback mare the color of a midnight scar. Mira has a mixed history herself, with one foot in the Negro world and the other foot in the land of a cotton field master who took his pleasure at Mira's mother's expense. If anyone would understand my plight, it is Mira. She is a rare breed, blessed with the will made of iron, and the ability to deflect hate like no other woman I have ever met. She has been beaten, threatened, and raped herself, and yet, there is never a moment when she does not wear a smile. Especially when there is a new life to bring into the world. She says it is her calling from the lord to see to it that babies arrive on this earth as safely as possible. Mira does carry a fault, though, and that is her lack of ability to be discreet. She is a talker, a storyteller of great renown. She has that wonderful voice that warms a soul like a stew warms a stomach on a cold night. It is from her tongue that most all of Markleburg County has learned of my return, and of my condition.

As my time grows near, so does the fullness of the moon. July days are long, hot, and miserable. The nights are no different. Harvest time demands that Titus and I work the field, picking cotton and placing the heads in a drag-bag that grows to an unbearable weight. This task is difficult for both of us. My belly is swollen to a girth that I could hardly imagine. It looks like I have swallowed two watermelons.

Titus steadies himself on one knee and his stump. Our progress is slow, but each day, we work from sunup to sundown. We cannot afford to hire labor, and we both fear that the profit of our efforts will not see us through the coming winter. If it weren't for the perennial plant, we would have no hope at all. Sadly, midway through the month, Titus is left to work the harvest on his own. As I pull myself through the field, my water breaks and floods under me. Titus tears out after Mira Smoot, and in the coming of night, I am racked with such pain as I have ever felt. I scream into the night, cursing every man who has walked the earth, but especially one. I will always curse him. Mira knows of my fate; my worst living moment. I confess to her under the duress of pain and fear that a renegade group of soldiers overwhelmed the surgeon's tent. They killed every man, and left the three of us who were nurses to live and take their pleasures with. Minutes seemed like hours. The catastrophe of childbirth brought forth a torrent of liquid memories. Mira cradled me, rocked, told me that she understood my pain. She has suffered the same disgrace. After it is all said and done, a bloody, hollering, healthy boy is placed in my arms, and for the first time in my life, I don't know how to stop the cries of another human being.

6
THE FALL

I named the boy Charles Emerson Clendon Harrow. Titus didn't seem to mind the omission of his name. He still lives while our father and brothers have perished under the call of duty. I hope that the legacy is fitting, will somehow find its way to encourage the child to aspire to honor. It is the only good start I have to offer him.

"My only objection is the surname. He is not a Harrow," Titus says.

We have arranged our meager furniture in the shack so that a bassinet stands next to my bed. Charles sleeps peacefully nearby. He is not a fussy baby, which is a great relief for us all. "And what else would you have me call this child? He is as much a Harrow as you and I."

Titus's face flushes red. "People will know."

"How can I prevent that?"

"I worry for him, for you."

"And yourself?"

"For us all, living and dead."

"So I should not have returned home?"

Titus exhales deeply with the knowledge that he cannot win the argument that he has provoked, then heads to the door, and stops. "I will not speak of this again."

"He will need his uncle," I say.

Titus looks to the sleeping baby, then to me; the anger melts from his face. For a moment, I see his sensitivities. I am relieved that not everything good has been amputated.

"And I will need him," Titus says, then exits the shack, the fall of the crutch as solid and determined as his footstep.

Mother, to her credit, has remained tight-lipped during the exchange with my brother, but she cannot restrain herself any longer. "He is right, you know?"

"What else am I to do?"

Mother looks away from me because she has no answer to my question. Silence invades the shack, and I am suddenly hot to the toes. When I look down to Charles, he is staring up at me with his droopy deep brown eyes. The Harrows are all blue-eyed, and this is yet another way that the boy will be different from us all. If there was any woodland herb I could eat and change the flavor of my milk so the color of his eyes would change to blue, I would, but there is no such magic in this world that I know of. I want him to be like us more than anything.

I am still in search of recognition of his face. Sadly, there is none. Maybe the fact that he has the face of a stranger is another blessing. What if I see the aggressor every time I look at my son's face? Would I hate him? Fear him? Loathe him? I am safe from that for now. I hope the memory of that face has been permanently erased from my mind, replaced with the subtly of love and the connection of blood. I am sure of the connection. The being erupted from my body; I felt it, saw it, whether I could believe it or not. I fear the love, though I feel it, know it exists. My heart aches when I am gone from Charles for any length of time. I worry for his welfare, for his every breath. It is a kind of love different from any I've ever known.

I am back in the field now, still offering my contribution to the harvest. My body recovers slowly, and my strength is only half of its normal gauge, but Titus cannot do all of the picking on his own. We both fear a loss of the crop. Weevils have been reported in a nearby county. Destruction is at hand if we don't hurry. I have no choice but to leave the baby in Mother's care and spend as many hours in the field as I am physically able. I have no choice but to leave Charles's side, no matter how much it pains us both. He cries out in separation, and that binds us even tighter.

7
THE RISING STORM

I have resisted going into town for as long as I could, but Titus is ill, and we need grain. Milk must be bartered with the Fergusons outside of Allwhich. I will ride past the farm on my return. I have no choice but to take Charles with me. He needs to suckle, and there is always chance of delay. If we are going to face the world, it will be together.

I drive into town on our buckboard, pulled by a gray work horse named Jimbo. The gelding is the progeny of horses that have served the lands of Harrow House since my grandfather took the mortgage. I trust Jimbo implicitly. He is a fine horse with an amenable personality. It is a smooth ride into the realm of the populated, and Charles sleeps most of the way.

I do not dillydally. I head straight to Maxwell's feed store, park the wagon, and ignore any looks my arrival has provoked. It is with great relief that Vern Maxwell has other business to attend to, and his wife, Marletta, tends to my needs. The owner of the general store is a died-in-the-wool believer of the cause. Vern was too old to take up arms and stayed behind to serve those, like my mother, who were forced to wait out the war. Men like him found power in the operation of the town that they did not hold before the war. His store is my only option, otherwise, I would have found a different outlet from which to purchase my grain.

Marletta Maxwell is a mouse of a woman, and I can hardly remember the sound of her voice. I cannot hide that I am pleased to see her, and she seems so of me, when I enter the store. She barely says a word during our transaction, outside of the requirements of business, until I prepare to leave.

"I heard you was back," Marletta says. "But I didn't believe everything that I heard." She had obviously found a power in the war she did not possess before, too.

I had turned to leave after depositing my money in her palm, but her words stop me. "And what was it you heard?" I ask as I spin around to face her.

Marletta's face blushes red, and she looks away from me. "I cannot speak of such things."

"But you just did." I pull Charles tighter to me, and force his face to my shoulder by cupping the back of his head with my hand. "What did you hear?" I want to protect Charles, put my fingers in his ears, but I cannot.

Marletta looks past me as if she is in hopes that a customer will enter the store. Outside, I hear the bags of grain being loaded onto my wagon. I could walk away, but I can't. Not now.

The storekeeper's wife exhales and says,

"I don't believe it. I don't believe any of it."

"Tell me."

"They say you gave yourself to the soldiers in exchange for your life. That the boy is willfully Union blood."

"They say worse than that." I knew it was Mira Smoot who had told the tale of Charles's origin, but I was also smart enough to know that a tale takes on a life of its own, just like that of a lie. Mira would not attach that embellishment to my story, I am sure of it. People add and subtract what pleases them for their own benefit, for their own purpose. Charles has been anointed with the hate against the victors. He would always be a bluecoat, a betrayer of the cause. Men would blame him for the loss of their legs and pass down the rage to their sons and daughters. Life in school would be a misery. No matter the talents that Charles inherits from the Farrells and Harrows, beauty, mechanics, a healing touch, it will be overruled by the unknown blood that runs through his veins.

"They do say worse than that," Marletta says. "I thought you should know."

Footsteps on the boardwalk and the ring of the bell save me from saying something that I would regret for the rest of my life. I want to scream at Marletta and her husband, in his absence, for helping to spread such falsehoods, even though I know I will only make things worse for myself and for my son.

I spin, and hurry past Caroline Renny as she enters the store. Caroline, who lost two sons in the war, doesn't say a word to me. Disapproval and hate anchor her chin upon seeing me holding Charles tight against my chest. I worry that she is building a ball of spit to throw my way. If not now, it will come soon. I am sure of it. She has already heard the tale of my duty, of my time away. It matters not how much relief of suffering I have provided to the boys on our side. All that matters is that I was overrun, did not fight back hard enough, that I brought back that shame with me — which is hardly the truth. But people like Marletta and Caroline are not interested in the truth. They are only interested in distractions from their own pain, from their own shame — and my son is the repository that they have chosen for such a thing. Over my dead body.

I see judgment and ugliness everywhere I look as I leave town. In every eye, in every face, in every soul, I see a story that is not true but cannot be controlled or changed. I am grateful that Charles is only a baby.

I refuse to allow tears or rage to drive me

home. Even though my worst fears have come true, I am relieved. Relieved to know what I must do, how I must proceed. The only trouble will be convincing Mother and Titus that our time on this land is past. Charles is not safe here, and neither are we.

8
THE WIND AT OUR BACKS

Mother sits inside the shack watching as I pack the last of our belongings into the wagon. She has been the most difficult to persuade to leave. In the end, I challenged her to a ride into town to see for herself what lives we face, but she declined. Mother knows how she would be looked upon, scarred, burned from trying to save her home, her beauty taken by the flames — she is a monster who cannot look at her own reflection in the mirror. But it is not her appearance that kept her from the trip. It is her love of Charles that prevents her from experiencing the hate that she knows exists, no matter our good name or the former standing in society. She cannot stomach seeing the last of the Harrows spit on, sworn at, begrudged for a crime that he did not commit.

I hoist Charles's bassinet onto the back of the wagon, tie it down, then face Mother and Titus. Charles is cradled in Mother's arms, sleeping amid the racket of packing. He is too young to remember this day, and for that I find another feather of gladness to add to the wings that will carry us away.

"That's it, then," I say.

Mother nods. "No tears." She looks up to the clear autumn sky, blue as the China her father bought in Williamsburg and gave her for a wedding present, then to me. "We won't get far."

"We have a good month," I say. "If we have to hole up in St. Louis, then so be it."

Titus exhales. He is glad to leave Harrow House behind more than any of us, I think. He knows, like we all do, even if the house could be rebuilt, that we will be haunted by the past, by the war, by the aftermath. He was the first to say that we all need a fresh start, a place to remake ourselves, to build another life. "And then to California," he says.

"Yes, as long as it takes," I answer. We have sold our property to Mister Byles for pennies on the dollar, and scrounged up every cent we could find for the journey, selling what survived the fire and our sad bank account. Mother wouldn't sell her gold wedding band that father had placed on her finger, and I couldn't blame her. Its value wouldn't have got us much farther as it was. It will take everything we have to finish the trek, and there will be times when we may well have to stop and work, or hunt the land for a season, but we are determined to finish what we start. We are determined to start over in California.

Titus nods. Mother nods. We're all ready to go. Then she covers her head with a light hood, walks out into the sun, hands Charles to me, and climbs, with the aid of Titus, to her spot in the rear of the wagon. We follow suit with Titus in the driver's seat, and me next to him, holding my son.

Titus knickers Jimbo, and we start our journey in silence. I take the direction of my mother, offering no tears to the wool. But inside, I am in a panic, knowing that I will never see this beloved land again. I know I will never smell the air whipping through the oaks on a stormy spring day, or embrace the hickory burning in the hearth. The voices of my family have been silenced on this land as we roll along; our war with it is lost. I can hardly bear to say good-bye, but I am glad for the leaving as much as Titus and Mother. Maybe more.

We will have a chance to become ourselves again in California — if we get there — have a life far away from the war, the memory of it, the pain of it, the sight of it. And in doing so, in going west, Charles will grow up as my son, a Harrow through and through, without judgment and hate, until that fateful day when he is old enough to ask about his father. When he can understand my words, digest the tale, I will tell him the truth. I hope I can heal his pain. I hope my own pain is healed by then. Perhaps, if luck smiles on us all, our journey west will be the best thing that has ever happened to us.

The Prairie Fire

The Wapihanne ran so slow it looked like it was standing still. Rain had been sparse of late, but the river's current continued to push underneath the surface, invisible and deceptive at first glance, but it could drown a weak swimmer even though it looked harmless. Naxke held a secret fear of water, of the power it held over her. She never told anyone of her fear, and she only stood on the edge of the Wapihanne when she had to. Even when it was calm and peaceful, the water could take a life. She had seen it happen more than once when the river raged, after the spring rains.

At the right angle, and in the right light, the water looked like a white cloth cutting through the flat, grassy lands of the koteewi. The air wasn't cold enough to freeze the river, the leaves still pulsed green. Naxke knew that what she saw was the river bottom reflecting upward.

A blue jay chattered, and a chickadee fluttered inside a berry bush searching for insects on the leaves, not the fruit. It was a perfect day, at least on the outside. The sun poured down on her stiff shoulders, though there was nothing the bright orb could do to encourage or warm her. Kitha was late. That was something that had never happened before, not in all of their life together. Kitha was as reliable as the moon and the stars, and now he wasn't where he was supposed to be.

"You look ill." It was her sister, Seke's, voice.

Naxke was the younger of the two, her hair the color of a blazing maple. She had hated her hair and fairer skin when she was young. It made her different, made her stand out from the others, but as she had grown into a woman, she had become accustomed to the tresses, to the differences. Oddity was the curse of her family. She longed to look like Seke, to look like the rest of the tribe, though her sister had her own otherness to deal with, too.

"I am only worried," Naxke said. "Kitha has me in fits. The sun falls again and the ground underneath my feet grows cold."

"I warned you."

"You warn me about something every day.

How do I know which of your words to hold on to? You are sitting on the edge of a storm, meddling under the thunderclouds for something to gossip about."

Seke cast Naxke a childish glare and turned her back to her. Seke's black hair glistened in the soft light of the setting sun. There were whispers that she flew with the crows at night, listened to the dead speak in the wind, but it was only because Seke could read shadows and was a teller of sad tales. The others treated her as if she had a stink on her, and she did nothing to discourage that way of thinking. Seke liked walking alone. That was her *difference.* The stink made Naxke glad of her fire hair on better days.

"I worry, too, that's all," Seke said.

"What do you know?" Naxke stared downriver, her eyes suddenly hopeful at the promise of movement, but it was only a drifting log, not a pair of canoes. Her heart sank quickly back into its thick pocket of despair.

"I only know what I told you. He should not have gone. You should have stopped him. I know nothing more than that or I would have told you. There are men not to be trusted beyond our village. The world is changing faster than any of us know."

"The whites?"

"Perhaps."

Naxke sighed, nodded. "You know there is nothing I could have done to stop him. You know him as well as I do."

Seke turned back to her sister. "I do. You are right about that. I know Kitha's will is as strong and pure as the current underneath the river."

The scream for help came at the first sight of a blinking star in the sky. Naxke didn't stir, didn't run to find out what was wrong. She knew what she would find, knew her fears were about to come true. Seke had been right. It was a far more dangerous world than it used to be.

Naxke pulled a blanket over her head and could hear her own heart beating loudly. She wondered if it were possible to suffocate herself, drown in her own breath, so she didn't have to face what was to come next. There was no water nearby to dive into; she had only air and the emptiness and silence of her empty bed.

Stamping feet rumbled the ground underneath her, the rush of the tribe. Naxke roused and pulled herself from under the blanket. She could hear words and murmurs beyond the wigwam, through the woven reed walls, down the open smoke hole. The fire had long since gone out; it smoldered in ribbons then wafted away, out into the world. From the outside, her life looked normal.

"He's dead." It was a whisper and truth that she had felt in her heart when she was talking with Seke. Kitha no longer walked in this world. She had felt him leave two moons ago. She had told no one. Not even her sister.

Naxke stepped out of her wigwam and her eyes met the gray mist of evening. Light had drained from the sky but had not completely disappeared. The one star had now become two. Darkness supped on what light remained. She could barely breathe. Everyone was running toward the river. She walked slowly, forcing one heavy foot in front of the other.

Seke joined Naxke at the bank. As they walked to the canoe, the people parted, lowered their heads, and said nothing. An owl hooted in the distance. The hoot quickly faded into silence, dread, and the uncertainty of what had happened, of what had led them all to the edge of the river.

Tu-Co-Han, the chief's son, stood at the front of the canoe, his arms crossed and his head lowered. Beyond him, a white man, a familiar fur trader, sat at the bow with his head lowered, too, his arms pulled captive behind him. The other canoe was empty, full of deerskin blankets. Sadness hung in the air like a stray rain cloud.

"Where is he?" Naxke said.

Tu-Co-Han raised his head and met her gaze. "There, covered up. He is dead, Fire Woman. I could not save him from Galligan's greed."

So it was the fur trader, Galligan, the white man with shifty gray eyes. He looked up when Tu-Co-Han said his name, then looked away from Naxke's glare, from her teary eyes. *"He's dead."* She had heard those words already, but she didn't want to believe it, wouldn't believe it until she saw Kitha's face, even though she had felt his death in her bones, in her heart. Seke had confidence in black wings and uncertain things, not her.

Tu-Co-Han reached out to comfort her, but Naxke pulled away. She could offer nothing in return other than a sob. Her cries immediately erupted into an uncontrollable, guttural scream.

The owl lit out of a nearby cottonwood, startled, its own voice caught in its throat as it disappeared into the night, silently, with the quick flap of a wing as if it had something urgent to tell the others.

The council house was ablaze in light. Naxke stood outside, her back against the north wall, braced, keeping her from falling to the ground and collapsing into a useless heap.

"They will kill him," Seke said. "Or banish him after punishment. Either way, he will be gone."

"It is the way," Naxke answered.

"Unless he is innocent."

"Why would you say such a thing?"

Seke pulled back and hissed at her sister. "The way is not always the bearer of truth."

"He killed Kitha," Naxke said.

"We have not heard his story."

"He has not said a word."

"He is afraid for his life."

"He should be."

The men of the village rose to their feet as Naxke and Seke entered the council house. The same reeds as her wigwam were used to build the house, but it was five times the size and the roof was covered with pulled skins. A fire burned in the center of the house, warming it beyond comfort. Naxke broke into a sweat at the sight of Galligan. His face was swollen, his eyes black and blue. She wondered when he had been beaten. She hadn't noticed any bruising at the riverbank.

The sisters sat at the front of the room on an empty wood bench. Tu-Co-Han sat opposite Galligan. Kitha's brother, sister, and mother sat directly in front of the chief, Matheundan. No one spoke a word, only the fire had a voice, and it only offered short snaps and pops from green wood.

Finally, after everyone was settled, Matheundan stood up and spoke, "We have come here tonight to face a tragedy brought upon us by a man we once called friend." The chief looked weary, his face worn with time, age, and worry. This was not the first time they had lost one of their own by the hand of a white man. "Tell us, Tu-Co-Han, how this came to be. How did we lose our brother, Kitha?"

Tu-Co-Han stayed sitting for a long, deep breath, then rose up and stood stiff, his shoulders squared, almost as if he was a proud warrior ready to go off to battle. "We came across Galligan at the forks. He told us of many new beaver lodges he'd found beyond a swampland. It was a lie."

Naxke shivered, said nothing, stood up, and walked out of the council house. She heard whispers of disapproval follow her, but she didn't care. There was nothing for her to hear. There was no use in reliving Kitha's death. She didn't need to know how he had suffered, whether it was for one minute or one hour. It didn't matter. He was dead.

The air had cooled and night had completely fallen. The sky was full of silver beads on the black cloth of forever. Most everyone was back in their wigwams. All except the men; they were seeing to Galligan's fate. No good would come of it. He would die, too. It was the way: a death for a death. Only then would the wrong be settled, be even. Oddly, Naxke felt sorry for the fur trader. He looked afraid, as sure of what was to come as Matheundan, Tu-Co-Han, and the rest of the men. She could do nothing to save him. She wouldn't, even if she could.

Tears streamed down her face as she walked. Naxke did not slow her pace when she heard footsteps coming after her. She expected it to be Seke, but she was wrong. A strong hand reached out to stop her, then spun her to face him.

"You must hear what I have to say," Tu-Co-Han said.

"Let go of me," Naxke said. "I do not have to hear anything."

"You must know the truth. You must accept it or no one else will."

In that moment, a bitter taste spread at the back of Naxke's throat and a tremble of recognition rocked her feet. She didn't know what she thought, but something was wrong. Tu-Co-Han's eyes had never been so hollow.

There was little time to mourn. Kitha would be buried inside tree bark in a deep grave. The burial would occur the next morning as the sun ate away at the darkness. It was the Between Time: when the sun, the moon, and the stars shared the sky with their wonder and knowledge. Naxke's people believed it was an opening, a spirit path to travel safely.

Naxke could hardly think of Kitha being gone but still so close to her. She longed to see him one last time. Death was like Seke's differences. It had a smell that stuck to you, threatened to take you, too, if you got too close to it. Touching a dead person was taboo.

A soft tap came from the outside and Seke eased into the wigwam, her head lowered, the shadows following her like they were beloved companions. "I am still worried about you, sister."

The last word stung, called Naxke away from imagining Kitha in his grave, then on his way into the sky. "Why do you say such a thing? Call me sister now?"

"There's no need to be angry. I offer comfort, that is all."

"What do you want?"

Seke had stopped inside the door. She hesitated, "I think you should speak to Galligan."

"I have nothing to say to him."

"You know he is to die under the next moon."

"I know what they will do." Naxke frowned and looked away from Seke.

"His hole is dug, too. He waits for death to rescue him from his troubles."

"I can't save him."

"You are the only one who can."

No wind spoke and a thick blanket of clouds covered the stars. A thin fog hovered over the tops of the drying grass. The koteewi thirsted for moisture. Fog was not enough to save the land, to turn it green again. That season was over, even though fire still danced in the sky, distantly, above the clouds, threatening to jab the earth and set it ablaze. Grass snapped under each step. The whole world felt fragile, about to break or burn at any second.

It was the middle of the night. All of the tamed flames in the village had fallen to embers, guarded from spreading by fear and watchful eyes. The air smelled of woodsmoke and slumber. Nothing stirred. Not animal or man. Only the Creator watched, and Naxke hoped He was looking away as she slipped out of the wigwam.

Her heart raced as she padded quietly to the edge of the village. Her eyes welcomed the darkness. She was glad she knew the way, but it wouldn't have mattered, her heart would have pulled her to her destination. Seke had been right. She had to know Galligan's side of the story.

Naxke had to know of Kitha's last moments, that he had not suffered, that his death was quick. She hoped she remembered enough of the language to understand what the fur trader had to say.

Galligan's place was in the bottom of the hole. The ground was so dry the walls threatened to crumble and cave in. A strong grid of oak branches barred the top of the hole. There was no escape for the white man.

Tu-Co-Han's best friend, Lo-te-Kay, guarded the hole. The sloppy man slept deeply, his snores rising into the night air like Naxke had been counting on. An owl answered the man's nasal grovels in the distance.

She stared at Galligan's hole but avoided the other one at the edge of the hickory grove. That hole was empty for now. It existed for Kitha's body, nothing more.

Naxke crawled to the edge of Galligan's prison, hugging the ground, hiding from the sleeping guard, hoping that she was nothing more than a shadow. "Galligan, do you hear me?" she whispered.

Something stirred behind her and Naxke froze. She feared being caught speaking with Galligan more than anything else. Lo-te-Kay had not moved. It must have been a night creature that had roused.

"I am here," Galligan said. "Go away. My presence has caused you enough pain."

"Tell me of his death. Tell me that Kitha was brave and faced the darkness without fear."

"He was already dead when I found him, attacked from behind with a rock or a tomahawk, I cannot be sure. I saw no weapon lying about."

"Did you stand for yourself?" Naxke said.

"Who would believe me? There were many ready to speak out against me even though they were not there. My fate was sealed before I arrived back in the village."

Naxke buried her face in the earth. She wanted to scream, to lash out, but she knew that would do no good. The dirt was freshly turned; dry as a maple leaf in winter. It tasted of secrets. Finally, she said, "Tell me, did Tu-Co-Han kill my beloved? Did he? Is that what you say?"

"I cannot know. I saw nothing to say so. He was my captor, but perhaps only because he wandered upon me when I found Kitha. I had blood on my hands. I was trying to save him by stopping the bleeding, but it was too late."

"Why should I believe you?"

"Why would I tell you a lie?"

Naxke slid into Seke's wigwam, still hoping the shadows would protect her from the Creator's eyes. "What do you know?" she demanded. Dirt was smeared across Naxke's face, striped in crumbles under her eyes, like war paint.

Seke stood beyond the fire; her eyes shone like polished black agates. "I know many things, but nothing of which you ask."

"Did he kill Kitha?" Naxke said.

"Galligan?"

"No. His brother? Did Tu-Co-Han kill Kitha for his place next to his father? He will be chief now."

"It is an old tale."

"That doesn't matter."

"It does. One man will do anything to have what is not his, while the other man who has it does not want it, and does everything to lose it. Kitha had no interest in being chief, you of all people know that to be true. Yet, he would not step aside. How could he? He loved his father and our people too much. There was no trade, no bargain between the two brothers. Their resentment had grown from day to day until the years mounted a campaign of hate. You know this is how we all saw Tu-Co-Han."

Naxke twisted her lip as a tear slipped down her cheek. "You knew Kitha's fears."

"You knew his heart."

"Are you no different than Tu-Co-Han?"

"We share no blood."

The twist of Naxke's lips turned to gritted teeth. "I did not choose to be here. Our parents did not leave me to the beasts when they found me. You know that. I was alone, orphaned by the cruelty of others and weather. I would have died if I had not been rescued and brought here."

"We share their love, sister. I meant no harm. It is true, I loved Kitha, but not in the way you do, or did. He would have been a wise chief, regardless. He found discomfort in my presence, but he came to me for counsel like his father came to our mother."

"It is the way," Naxke said, relaxing, putting her own stories of resentment to the side. "What do you know?"

Seke walked across the wigwam and embraced her sister, kissed her forehead, then pulled away. "My heart tells me to believe Galligan."

"That only means that he did not kill Kitha. We don't know what happened to him. We don't know that Tu-Co-Han is guilty of anything. Is that true?"

"That is true. However, we must find out. We have little time. They will begin to fill in Galligan's hole as soon as the first light cracks the sky. He will know true darkness once the moon rises. They will make sure he suffers until he takes his last breath."

Both women knew there was only one person that they could go to for the truth: Tu-Co-Han himself. It was better to seek him out together, not alone. There was a risk to their plan, making an enemy of the chief's only remaining son, but they agreed that there was no choice. Naxke had to know if Galligan was lying or telling the truth.

"Why are you here?" Tu-Co-Han said.

"I seek answers," Naxke said. Seke stood behind her, nearly out of sight, almost hidden by the darkness.

"You should not have run out of the council house. I had my say then." Tu-Co-Han turned away, intending to go back to his bed of furs and blankets.

"Galligan claims innocence."

Tu-Co-Han stopped and stomped his foot. "You are forbidden to use your language."

"I am not forbidden from searching for the truth."

Tu-Co-Han growled. "Come in. We must put an end to this."

Naxke hesitated. She had never been inside Tu-Co-Han's wigwam.

Tu-Co-Han was tall, like Kitha. As the younger of the two, he'd had more time to play and to hunt, to develop muscles and endurance. Kitha had been softer in body and spirit. Tu-Co-Han's face looked as hard as the stone at the bottom of the Wapihanne, but not white, dark, bronzed by the sun and a beating heart. There was nothing gentle about his ways. Even his wigwam was sparse and cold.

"Sit," he commanded. There was no one else inside the wigwam. Tu-Co-Han had not taken a wife, had not fancied one woman enough to share a blanket with her.

Both women obeyed.

"Did you see Galligan kill Kitha, Tu-Co-Han? Did you see him strike out in rage or greed?" Seke said. Naxke had fallen pale, her eyes teary and suddenly afraid. She realized what she had done. Spoke the white man's words and accused the chief's son of something no man should ever consider.

"I did not see the kill," Tu-Co-Han said. "But Galligan was there, next to Kitha. He wore my brother's blood on his hands."

"That much we know," Seke said. "Galligan said as much. The wind and owls have other stories to tell."

"Do not threaten me with your false magic, Dark Sister. I do not believe in your skills any more than my father does."

"Kitha came to me. He feared you. Did you know that?"

Tu-Co-Han circled the two women like a bobcat on the prowl. His face was void of any feeling. He was stalking nothing that Naxke could see, unless he couldn't find the words to say.

Tu-Co-Han stopped near the center of the wigwam. A little fire struggled to give light and warmth to the wigwam, but there, Tu-Co-Han's face was visible. He was angry.

"Kitha chased many ideas, dark and light. He had nothing to fear from me."

"Many of us believed otherwise," Seke said. "Your father's time here grows short. If a change was going to take place, it would serve you best if it happened before the chief meets the Creator."

"What are you accusing me of, woman?" Tu-Co-Han demanded.

Anyone else would have recoiled, shivered at the tone, but Seke didn't waver. "It will do me no good to accuse you of anything. I know my place. I am telling you that there are stains you carry. Killing Galligan will not remove them. If you both claim innocence, then it is possible that Kitha stumbled, fell, and hit his head. Did you consider that, Tu-Co-Han? Or did you need to prove yourself so badly, that you are willing to let a man die?"

"A white man," Tu-Co-Han sneered.

"A life is a life. Only the Creator has the power to take that away."

Tu-Co-Han maintained the sneer, the anger, but there seemed to be a consideration of Seke's words. His voice dropped, was quieter when he spoke. "There are things you do not know, Seke. Change is coming. Kitha's death foretells of a darker time for our people."

"Now who is dabbling in shadows?" Seke smiled when she spoke.

"I speak the truth. Naxke knows of which I speak. News of a treaty with the white man has reached our place in the world. It will move us from this land. Kitha was heartbroken and begged to go on the journey with us so he could heal his anger at our father for not fighting. I am not the one with war in my heart," Tu-Co-Han said. "It was Kitha who longed to fight, to rise up."

Seke looked to Naxke, confused. "Is this true, sister?"

"Yes," Naxke whispered. "Yes, it is true. We must all leave here. We are ceding our lands and dreams. No fight will stop it."

"And you didn't tell me?" Seke said to Naxke.

"It was not my place. It was Matheundan's place to tell his people of their future. That time has not yet come," Naxke said. "The sun will rise soon and everyone will know of the destiny that awaits us all."

"This changes everything," Seke said.

"It does," Tu-Co-Han answered. "It does."

Naxke drew in a deep breath and said, "Swear to me, brother, that you brought no harm to Kitha. That you speak the truth."

"I speak the truth."

"Then I will believe you."

■ ■ ■ ■

The horizon shimmered with a thin, gray line. It was a thin peek of light, enough for the proceedings against Galligan to begin. The men of the village had begun to gather at the hole, waiting at a respectable distance. Naxke and Seke stood next to one of the towering oak trees, lost in the shadows, though everyone knew they were there. There was no need for them to hide.

Once all of the men assembled, and dawn engaged the night, Matheundan and Tu-Co-Han made their way to the crowd.

Matheundan walked cautiously with a stick, stooped over with age, in the dim light. Tu-Co-Han followed close behind, his head lowered, the emotion on his face impossible for Naxke to read. She held her breath and tongue. Seke did the same. They had done everything they could do. There was nothing left to do but wait and see what Galligan's fate would be.

The chief stopped short of the fur trader's hole and Tu-Co-Han eased to his side. They exchanged whispers and nods then turned to face the men of the village.

Matheundan cleared his throat and spoke as confidently as he could. A crack in his voice echoed across the dry grass. "On this solemn day, we send my son on his final journey and decide the future of the man accused of killing him. It is a day a father never wants to see come."

Tu-Co-Han stiffened and looked over his shoulder. Even in the darkness, Naxke knew his intent to search her out. She stepped out of the shadow of the tall oak and showed herself to the village. It was her right to be there. No one would deny her that. Seke stayed back.

"Come closer, sister, so that you may hear what I have to say," Tu-Co-Han said to Naxke. Matheundan nodded with a gentle urge.

Naxke made her way to the two men slowly, aware that every waking eye was on her. She stopped behind the chief and his son.

Tu-Co-Han turned and faced all of the men of the village. "I am the accuser of this man, Galligan, and have called into question his intentions. I do not deny anger at all white men. Our lands are lost to us. Our lives have changed for the worse by their presence. When I saw my brother, Kitha, lying in stillness, blood on his head and blood on Galligan's hands, I allowed rage to blind me. I believed he had killed my brother out of greed, that he wanted all of the pelts for himself, that he was no different from other men who kill. I did not listen to Galligan's protests, but now that time has passed, I have to reconsider what I saw and why I saw it the way I did. This is no easy thing for me to say, brothers, but I now think Galligan should be free. I believe Kitha died by accident and not by the hand of a white man. Putting Galligan to death will not bring my brother back to this earth or return our lands to us. This Treaty of St. Mary's has been signed, and our time here is short. Another death will not heal our pain."

Murmurs of disapproval rippled through the crowd of men. Naxke watched them all closely. Tu-Co-Han's words were not what they had expected to hear. Setting Galligan free was the last thing anyone — even her — expected to come from the man's mouth. The bigger blow was the confirmation of the fear they all had: the treaty was real. There was no turning back. A new, unknown land awaited them all, not only Kitha.

No one outwardly protested, but voices were raising higher at each breath.

Matheundan raised his hand and every voice went silent. "My son has shown great wisdom in sparing the life of our friend, Galligan, but he alone cannot set the man free. Naxke's voice must be heard."

Another eruption of grumbles broke out. Naxke knew why. It was not only because of the color of her hair, the color of her skin — the same as Galligan's — but she was a woman casting a vote in a matter she held no power in. She knew better than to utter a word. Naxke walked forward and stopped in front of Matheundan, then nodded.

Galligan would go free, but Naxke wondered what damage Tu-Co-Han had done to himself. Had he shown wisdom or fear? Only time would tell how the people would see the outcome, and ultimately, how they would see Tu-Co-Han. Was he a true leader, or a shadow of what Kitha might have been? Naxke saw the path open, and knew she had to walk on the side of wisdom instead of fear. That was the way Kitha would have wanted it.

The day of Kitha's burial and Galligan's release, Matheundan put out the word that they would move before the winter winds set in permanently. There was much sadness in the village. Many of the people had never known any other home. Naxke had joined the people as a scared child and Seke had been born to them. Neither of them wanted to leave, but there was no choice. The land was no longer theirs to live and die on.

Later in the evening, as the sun set on the day, Galligan called on Naxke in her wigwam. He was on his way out of the village. "You can come with me," he said.

"That is kind, but this is my home," Naxke said.

"But it is not. You don't know what awaits you on your journey."

"What awaits me with you? I know nothing of your ways, of the ways I am expected to behave and talk, and be with people I do not know."

"You can learn. I will help you. It's the least I can do. It was you who saved my life."

Naxke studied Galligan's earnest face, cleaned of his prison dirt. His eyes were sincere. She was certain that he believed what he said, that he would care for her in the white world. She had considered leaving once upon a time, thought of running away, of finding people of her own blood. The others had made life hard when she first arrived, even Seke had been difficult, but Kitha had shown her a love like no other, and once he had done that, so, too, did everyone else. In the end, Naxke had spoken when she'd had no right to. This was her home. She knew her place. Her heart would remain buried under an oak tree.

"The people are my home, Galligan. Wherever they go, I will go. It is the way."

The fur trader sighed in agreement, acknowledging that Naxke was right and there was nothing he could do to convince her otherwise. He left the wigwam, never to be seen or heard from again.

The clouds were angry on the day of the leaving. Lightning danced across the sky, but no rain fell. People walked along the Wapihanne, and others eased their canoes into the water, drifting with the slow current. There was no turning back; there was no place to seek shelter. They had no home, only the way ahead of them to some unknown place.

Naxke and Seke walked shoulder to shoulder behind the chief and his son. They did not speak, did not cry.

The thunder clapped so loud that the earth shook. They both heard the lightning strike the ground, heard the sizzle of dry grass erupt into a fire. They smelled smoke, but they did not quicken their step or look back. Everything would burn, the wigwams and the memories of life left behind. The earth would erase their presence, and before long, no one would remember that they had been there at all.

The Buffalo Trace

1

April 1, 1807, Indiana Territory

I held the paper behind my back, trembling with excitement, like it was a secret I couldn't wait to share. Pa looked at me sideways with deep summer-blue eyes over wire-frame glasses, then smiled. "Well, there you are young miss. To what do I owe the pleasure of your company?"

He called me young miss — whether I liked it or not — instead of by my name, Hallie Mae Edson, when he was in a good mood. Whenever I heard my full name come out of Pa's mouth, I knew I'd done something that had riled him. A rare occurrence most days, but I was more than capable of turning his face beet red with restraint on my stormy days. Today, however, was not that day. I was young miss, the apple of his eye, his one and only favorite daughter. I dared to hope that I had half a chance of getting what I wanted.

I stepped inside his workshop and ignored as best I could the strong smell of sheep tallow simmering in the iron pot. Pa was a candlemaker, a trade most often pursued by womenfolk. He had taken up the task after the death of my mother and found more success at it than he'd planned. With new folks moving into the territory every day, he was busier than a bee working a field of bloomin' spring flowers. He had six broaches going, long pieces of planed wood with multiple cotton wicks that were hand-dipped and trimmed over and over again until the candle was formed. I was glad that the tallow was sheep instead of pig. The stench of pig fat made my stomach roll, and the smell would never leave my clothes. School days had been troublesome enough without me smellin' like a market-ready hog. Numbers and letters bored me. I longed to shoot and hunt with my brother, Tom, so it was those things that I took to. Learnin' inside a schoolhouse made me feel like a goat bein' pulled around on a leash.

"I got a question to ask you, Pa," I said, fightin' to hide the paper behind my back. I had never wanted something so bad in my life.

Pa stopped the dipping and studied me

right close. "What you got there, young miss?"

"I know you need help here in the shop, Pa, and I can still dip for you. Me and Tom both. We won't be slackin' in our chores none. I promise."

"You're acting like you got ants in your pants on Christmas morning, Hallie Mae. Now why don't you calm down and tell me what has got you all possessed. You haven't been sneaking glances at Will McIntyre again have you?"

My face flushed red. I could feel the color change rush to my cheeks then dart to my toes. The mere mention of Tom's best friend's name gave me a head twirl and an instant sunburn. "This ain't got nothin' to do with no boy."

Pa's face tightened and he settled back in the chair with his spine so straight I feared it might snap. "We don't say *ain't* in this house, Hallie Mae. You know that. We're not barefooted, uneducated Hoosiers. We're proud, hardworking folk who respect our language and ourselves. I've had this talk with you before and I don't expect to have it again. You're not an ignorant girl. A sloppy one sometimes, but not ignorant. But I figure you'll grow out of that with time and training. Now, tell me what this all about. I've still got two hundred candles to dip before the moon rises."

I looked down to my toes to avoid his glare. Regardless of what Pa had said I *was* barefoot, since it was spring. Any thrill of the mention of Will McIntyre had left my entire body with the tone of admonishment given to me by my pa. I sure did hate to disappoint him. My mouth got ahead of my brain some days. Now it was so dry I couldn't utter a clear word. I had no choice but to hand him the paper.

Pa looked down and read it silent with his eyes, not giving me a clue to what he was thinkin'. I moved my lips when I read. His index finger shivered, giving the announcement an unintentional tap. It was the sign I was looking for. I lowered my head in defeat before he said a word.

"Tom wants to do this, too?" he said, still eyeing the paper like it was the devil come to take me away.

"Says so," I said to my feet.

"You're just a girl, young miss," Pa whispered.

I shook my head. "I'm nothin' like Abagail Peterson, all frilly with ribbons and bows, and acts like she's gonna grow up to be the Queen of England."

"She might be."

"Impossible. Just like it's impossible for me not to be nothin' but what I am. You say so all the time. 'Be yourself. That's the best you can be.' So, I am. I can skin and gut a squirrel faster than any boy around, including Will McIntyre, whose face goes pale at the first sight of blood. I can outshoot him and Tom and the rest of the boys, too. You made sure that I could fend for myself. Didn't you?" I exhaled to calm myself down, to keep from getting ahead of myself and overstepping my bounds with Pa. I was shocked he hadn't said so yet.

"I know everyone's upset about that Larkin baby," Pa said with a long sigh. "I know the troubles that incident has sparked. I hear it every day I step outside this shop. The mister is dead with the Indians taking the missus and their children captive. All five of them, including the baby. Cries of fear have washed up and down the Trace louder than a mob of blue jays pursuing a marauding hawk." He stopped and looked at the paper again. "I fear this struggle with Tecumseh and his brother, The Prophet, will fall to no good for us all. So, this is the response from Governor Harrison? A call to arms putting our young men on the road to make the travelers feel more secure?"

"Young women, too. Calls for us all. Says

so right there." I pointed to the paper knowing full well that Pa had read the words I was referencing. He'd chosen to ignore them for as long as he could.

"You're just a girl," he said again.

"And that's all I'll ever be if you keep on saying that." The words jumped out of my mouth unbidden. I wished I could take them back by the cause of pain that flashed across Pa's face, but I couldn't. What was done was done.

"A militia?" he said, relaxing his spine. My heart raced. I saw an opening.

"The Indiana Territorial Rangers," I said with so much excitement my fingers curled around an imaginary trigger.

"And they want you to patrol the Buffalo Trace from Vincennes to Louisville?"

The Buffalo Trace was a wide path pounded into the ground from migrating buffalo making their way to the salt licks in Kentucky. It was a timeworn trail that offered an easy ride from the Ohio River city, Louisville, all the way to the capital of the Indiana and Illinois Territory, Vincennes. Except when whites crossed paths with Indians, and they took it upon themselves to cause troubles and fear. We lived right square between Vincennes and the river, outside of a small dot in the Trace called Cuzco.

"There's to be three divisions," I said, giving Pa more information than was on the paper. Tom had filled me in because of what Will had told him. "Captain William Hargrove and the First Division is gonna patrol from the Wabash River to French Lick. Our own Samuel McIntyre is dustin' off his uniform and will head up the Second Division, based here in Cuzco."

"So, that's how you know all of this, tagging after Tom?" Pa said.

I wasn't going to let my feelings show anymore than I already had. I never tagged after Tom. I was with him is all. And joinin' up with the Rangers had nothing to do with Will McIntyre. At least that's what I was telling myself and tried to convey to Pa. I could help. Make a difference. Have an adventure that wasn't full of side-mouth gossip and silly giggles.

"Couldn't say," I answered. I rushed past the thought of Will and continued on with what I knew. "Second Division will patrol from French Lick to the Falls of the Ohio, and the Third Division has the east route along the river from Lawrenceburg to the Ohio border."

"You'll be gone for days at a time," Pa

said, setting down the paper next to him. He stirred the tallow without looking at me. I wasn't sure what was to come next from him. "Paper says the pay is a dollar a day. That's a fair wage even though you have to supply your own horse, ammunition, and a tomahawk."

"Gotta have a belt and two knives as well. A long and a short."

"You don't have a long knife."

"Tom's out fetchin' one for me. At least finding out if he can find one that's fittin' for me."

"And how do you expect to pay for such a thing?"

"I was hopin' you'd loan me the money against my wages. I'd pay you off first thing before anything else, once I got my first dollar."

"You really want to do this?"

"I do. More than anything. It's the first thing that's come along that I can stand shoulder to shoulder with Tom and the rest of the boys and do what I do best. They haven't found that Larkin baby yet. Rest of 'em escaped the Indians, but if somebody don't find that child, he'll grow up a savage, or worse, not grow up at all. I can track a coon on a moonless night better than anyone around. You know I can. Meat's on the table more from my efforts than Tom's."

"That's because he's pining after Nell Jenkins."

"And he's lazy."

"Be nice to your brother."

"I am most days."

"I've thought of that baby, too," Pa said, then stood up and walked toward me, "out there all on its own." He stopped and put his hands on my shoulders with his elbows extended all the way so we was face to face. "You know I couldn't bear losing you. Your pride, confidence, and beauty remind me of your mother every day. I see so much of her in you that it makes my heart ache sometimes. Just the thought of something happening to you shatters my spirit. Tom, too. But especially you."

"I know I got chores to do, and I'll do my best to keep 'em up, but please don't say no," I whispered, trembling all over.

He shook his head. "I won't tell you no. Tom, neither. I'll get some help with your chores if need be. If your mother was still alive, she would do anything she could to help find that baby and help keep everyone safe. She would have been out the door so fast the wind couldn't have caught up with her skirt. If you want to do this, then go ahead, but you have to promise me that you won't do anything to put yourself in harm's way, and you'll come back to me as soon as you can."

2

When breakfast came, I was giddy as a ten-year-old on the last day of school. I wasn't sure that Tom had slept any more than I had, which had been about two winks. I knew I wasn't doing myself any good, but I was so ready to start Ranger training that I went to bed in my clothes. All I had to do was wash my face, grab my bag, and walk to the breakfast table like it was any other day. Pa looked like he'd tossed and turned all night, too.

Tom glared at me when I sat down across from him at the eatin' table. "What's the matter with you, you old grouch?"

"I ain't speakin' to you," Tom said. He was a shorter version of Pa, except he was gangly, hadn't grown into himself yet, and clumsy as a mule drunk on soured corn. His curly brown hair was unwieldy, and his eyes — the same color as Pa's, all full of summer and clear skies — were most often tinged with kindness. Except when he was mad. Then they was as dark as granite.

Pa looked over his shoulder from the fireplace but said nothing. He didn't have to. Tom jumped in and corrected himself before anybody could utter another word. "I'm not speaking to you, sister."

Sister. That was my angry name from Tom. Between his pet names for me and Pa's, sometimes I had to wonder who I was. "And what, pray tell, I have done now, brother?"

He started to say something, but clamped the corner of his lip to contain the words inside his mouth.

"Well, what is it?" I said. "A horse step on your toe? A fly slip down your throat?" Tom was easy to goad and I couldn't help myself. My excitement for the coming day was bubbling over.

"That's enough, Hallie Mae." Pa stopped the fun and sat down two bowls of boiled oats on the table. His eyes looked tired and his face held a grimness that was usually reserved for funerals. His tone snapped the joy out of me as quick as it had come on. "They found the Larkin baby," he said, turning his back to us, tendin' to the fire. We didn't have to ask what the outcome was. Pa's gray face was a shroud of grief.

I was sad before I knew it and I couldn't eat one spoonful of the oats. Tom, on the other hand, ignored the heavy pall in the room and dug into his breakfast and ate like another meal would never come. I let the silence settle between us the best I could. All sorts of songbirds were singing outside the door, welcoming the bright, sunny day that had been bestowed on us. Cardinals, blue jays, sparrows, and yellow canaries were celebrating their wings. They didn't know no better than to be happy at the sight of the sun.

"Why are you mad at me?" I whispered to Tom. Pa was six feet away from us. It wasn't like he couldn't hear me. I was trying to get Tom to answer me.

He took a big swig of milk to wash down the porridge, licked his lips, then returned the glare that had welcomed me when I'd entered the room. "Are you deaf?"

"I can hear you fine."

"I'm not talking to you."

"Yes, you are."

"No, I'm not."

"I guess I'm hearing things."

Pa turned around from the fire and stalked out the front door. He'd had enough of us. I couldn't say that I blamed him.

Tom watched the door pull shut, then said, "You told him about the Rangers. You was supposed to wait till I got home."

"Did you get it?" My excitement rekindled itself, sparked by my craving for a new knife.

"Get what? I don't know what you're talkin' about."

"Yes, you do. The long knife. It's all I need."

"So if I say no, then you'll have to stay behind?"

I leaned forward with my chin over my untouched oats. "So that's what this is all about. You're afraid you'll get shown up by a girl."

"Am not."

"Are, too."

Tom exhaled, sat back, and crossed his arms. "I got it."

"Good. 'Cause it sounds like we got some Indians to go after."

"They're long gone."

"You sure?"

"Or hidin' out with the British. Ain't no justice gonna get served to those heathens and everybody knows it."

"You shouldn't say . . ."

"And you shouldn't tell Pa things you promised not to." Tom bit his lip again. There, he'd had his say. He was pleased with himself. But he was still mad at me.

"I'm sorry," I said. "I was wrong to do that. I couldn't help myself is all." I meant every word I said, too.

"Well, I guess it's my own fault. I know

you can't keep a secret any better than an owl. You're always goin' about sayin' who, who, who?" Tom cracked a wry smile then, and I knew we were all right, that he wasn't mad at me no more. "You better eat up. Captain McIntyre don't like recruits bein' late."

I took Tom's advice and started to eat. He did, too. I eyed Pa through the window, standing outside the door, staring off into the distance, toward the cemetery where Mother laid in her eternal rest. I saw him there sometimes, talking to her, asking her opinion, nodding as the squirrels chattered above him, as if they were giving him the answers he longed for. I understood his melancholy, his newfound sadness even though he tried not to show it to me and Tom. The loss of the Larkin baby weighed on him, touched his skin like fire to an open wound. Death gave him the shivers. Me too, but I tried hard not to think about it too much. Losing Mother knocked me off my feet, and I've struggled to stand upright ever since she died.

For every bite Tom took, I took two. It was only a few seconds before he caught on to what I was up to, then the race was on. Even though he was a year older than me, he was always trying to catch up to me, beat me at every task. But like most challenges, I won this one easily. I jumped up and washed my plate before Tom could set his spoon on the table. I didn't want Pa to do any more of my chores than he had to if I was gonna be a Ranger.

3

We assembled outside of Cuzco at the McIntyre place. The morning air was cool and fragrant with the ripe possibility of spring. What was once brown was now transformed into a vibrant, showy green. Grasses shot up in the paddocks, dotted with the spiny leaves of dandelions yet to sprout a bloom. I always thought the flowers looked like tiny suns. All sprinkled together they made a bright yellow blanket that glowed at night. Some folks, like the McIntyres, tended the dandelions to make wine. Pa never took to drinkin' any kind of liquor, but I worried he might get a taste for it after Mother's untimely death. He held out, though, I think for Tom and me. Mushrooms were abundant in the woods that skirted the McIntyres' well-kept farm; spongy brown fungus that had to be soaked overnight in saltwater to rid the holes and crevices of bugs and dirt. Fried in butter the mushrooms sure were tasty. Titus Findlay ate one of those brown ones with a thick stem and nearly died. You had to be careful which ones you put in the skillet. I heard tell he suffered mightily from stomach pains, producing gas so rank that a new litter of pigs fainted when he struggled to the outhouse. Will McIntyre told me that. I don't know if it was true or not, but I believed everything he told me.

The McIntyre family had come into the territory as soon as it was opened up from somewhere in Virginia. Where exactly never mattered much to me. I was only glad that Will and his family lived close enough for me to see him with some regularity. There wasn't a girl around who didn't stop talking and take notice of Will when he passed by. He was tall with well-formed muscles from hard work, skin bronzed by the sun, and blue eyes that could look right through you and see what you was thinking. To him, I was Tom Edson's little sister, a tagalong that never seemed to annoy him. He hardly acknowledged my presence except when it came to shootin' or knife throwing, then he tried to beat me like I was any other boy. I was glad of that, but sometimes, as long as those times was secret, I wished he would look at me like he did Abagail Peterson — who, to my surprise, had gathered up a horse, long knife, and all of the requirements to be a Ranger, and showed up in the paddock with the rest of us. Of course, she had pink bows in her hair and a tiny bit of rouge rubbed on her cheeks, like she was gonna get all gussied up and be whisked off to Paris, France, instead of protectin' travelers on the Trace. I had to say, I hadn't never seen her in pants before. I had to put my hand over my mouth to keep from laughin' out loud at the first sight of her. She looked like a ragamuffin in the school play from the neck down. I figured it was her brother, Miller's, pants she was a wearin'. They were twice the size of her waist and the cuffs were rolled up on the legs so she could walk without trippin' over her proud self. I wondered how long she was going to last in the hot sun. I figured she'd wilt like a dandelion set to boil.

"I bet you could wrestle her to the ground in two shakes," Tom whispered. He was as amused as I was by the sight of Abagail Peterson lookin' like a toad tryin' to be a frog.

"One shake," I said after seeing Will take notice of Abagail, too.

"You're probably right."

Captain Samuel McIntyre was father to a brood of six boys and two daughters, all younger than Will. They all stood watch from the porch, drawn out by the excitement and most likely the relief of not being under their father's command for the rest of the day. Samuel was an organized man who shared in Will's good looks and strong build, but unlike his son, he took himself serious. He was dressed in the remnants of a Virginia militia uniform and stood straight as a broomstick, watching the dial of his gold pocket watch tick away the seconds, tappin' his foot in wait to call his assembled troops to order.

There were ten of us who had answered the call to arms. Eight boys, me, and Abagail. The boys congregated in the middle, jabbing elbows, guffawing, actin' like the fools they were without taking direct notice of us girls. Abagail stood on one side of the mob and I stood on the other. She ignored me and I offered her the same slight in return. I figured she'd realize what she got herself into once the real training started. I had never seen her run, much less fire a long rifle. I wondered if she'd faint at the first sight of blood like Will McIntyre.

The captain looked up from his watch and yelled, "Assemble!" His jaw set hard and he stared in front of him without offering any more instructions.

A few boys kept on talking, Jacob Hopmeyer and Edward Vance in particular, troublemakers since the day they'd arrived in the territory. My guess was their fathers had sent them to join the Rangers to gain some discipline. Lord knew they needed it. The rest of us jumped at the command, forming a wiggly line five feet in front of the captain.

"Straighten up!" Captain McIntyre said. I had never heard him yell before. His voice sounded like a booming drum, and gave me a quick learnin' not to cross him. I didn't want to catch the full force of his attention. No, sirree, I was gonna do everything he said.

Everyone but Jacob and Edward obeyed. They were still engaged in some kind of finger wrestling contest. Captain McIntyre didn't take kindly to being disobeyed. I heard Will let out a slight whistle, which in my experience, meant those boys were about to get a thrashin'.

The captain lurched forward and grabbed Jacob by the ear faster than a frog's tongue snatchin' a dragonfly out of the air. "You listen to me, young man," he said. "When I say move, you move and keep your mouth shut. If I have to tell you again, I'll send you straight home to your pa and he can deal with you because I won't. There's too much at stake here. Do you understand?" To emphasize his seriousness, the captain gave Jacob's captive ear a good twist. He offered the boy a look that dared him to yell out in pain.

To my surprise and relief, Jacob mumbled a, "Yes, sir," and stood there and took the ear twist like a man even though he was a few years from that in my mind. We all were under the age of twenty.

Captain McIntyre let go of Jacob, then returned to his place, heading up the middle of the line. "That goes for the rest of you, too. Do I make myself clear?"

It was as if we all had been joined at the hip and sung in the church choir since we was nothing more than babies. "Yes, sir!" we all said in unison. Even Abagail showed enthusiasm.

"That's more like it," the captain said. "Bein' a member of The Indiana Territorial Rangers is serious business. There's Indians out there heartless enough to leave an infant to fend for itself against the bears, and we're gonna put a stop to that. Understand?"

"Yes, sir!" Our voices reached heaven on wings forged of disgust and anger. Pa hadn't told us what had happened to the Larkin baby, but the captain saw fit to make it our business now that we had an official reason to know.

"Good," he said. "We're gonna train hard and fast for two weeks, then you'll be set to the road. One on horseback, one on foot, carrying the long rifle. Don't matter if you're a boy or a girl, everybody that signed up has to qualify in both tasks. Looks like we'll have five sets, that is if the lot of you don't go runnin' home like whimperin' pups shoved off a teat. This is tough work and you'll earn your dollar a day twice over. Understood?"

"Yes, sir!" Even Jacob and Edward wore serious faces now. There was a reason the captain took himself serious and the McIntyres were some of the best-behaved children in the territory. The captain said what he meant and meant what he said. I liked him.

It wasn't long before we were lined up single file, waitin' to show off our horse ridin' skills. Me and Tom had been riding since we was old enough to stand. I wasn't sure about anyone else other than Will. He was as good as they come on a horse. He rode a roan mare who listened to him like the rest of the girls. She was as captivated by him as any human, and sometimes I thought that horse could read his thoughts, for there wasn't a move he needed to command her to make. She knew ahead of time which way he wanted to go and how fast he wanted to get there.

Will was up last, so I would have to wait to watch his grace on that mare. Jacob Hopmeyer was first up, directed by the captain to run a route around four rain barrels front to back, then opposite. Fast, then slow, counted off by Tom, who had been appointed as the timekeeper. Captain said it wasn't no race, but if there was time involved, it sure seemed like a race to me. I couldn't wait to get into the saddle of my ride, a trusted brown I called Ol' Hank. He was a hefty boy, up to pulling a plow as much as he was made for ridin'. Considering Pa was a candlemaker, there wasn't much need to farm other than the fresh garden we needed to get through the seasons. Ol' Hank had a mind of his own but he liked me well enough, as long as I didn't yank too hard on his bit. He had soft teeth.

Jacob rode a draft horse that was as slow as spring comin' on. Good Lord, you have to wait forever for the cold and snow to go away. That horse didn't know the word hurry. Captain McIntyre frowned as he watched Jacob traverse the barrels.

One after one we went. Edward, Abagail,

then me. Abagail was a better rider than I thought her to be. Her horse, a skinny little black mare, cut low and fast on the turns, and for a second, I feared she was gonna get a better time than me. That mare kicked up some dust, and gained a nod of approval from the captain, until she took a straight run and failed to give the horse its head. It fought her then, and went into a braying fit. I was relieved even though I knew better than to celebrate someone else's failure. I had something to prove.

I whispered in Ol' Hank's ear askin' him not to be his stubborn self. I needed a win. Can't say for sure if he understood or not, but he didn't moan when I took to the saddle. I ran him hard, cut deep myself, then freed him to run on the long stretch. Wind in my face, eyes focused on the barrel, I didn't think a whit about that Larkin baby, or why those Indians left him to die. I rode to win, to be free, to become something I wasn't. When I crossed the finish line, Tom quit his countin' and a bead of sweat slid down the side of my ear. I swear it hit the ground and cried out in pain. Captain wasn't givin' out times 'til the end, but when I ran past, I could tell he was impressed with my turn at the barrels. That was all I wanted, other than beatin' Abagail Peterson.

Tom went then with Will takin' over with the timin'. He ran a good lap, but didn't illicit any kind of response from the captain. Neither did Will when he ran, even though it was obvious to everyone — grace married to the speed of thunder — that he was the best of us before he came to a sidestepping stop. If it had been anyone else, I would have thought they'd cheated, run the course before anyone else had had a chance. But it was Will McIntyre, and he weren't no cheater.

The captain didn't announce the winner, which relieved and disappointed us all. He said there'd be another chance tomorrow. Then the day after that. We was gonna run to the end, then we'd have one race to set the winner in stone. I liked that idea. Gave me time to improve, to watch Will's line as he curved around the barrels.

All the trainin' was gonna be like that. Short knives. Long knives. Rifle shootin'. We'd all compete with ourselves day after day, until the end, then we'd find out who was who, and what we was gonna be on the Trace. Captain said a flower didn't bloom in a day and he was right about that.

4

Every night before I fell asleep, I wished to dream of my mother. Her voice was like the distant wind. I had to strain to hear it in my memory. Some days I dropped my own voice a might deeper, hopin' to hear something of her words come from my own mouth, but nothin' ever did. I missed her something fierce. I knew Pa and Tom did, too. They didn't say so, but I could see it in their faces and on their shoulders. Other days, I tried to catch a glimpse of Mother in my own reflection. I suppose it was there as much as it was in Tom's eyes, too, but it was like I was blind to her. It was, however, my good fortune to have her blanket in my possession. I didn't sleep with it or use it for warmth. I kept the soft blue wool cover in a wood box under my bed. Along with my wish, I'd sneak a deep sniff of the material and try and breathe in her scent as much as possible, then I'd lay flat on my back and try to conjure an image of her. Sad to say, she never came to me in the middle of night to offer me comfort or love. After a dreary long winter and a few short months of spring I had started to understand that dead was dead. She was gone forever and there was nothin' I could do to bring her back. My heart broke for those

Larkins and I couldn't help but cry myself to sleep one more time.

Trainin' days wore me out, but I had promised Pa that I would still dip for him in the evening. The flood of folks comin' west needed candles to light their way. After twelve-hour days in the sun, if it was nice out, or in the rain if spring was bein' spring, I'd head straight out to the shop after eatin' a bit of supper. The McIntyres put on a big dinner spread in the midafternoon after a mornin' of marchin', shootin', knife-fightin', and the like. Will was a lucky boy to have a momma who could cook for her own brood and ten more mouths, and not notice or complain about the extra effort. She said she was accustomed to cookin' in oversized batches, and I suppose that was the truth. She made fatback and beans, corn bread, young-nettle salad picked straight from the woods behind the house, and baked a rhubarb pie that was near the best I ever remember. There wasn't a thing about Missus McIntyre that reminded me of my own mother, other than the joy she took in the care of her children and all of us Rangers that were donned on her to look after now that we had come under the captain's charge. Missus McIntyre was thick and wide as a milking cow and wore the same kind of soft, understandin' brown eyes. She smelled of flour, salt, and freshly turned garden soil, and like the captain, I was enamored with her, too. It was easy to see in her perpetual cheerfulness that at some point she had been a pretty girl. Time and birthin' children had dimmed her looks, but not her spirit. She was the sun in the house and her light touched everyone around her. Even the captain, who I wouldn't have thought liked playing second fiddle to anyone. But he did to her, to My Lady as he called her, with grace and kindness. Will was a fine combination of them both, and it wasn't no surprise that he had a glow of his own.

With all that went on in my days, it was surprisin' that I didn't fall asleep standing up with a broach in my hand and thirty more candles to dip. But somehow I managed to meet the demand of my days as a Ranger and my nights as a candlemaker's daughter. Tom, too. We both worked harder than we thought we were capable.

The days passed through rain, sunshine, and a baby's funeral. His fragile body given back to the soil and his soul offered up to heaven. It was a sad, gray day, and all of us Rangers stood together in a tight formation, shoulder to shoulder, our faces washed of youth and replaced with the hunger for justice, and revenge — until Elvira Larkin stood and begged us to give up our arms and any thought of continuing violence. She was a Quaker and did not believe in an eye for an eye. For a moment I considered heeding her words, but I couldn't help the feelin' I had, that Baby Matthew had been robbed of seeing a full life only because his family had set foot on the wrong side of the Trace. Even in the deep hours of the night when I laid awake in my comfortable bed, all I could hear was dirt cascading down on that small wood coffin. I knew I couldn't do anything to bring that baby back any more than I could my own mother, but maybe I could stop a tragedy from happenin' to someone else. I would wake more convinced that my longin' to be a Ranger was the right thing, a good thing, and that would spark my feet to the ground into a run straight to the McIntyre's place.

It was hard to believe that time had passed so quickly. Our two weeks of trainin' was almost up. Three more days, then we'd be out on patrol, ridin' up and down the Trace doin' our best to bring peace of mind to the near constant band of travelers who were on their way to one place or the other. Edward and Jacob had fallen in line, goofin' around only when time called for it. Jacob turned out to be a fine horseman and it was pretty easy to see what job he was gonna get. The rest of the boys learned pretty quick to take me as a serious threat to makin' them look bad when it came to shootin' and handlin' a short knife. The long knife was my bane. I'd never toyed with one much. Well, not at all, until Tom brung me home one. I wasn't the worst skilled one among us, but pretty close. I was near top of the pack with the rifles, tight behind Will, which was no surprise. The greater surprise was that Abagail was still holding her own. She was a fair shot, a decent rider, and capable of fending off attacks with both knives. Her momma had taken her clothes more serious since Abagail had put herself forward into the heap of Rangers. She spoke to me when she had to but most of the time she shadowed Will, hopin' to catch his eye. I tried to hide my jealous tendencies, but I was a duck out of water when it came to that. There wasn't no foolin' anybody about how I felt about Will McIntyre, and that uncontrollable emotion caused me a great deal of grief and embarrassment. Tom teased me unmercifully. Even the captain took time to note my infatuation with his son, warnin' me to focus on duties at hand and quit searchin' for rainbows over Will's pretty head. I didn't shoot worth a darn that day.

5

"Where's, Tom?" I said to Pa. Tom was nowhere to be seen, his spot at the table empty and untouched.

Pa was stirring the oats, had his back to me, his shoulders sagging with permanent exhaustion, dressed for his day in the shop. "He went on without you."

The quick response struck me as odd. Me and Tom always walked to trainin' together. We talked about the day before, what we had to do, how things were goin', that kind of thing. Bein' a Ranger had brought us closer together, put a lid on our sorrow, gave us somethin' in common we'd never had before. From what I could tell, we was matched as even as the tassels on summer corn; only the wind made one higher than the other. I hadn't said anything wrong or done nothin' to shame Tom that I knew of, so I was bewildered by his absence.

"He say why?" I said.

"No." Pa was stiff, didn't move a muscle other than what was required to attend to his duty in the fireplace. The cabin was stuffy, humid, like all the air had been sucked out of it when Tom had left. My gut said something was amiss, but Pa's tone and attitude warned me off of pursuing the question any further. I was sad for a second longer, then I realized I was more hungry than anything.

"That's all right," I said and sat down in my spot at the table.

Pa served me my breakfast and left me to eat it all on my own. I wanted to rush out after him as he hurried to the shop, but I knew he was focused on his work, had to ready the dipping pots for the day. He's weary from all the work. That's all it is. Nothing is wrong. I told myself all of this even though I didn't believe it. After Mother passed, I saw a crack of gloom in every ray of sunshine. So did Pa and Tom.

It wasn't long before the air hung low with the faint smell of sheep tallow, a new fire, and the curiosity of a sour mood held familiar court over the world. Even the clouds drooped with grayness and promised turmoil in the hours to come. A spring storm was brewin' over the trees; thunderheads reached and roiled in the tumultuous sky, growing by the second. But that didn't mean that trainin' would stop. Just the opposite. Captain said we had to be versed in all kinds of weather. Danger and travelers didn't stop 'cause of the threat of rain or discomfort. If that was the case, none of us would be here.

I finished up my breakfast and gathered myself together quicker than I usually had to. Tom's absence had caused me to linger longer than normal. I rushed to the barn, saddled Ol' Hank, and made sure I had my short knife secured in my belt. It was the only weapon I carried at the moment. Captain's tack stall served as an armory for our rifles and long knives. Once I was settled in the saddle, I hurried away from the cabin, leaving the smell of candles and Pa's sullenness to hisself.

Ol' Hank took pleasure in the early mornin' run. Our cabin was a good ways away from Cuzco and even farther from the Trace. To get to the main road, I had to go north about half a mile, down a ravine and up another, then rush a stretch to the McIntyre place.

The path to the trainin' field was nothing more than that, a deer path worn wide over the years as folks came and went to buy candles, peddle wares to us, or visit during happier times. I knew the dirt and turns like the pores in my skin. A hard right here. A run through a good fishin' creek there — fingerin' off the Wabash — dotted with monstrous sycamores spotted white and brown by thin, peeling bark that seemed to glow in the summer sun. The leaves on those ol' trees were as big as plates, and with the wind riled up they flapped like fans, pushing the air against my face like they were born of a distant tornado. To make things even worse, the light had dimmed deeper, grayed by the storm clouds and the new batch of leaves that had already began to deprive the ground of a constant source of light. Thunder clapped in the distance and I urged Ol' Hank on. I sure did wish Tom was with me.

I wasn't afraid. At least I thought I wasn't until I took a turn on the edge of the Russells' cow pasture — our nearest neighbors. Once I cleared the curve, I came full on into a roadblock. I had to pull Ol' Hank to a sudden stop, which he complained about with might and disdain; whinnying and snorting like he'd been gouged with a red-hot poker. Poor horse gave me a spiteful look, but obeyed the evil bit in his mouth.

Two men dressed in travelin' garb, one tall and the other short and round, stood with horses nose to nose, blocking my way past. More thunder roared in the distance — but it was growing closer. Wind slapped my face and I could hear my heart beating in my chest. They didn't look friendly, not friendly at all.

"Well, well, looka here, Miles, we found us a girl in a hurry that ain't goin' nowheres," the tall man said.

"Looks like," the short one said. They both wore dark, hooded cloaks, had scraggily beards, onyx eyes, and faces I'd never seen before. Neither of them had a welcoming tone. They looked at me the way a cat looks at a mouse before it claws in for the kill.

The hair on the back of my neck stood on end and I didn't like the way I felt. Ol' Hank felt the tension through the reins and danced to the right a bit.

"Best get that horse under control, girl," the man called Miles said.

Ol' Hank snorted and lifted his tail to drop a load. I liked his response. My instinct said I should make a run for it. These men were up to no good. Pa had found opportunity in the flood of travelers makin' their way into the territory, and so had men like these. Bandits. Robbers. Thieves. Call 'em what you want, but they was the reason there was a need for Rangers. Them and Indians. As if we didn't have enough to worry about. . . . Illness took Mother, not men with evil intent.

I looked over my shoulder to check for a way free and my heart dropped. Two more men had appeared, dressed similar in clothes and demeanor as the two in front of me. Something told me they were all together, working as a team to trap me.

With the way behind me taken away as my way of escape, my eyes darted to the right, then to the left. One side of the road offered a deep wooded ravine peppered with blackberry thickets, and the other side dropped straight down to a shallow creek, the sides sandy and unstable. The four men had picked their spot well. I wasn't going anywhere.

Miles handed the round man the reins of his horse, a young gelding that had midnight eyes like its rider. I had to make a decision quick. He was coming for me, I could tell.

With that thought in mind, I spun Ol' Hank around and jumped off him. We were heading back the way we came. I slapped the horse's solid behind and yelled at him to run. He did exactly what I told him to. I knew with a distant whistle, the horse would come back to me like a loyal dog. Ol' Hank ran straight through the two horses, pushing the men to the side of the road, saving themselves from being trampled. I darted to the sandy side, jumped over the edge, and slid down to the creek before any of the men could gather themselves to come after me. I disappeared into a thick stand of grass that was unaware that the new leaves and shade overhead would drown out the sun soon — but at the moment, I was glad for the presence of it. I could hide, wait for the men to make their next move. Which didn't take long. Two of them came after me, Miles and the round man.

I scurried across the creek and pulled out my knife. I ran faster than I ever had in my life, heading north, toward the safety of the McIntyres's land. I was close, but I didn't know these woods like I knew my own. I did know my way in the woods, though, since I'd spent a good part of my life under the canopy of elms, oak, and sycamores. Spotting a game path was second nature and I found one quick. But the bad thing was the weather. Morning had turned into night; the sky was black as the rot on a pig's foot and thunder brought forth more lightning than I wanted to see. I feared a tree strike or worse. A bolt needlin' to the ground and catchin' me on fire. Death would be quick, unlike what faced me if I let myself be caught by the men giving me chase.

I ran fast, but Miles ran faster. I was on a

climb upward, close to a paddock or field, one that I hoped would lead me to help. I started screaming my fool head off. But it didn't do me any good. Most likely, it slowed me down. I felt a hand on my shoulder, then pressure that forced me to stop. I was spun around against my will. Caught. In danger. I didn't have time to recall everything I'd been taught in the last two weeks. I couldn't think. It was all I could do to push away my fear so it wouldn't paralyze me.

I was panting, he was panting, but I had my knife out, ready to fight, and the man wasn't about to let me go after workin' so hard to catch me. Before I knew it, he had both his hands on my wrists, binding the movement of my hands with his power and strength. I could have given up, since the threat of the knife — which I still held — had been rendered useless. But I knew better. I stepped back and with all of my might, I jumped up, raising my wrists to my chest with all of the strength I had. The move, showed to me by the captain, proved effective and gave me my freedom as I broke out of the man's grasp, though not without a cost. My knife fell to the ground.

I had another quick choice to make. Stand and fight, or run.

I chose to run. There was no way I could survive four against one. That's what the captain said. "First order of business is to keep yourself alive. Do whatever it takes. Stand and fight if you only got a chance of winnin'." Seemed simple at the time he said it. Not so much now.

I tore away from Miles as quick as I could and headed toward the field.

Once I was at the top of the ridge, facing blowing wind and rain, I came face to face with another man. Only this time I recognized him. It was Captain McIntyre, still as a statue, eyeing me like he was judgin' a cake in a church bakin' contest. I was pale with terror, shaking with fear, but relieved to feel rescued. I stopped before him, trying my best to catch my breath and tell him that danger was on my heels, heading our way. I had never been so happy to see a man I knowed in my life.

He nodded, and said with a calm voice, "You did good, Hallie Mae, except one thing. You left 'em your knife."

"What do you mean I did good?" I said between heartbeats.

"This was a test to see how you'd fare on your own," he said, "how you'd react to an attack or bein' held up. Only thing you did wrong was let go of your weapon and give it to the enemy. I bet you'll be more careful next time, won't you?"

"Yes, sir," I answered as I came to grasp that what had happened had not been real, but an exercise, a test, to see what I had learned and nothing more. I thought I was going to die — or worse, be taken in by men who would do unmentionable harm to me.

Miles and the other men showed themselves, came up into the field as the storm came to a crescendo over our heads. They were friends of the captain's, no more a threat to me than a lamb was.

"Come on," Captain McIntyre said, "let's get inside before this wind blows us all away. Don't worry about your horse. The fellas will bring it back."

We all headed toward the house, equal in step and stature, relaxing from the fear of attack by the men, but still concerned about the weather.

6

Pa took time out of his day to come see Tom and me graduate into bein' full Rangers. It was a proud day, clear of storms, bright and sunny, perfect for a ceremony and a grand feast put on by Missus McIntyre. Roast chicken, new potatoes, fresh cream gravy, asparagus, bread, and rhubarb pie. All the other women brought a dish share. All Pa had to offer was his presence and a free candle for all the graduates and the captain. It was enough, I think, since I'd been busy with trainin' and couldn't make somethin' myself. The table sat out in the air in front of the house was so pretty I almost hesitated to take anything and put it on my plate. I'd never seen so much food in my entire life.

All of us, in one way or another, had been tested by the captain. Our worthiness to take to the Trace judged as capable, or not. Eight of us had made the grade. To no one's surprise, Edward and Jacob had failed to stand up to the demands set forth to take on the Ranger way of life. But to my surprise and everyone else's, Abagail Peterson had passed with near honors. In my defense, she dropped her knife and was captured by Miles and his gang, but she had escaped after the round one took a swift kick in the you-know-wheres — somethin' I noted to remember. Her desire to stay in Will's company and impress him with her skills — still a shock to me — was higher than I had anticipated. So, six boys and two girls formed Captain McIntyre's Indiana Territorial Rangers division. Only two other girls had attained status in the other companies, with ours being the only one with a multiple of females. Even though my companion was Abagail, I was proud of that fact.

After our meal and a few kind words from Captain McIntyre, we was paired up in four teams. Tom was put with Abagail straight away, to my relief. I stood in wait to see who my partner would be, hoping on one hand it would be Will, and on the other that it wouldn't. I feared his presence would distract me from the seriousness of the business of bein' a Ranger, now that I was official. When it came down to it, I got exactly what I wanted. Me and Will McIntyre was gonna ride and walk the Trace together. I could tell by the look on Abagail's face that she had no plans to speak to me ever again. And that was fine with me. I didn't care if she whispered a song in my ear at that moment. She could fly away with Tom and be as silent as a polecat — and as stinky — for all I cared. It took all I had to contain my excitement and glee. Especially as the men folk walked off, taking to their smokes and small talk, and I was left to help Missus McIntyre, her brood of daughters, and mothers of the other Rangers to clean up. Oh, Abagail lingered back, too, but she was too sullen to speak with anyone. Her job was cleanin' plates in piles, savin' the leftovers and sortin' the chicken bones for garden fertilizer.

"You done yourself right proud," the captain's wife said. "Are you up to it?" She looked at me with concerned blue eyes, soft and penetrable, just like Will's.

"Yes, ma'am, I am. Wouldn't have come along to train if I didn't think I could hold my own."

She nodded. "I've watched you from afar. You have fair skills for the weaker sex." She held my gaze and something in her face changed. I wasn't sure what it was. A hardness of some kind. Jealousy, maybe. Or fear. I wasn't sure which or what. I didn't have much experience with readin' faces or words that weren't spoke.

"Pa made sure I had the skills I needed in case he wasn't around to look out for me. This ain't Philadelphia."

"Isn't."

"Yes, ma'am."

"Your pa has done a good job with you and Tom. Your mother was a dear woman. Bless her soul in heaven. I wonder if she would have been so enthusiastic in your endeavors?"

We walked along the table slow as snails, collecting plates as we talked. Our voices were low. No one was paying us any mind. I wasn't sure why the missus was concerned, especially now, after I'd won my place among the Rangers. If she had reservations about my welfare, I would have thought she would have expressed herself before now.

"Did I do something wrong?" I said.

Missus McIntyre stopped. There wasn't a spot of anything splattered on her bright white apron. She was put together in a perfect way from head to toe, but her face looked so hard that it was about to shatter. "No, dear, I'm concerned about you is all." She put her hand on my shoulder. "Out there in the hinterlands, on the Trace to protect folks with knives and guns. I worry that any of you are up to the task."

"You're worried about Will, aren't you?" I almost regretted sayin' such a thing to an elder, especially in the tone that flittered out of my mouth.

"Of course, I am. But I'm more worried about all of the dangers you two will face alone."

I examined my toes hidden inside my walkin' boots and hoped my face didn't flush red at her suggestion. It wasn't somethin' I hadn't thought about myself, but I didn't want to admit such a thing aloud.

"We got us a job to do, ma'am, and I 'spect Will and me can do that, like we was two boys, if that's what worries you. It was the captain's wisdom to set us together, and beyond that, it was Governor Harrison who had to give way to boys and girls bein' able to serve in a protection corp."

"You're a smart girl, Hallie Mae. I'll expect you to mind your manners is all. Am I clear?"

"Yes, ma'am." I stopped and looked past her, into Abagail's green eyes — who was standing close enough to listen — and said, "Am I dismissed now?"

Missus McIntyre didn't answer, she kept on walking.

I turned and ran to join up with the men and Tom. I needed to be where I belonged more at that moment than any other.

7

Me and Will had never spent much time alone. A moment here, when Tom had to go after something, or a moment there, when we was waitin' on one thing or the other — usually Tom. But never hours at a time. Much less the thought of a whole day, or days, as far as that went. The thought of such a thing made me giddy, but deep in my heart I knew I had a job to do and this adventure had nothing at all to do with spending time with Will McIntyre. Even though it did.

Me an Ol' Hank were teamed up and Will was on foot. Captain's orders. We started out at Cuzco, early on a fine April mornin' with the air fragrant with honey locust, Solomon's seal, and the promise of a new day ahead of us. The sky was streaked with clouds that looked like wiggly first-graders' lines, puffed on the sides by unseen and unfelt wind. Birds were busy building nests, or tending to their new broods of hungry mouths. Bluebirds sat atop trees, singin' their hoarse robin's song to the world, letting everyone in earshot know that everything was well and good even if they were a bit weary. Which was fine with me. I would have hated to have started out on a stormy day.

My saddlebags were loaded down with enough food from Missus McIntyre's kitchen to last three days even though we were only going to be gone for two. That was the plan. A short trip to start. Once we returned, Tom and Abagail would take our place. We would rest two days, or in my case help Pa catch up on the candle dippin' I missed out on. After a few trips, we'd extend our tours to three and four days, but never more than that. Three teams would be out at once with one in for a rest. It was a smart system, all managed by the captain, who took his own turn patrollin' the Trace with one or another of us. Along with the Rangers, there were four couriers, one assigned to each of the three divisions and one to the headquarters in Vincennes, to send instructions and communicate between all of the captains and the governor. I had feared being placed as a courier until I realized that none of them were girls. Couriers rode alone. That would never do for a girl. There was no escapin' special considerations for boys. I didn't say nothin' to no one about that. It was the way of the world. At least I was on the trail, on the adventure, keepin' the fine folks of the territory as safe as I could.

Will was outfitted head to toe with weapons and ammunition. Like all of the Rangers on foot, he carried a Harpers Ferry Model 1803 rifle. The same muzzleloader that Lewis and Clark had carried with them on their expedition west. Will was a fair shot, but I was better, and that was no empty boast. My targets shattered twice the number of times as his. He was a little clumsy with the load, which even to me was a complex series of maneuvers, but so was everyone else. Loading and firing took time, and one of our chores was to practice at least once a day while we was out on the Trace — even the riders. Along with the rifle, Will carried a measure, a powder horn, a pouch for the wads and gunpowder, his long and short knives, and his tomahawk. He had the heavy burden of carrying the rifle. Ol' Hank bore the brunt of my assortment of weapons and necessaries, exceptin' the short knife sheathed on my right hip. Put simply, we was cocked and loaded for bear, bad trouble, or a long boring ride, which was what we both hoped it to be. I wasn't quite up to a run-in with Indians or men like I had thought Miles and his gang to be.

Since it was still spring and the air prone to be cool, we both wore buckskin jackets and pants. I had on my floppy brown felt hat with my hair braided and stuffed down my back. Since I was a skinny girl, I could pass for a boy until you got close up on me, or I had to speak, which I left to Will if the need came. Wasn't nobody's business that I was a girl. I wasn't gonna show 'em what I was in case they thought me less, weak, or unfit to be a Ranger.

We was a load of miles down the Trace, headin' for the Falls of the Ohio, before we encountered our first travelers. It was nigh on toward the falling tilt of the sun. It wouldn't be long before we set out to find a spot to strike camp. They was a man and a woman, goin' the same ways as us, ridin' in a cart stacked with all of their earthly belongings, pulled by a muddied old gray ox that didn't look none too pleased at the chore he'd been yoked for.

We caught up with the pair easily, and they seemed inclined for a bit of company, so they pulled over to the side, and welcomed us to talk a bit.

"Where you boys headin'?" the man said with a wave. His arms were skinny as a broomstick and his head was as bald as a hairless and pink baby mouse. His wife was twice his size with a sad look painted across her blubbery face. She worried a wad of chew of some kind in her left cheek, and spit every once in a while.

I smiled inward, of course, at the deception of boys, other than it wasn't no deception. Not really. My disguise, if it could be called that, was more for my own safety than anything else.

"To the river," Will answered. "We're Rangers. Indiana Territorial Rangers, put here by Governor Harrison to keep you safe."

"You? And that gnat of a boy there?" the man said.

That didn't make me smile.

"Yes, sir," Will said. "Only she ain't no boy. That there's a girl. Governor Harrison seems to think the Trace is a fit place for us all. I'd be inclined to disagree, but I've knowed this here girl since I was a tot, and I'll tell you, she can outshoot any fella in the territory."

"Is that so," the man said.

"Yes, sir."

"Then how come you're carryin' the rifle?"

"Because she's better throwin' a knife."

It was a fine comeback and I was proud of Will for bein' so quick to my defense. I held the man's gaze, then dropped my fingers to the hilt of the short knife on my hip. He looked away real quick.

"Well, then, I'm glad to know there's a patrol on this road. Makes me feel better," the man said.

"Do you have news?" Will said.

"You heard of Tecumseh and that brother of his gatherin' in Greenville?"

"No, sir, I didn't."

I sat atop Ol' Hank and watched and listened. The woman in the cart looked bored, like she'd heard everything the man said a hundred times over.

"Well," the man continued. "I heard tell

there was a mass of Injuns there. A thousand from one man, while another said the number was closer to four hundred. Now, you know there's no good that can come from that many Injuns bein' in one place, no matter how benevolent Harrison is to 'em. That Prophet is fillin' their heads with all kinds of nonsense about magical powers and witchcraft of the like. I don't know nothin' about that, but there's concern all the way to Washington. I heard tell there's a half-blood Shawnee that took a letter from the president to Tecumseh to try and smooth things over. Tecumseh sent the man away and told him to tell the president to come there and meet him face-to-face. Can you imagine such a thing, a heathen tellin' the president what to do and where to go?"

"No, sir," Will said, "I cannot."

"That's all I know for now. There's a storm brewin' among the tribes. Miami. Delaware. Shawnee. All being pulled and played by the French and British. Like I said, I sure am glad that you two are out here, but I sure hope you're outfitted enough to take on what's comin' for you, 'cause I don't think ya are. Don't matter if that girl's a good shot or not. You gotta get the ball down the barrel and powder in the pan before one of them savages comes for your scalp."

Will nodded and took into consideration what the man said. "We're ready. And if you're not in need of our services any further, we'll be on our way."

"Are there more behind you?" the man said.

"There will be. Now, don't you worry. Something unseen happens, you send up some smoke and we'll come a runnin'."

"I'll do that. I hope you get there in time. I don't want to end up captured like those Larkins."

"That's why we're here," Will said.

8

We stood high on a ridge looking west over an abundance of treetops bathed in the fadin' light of the day. Fresh, tender leaves, tinted gold as if they had been touched by an unseen god, stretched out for as far as I could see. Striped clouds lined the pale sky overhead, drained of blue, almost white, touched by fire hot enough to melt gold. The sun was gone, tucked in under the horizon. There was a little breeze; a caress wrapped around us causing only the slightest flitter of anything tethered. A fire crackled behind us with a comfortable flame. Awaiting next to the spit made of fresh green sticks was a skinned and gutted rabbit. Will took it with one shot to the head. I was impressed. Of course, he could have blown the thing to bits and I still would have been impressed.

Will was transfixed by the view. One of the finest I had ever seen. I'd never been this far down on the Trace so it was a new world to me.

"They say a squirrel can go from treetop to treetop all the way from the Mississippi to the ocean out east without ever touchin' the ground," Will said. "It won't be like that forever."

"Why do you say that?"

"Look at the land around Cuzco. Every time someone moves in, they fell trees and plant a plot of corn. More people come, the less trees there will be. Less trees, less squirrels."

I looked at Will's face all awash in the golden light, his hard chin jutted forward, his summer-blue eyes glistening with an extra dab of moisture from peekin' into the future too hard. His brow was furrowed with worry instead of the possibility of youth. I had never seen him so serious. Ruminatin' on the state of the world was a side of him I had never seen before. It was almost like I was lookin' at a different person. For all the years he'd exchanged shadows with Tom, at that moment I discovered that I didn't know Will McIntyre at all.

"You sound like a sympathizer to Tecumseh and his like," I said.

"I'm defending the way of life I love. Aren't we the same, me and him?"

"You ain't spreadin' lies about magic powers like him and his brother are doin'."

"He don't know no better," Will said. "He's protectin' what's his and what's always been his. Now, here we come changing things that have been the same for hundreds of years. Look at this road we're a standin' on. Where's the buffalo that made it? You ever seen one?"

"No." I looked to the ground, to the Trace, and tried to a imagine what a herd of buffalo on a trek to a salt lick looked like. I couldn't see such a thing in my mind because I'd never seen such a thing before me. I'd never seen a buffalo in my life.

"They're all gone is why. Or near gone. How does that happen?"

I shrugged and looked away. I didn't want to think about such things. As much as I hated to give up the view, I turned and made my way back to the fire. It was past time to eat.

Will stood still as a statue for a long time,

looking out across the expanse, thinking thoughts I never knew he was capable of, seeing things I had no idea of, and dreaming of a life that included me and everyone one of us back home. If I had liked him before from a distance, I liked him even more up close.

After we ate, our night passed with one of us standing sentinel over the other. An owl hooted in the distance, and another hooted back. A coyote yipped. Something growled down the hill, its discomfort floating upward in the air, too far away to reach us with its claws. I watched over Will as he slept, and I eyed the Trace for any comers. Through it all, I wasn't afraid nary a bit. I was exactly where I was supposed to be. It felt right. And I knew bein' a Ranger suited me. I liked seein' folks take comfort in my presence.

The next day, another blessed relief of calm weather, with a sky as cheerful as a China doll's face, greeted us as we turned around and made our way back to Cuzco. We passed travelers, assured them that they were safe, gathered what news there was, and arrived home without any scars of confrontation or encounters with bad luck. Captain McIntyre was happy to see us and sent Tom and Abagail straight out onto the

Trace in our place.

I headed home to our cabin, knowing full well that I had work to do there, candles to dip, time to spend with Pa and assure him that this new way of life would work out for us. He looked even wearier than he had when I'd left. I wondered if it was possible for exhaustion to spread in two days, as quick as a fever?

"Are you all right?" I said, studying Pa's face in the dim light of the shop. His shirt was wilted and his face looked like it was gonna melt right off. I had also got the first whiff of pig tallow, and I wasn't real happy to be reacquainted with the smell. He must've used up all the sheep tallow and had to resort to the pig. He'd been a busy man.

"More orders keep coming in," he said, dipping and talking at the same time, solidifyin' my assumption.

"Maybe you could hire a boy. Jacob Hopmeyer's brother. He's a good worker. You said so yourself."

"I have two children of my own."

"We're not children any more, Pa. Some girls my age have done got married and brought a baby or two into this world."

"You're not gonna, are you?"

"Well, I hope to get married some day,

but not anytime soon, if that's what you mean."

Pa froze in his movement and stared at me, examined me from head to toe, still dressed in my Ranger garb; buckskins soiled from the road, my hair still in a braid, Trace dirt under my fingernails. No boy would look twice at me if he was in his right mind. After a long take he looked away, put the broach down, and sat down in the chair next to the dipping pot. "You're right, Hallie Mae, you're not a child anymore, and neither is Tom. Both of you have grown into fine adults while I've been standing over this vat of pig fat dipping away the future and the past. I'm sorry. I suppose it's natural for a pa to want his children to stay young for as long as they can."

I knew better than anyone that Pa had lost part of himself the day he buried Mother, that his work had occupied him through his grief. But I could see that it was getting to be too much for him, that what weighed on him was more than the unfilled orders stacking up on his desk. He was lonely and sad, bound to an occupation and a way of life that had grown into a heavy chain, while his children longed to see the world and have an adventure or two for themselves. Spring had passed Pa by and landed square on my shoulders.

"I'm thinkin' I might give up the Ranger days," I said. I didn't know where those words came from. It wasn't a thought I had considered until I saw Pa's face after bein' gone. I felt more selfish at that moment than I'd ever felt in my life.

"You don't mean that."

"Maybe I do."

He judged me one more time and shook his head. "Maybe I will go talk to that Hopmeyer boy. I think you might be right. I can afford to hire a hand. You're not giving up this Ranger business. I won't hear of it. Not on my account. Now, you go on in and wash up for dinner. I put a stew on the stove for you. It should be ready."

I started to protest, but Pa read my face like it was a well-worn psalm.

"Go on," he said. "Do as I say, and don't argue with me. You've helped me settle something in my mind. Go on."

I couldn't argue no more. I was tired and wore out myself. I did as I was told, and gladly found my way to familiar food and a soft feather bed. I know I was only gone for two days, but it felt like it had been a week.

9

My two days of rest passed like one deep sleep. I hugged Pa good-bye as I left for my next tour, but he was well into a lecture with the Hopmeyer boy on the right and proper way to stir tallow. I was relieved that Pa'd brought himself some help into the shop. It would be one less thing for me to worry about while I was away.

When I rode up to the McIntyre house, I was happy to see Tom and Abagail's horses hitched up in front of the porch. It seemed odd, though, that there were more horses than usual tied about this early in the mornin'. There were six, all told, beyond Tom and Abagail's mounts, peppered in front of the well-kept house. I wondered if the captain had called a meeting of some kind that I wasn't aware of. There wasn't any friction in the air that I could taste. It was as nice a day as you could ask for; pale blue sky lackin' any clouds or wind, and the birds were happy to go about their business tendin' to their early broods. I didn't think anything was wrong until I walked into the house and saw Tom sittin' in the parlor surrounded by a bunch of grim-faced men.

I stopped sudden, like I'd ran face-first into a wall. The men looked up, saw me, and stopped talking, allowing silence to cut my way and stab me with a dreadful feelin' I'd had before. Something was wrong. Death was afoot. I knew the look like it was a long-lost uncle come home to borrow money.

It took me a second to work up the courage to walk into the room, headed up by the captain, who had no interest in looking me in the eye. Tom, neither. One step in, someone took my shoulder from behind. Not in an angry way, but a gentle way, saving me from stepping over a ledge of some kind.

I spun around and came face to face with Will McIntyre.

"They took her," he said real soft. A forbidden whisper on the tip of butterfly wings. Not the sweet nothing that I had dreamed of, but the announcement of something I could not imagine. I had to strain to hear him, but I did. I knew what he'd said and didn't need the details, even though I wanted them in a desperate way.

Will's face was pale and his eyes were streaked red; a taint of no sleep in the corner of each eye. He was dressed and ready to ride, save his boots. He was in his socked feet. I had to comprehend for a moment that this was his house and the headquarters for our division of Rangers, too.

He led me away from the parlor, willing me to keep my mouth shut with a stern side-glance that meant nothin' but keep your trap shut. He'd inherited the talent for command from both parents, though he favored his mother. I didn't need a book on how to read his face. No, sir, I didn't. The last thing I was gonna do was bring any undue attention to myself.

"You're the last person they want to see," Will whispered, leading me outside. We stopped on the porch with our backs to the house.

I clinched my teeth with foreboding. "We have to go find her."

"You're not going anywhere."

"What do you mean?" I knew the answer to the question before it had left my mouth.

"They can't afford to lose another girl."

"You're sayin' that to get me good and riled up, aren't you?"

"It's the truth of the matter, Hallie Mae. Momma was gonna be the one to break it to you, but she lit out to comfort Abagail's mother and tend to her needs. She's in a dither and worried sick."

"While the men sit and talk about what to do instead of going after her? Who wouldn't be in a dither, Will? That's foolishness is what it is." I looked out to Ol' Hank and caught Will's eye in the process. He seemed to know what I was thinkin'.

"You can't go after her," he said, reaching out like he was gonna grab me and drag me back inside. That was the last place I wanted to be.

"Says who?"

"The captain. Me and you is to stay here while they go on the hunt for those savages."

"So, it was the Indians?"

"That's what Tom said. They stole her away while he was sleepin' and she was standin' sentry. He feels real bad and all, like it's his fault that she got took. Her screams woke him up, but the fire had dimmed and it was too dark for him to get a look at anythin' other than buckskin and feathers. And then they were gone. Off on horses, with the night as black as that ewe over there."

I let my vision follow his nod to a pen of sheep the captain kept for wool and nothing more. Something didn't seem right, but I couldn't figure it out. I needed to talk to Tom myself and get his side of the story, but that was impossible. He was trapped in an inquisition with far more threat than I could offer. I felt sorry for my brother. I knew how he must've felt. But I was more worried about Abagail, and the rest of the girl Rangers for that matter. This might be the end — just as it was gettin' started.

"Where'd they take her at?" I studied Will's face for the slightest hint of blame on my brother. I didn't see any judgment at all. Only concern.

"At the first switch that heads to the river," he said.

The river always meant the Ohio River. I knew of the switch, but I'd never traveled it. Tom had, so I wasn't surprised that he'd stopped there to set camp for the night. "He looked for her?" I said, noticing a rising chorus of voices from inside the house. Men argued a lot before they ever got around to doin' anything of value if you ask me.

"Says so," Will answered. I believed him.

"Okay. He's gotta fend for himself, then." I headed off the porch.

"Where you goin'?"

"Home," I lied.

Will knew a falsehood when he heard and saw it. He looked down to his socked feet, then to me as I hurried to Ol' Hank. I had to get out of there before he stopped me. There was no way that I was gonna sit back and let anyone else go after Abagail, especially with Tom's reputation on the line. If that girl turned up dead it would follow him all his life. Captive as he was to the head men, I had no choice but to save his honor . . . and Abagail's life, if I could.

With that in mind, I jumped into the saddle like I had a hard wind helpin' me upward. Ol' Hank shuddered at the suddenness of my arrival, but he knew the press of my legs and the hard grasp of the reins meant business. It was time to run, time to fly, time to do what I set out to do. Be brave, be on an adventure, be a Ranger.

10

It didn't take Will two shakes to grab his pair of boots, put them on, and rush after me. But if there was one thing Ol' Hank loved to do, it was run with his head all to his self. I had a good lead on Will, kickin' up dust like I was, and I couldn't see him clear enough when I looked over my shoulder. I didn't know whether he'd betrayed me and set off an alarm to the other men or not. I knew he was on my tail and that was it. I urged Ol' Hank to run faster than he'd ever run before. I was damned if I was gonna let Will drag me back to the captain and pin me down in the kitchen, or worse, the cellar. Pa wouldn't like my use of strong language, not even in my head, but I feared for Abagail's life, and I knew I could help. Nothin' nor nobody was gonna stop me.

Not even Will McIntyre.

I rounded a lazy curve in the road and lost sight of my pursuer. I chuckled at the thought. Of all times to get what you want, Will chasin' after me, I could have cared less. Now all I wanted to do was get away from him. Life sure does have a sense of humor that I don't think is funny at all.

Ol' Hank was havin' the time of his life gettin' lathered up, so I leaned forward in the saddle and joined him in the race. I gave up my worry about Will, the other Rangers, and the whatevers that was goin' on in that meetin' room. I was ridin' the high wind of desire. I had a taste of freedom and I wanted more. I didn't lose sight or thought of Abagail, neither. My run was about her more than it was about me.

Settled in on a good run, I turned over the hard part to my horse. He'd stay straight in the middle of the road as long as I held fast, and let me wander in my mind for a bit.

If you would have told me a month ago that I was going after the Indians to try and rescue Abagail Peterson because she was ridin' the Trace as a Ranger, I would've laughed till I fell over. But Abagail had proven herself worthy, more skilled with knives and rifles than I ever thought possible. Until then she had been the spoiled daughter and lone child of a traveling minister who came and went, leaving her home with her mother. Abagail was an only child, a rare situation on the frontier. Most folks had a load of children. But whatever the reason, Abagail's parents had only brought her into the world. They doted on her somethin' terrible. I don't know if that's a sin or not, but Abagail seemed to have an endless supply of frilly dresses, gewgaws, and the like. I haven't got a clue how she talked her mother into lettin' her try out for the Rangers, but my guess was what Abagail wanted, Abagail got. And it wasn't so much an adventure the girl was after, but Will McIntyre hisself. I swear she hated me for gettin' to ride with him on the Trace, but she restrained herself and her cat claws — which was a good thing 'cause if she'd a come after me, I'd a given her a lickin' like she'd never had before. Fightin' wasn't her way. Instead, Abagail worked harder at bein' better than me at everything. I liked her for that, but on my part, I wasn't about to cede my affections for Will McIntyre without showin' effort of my own. I'll have to give it to Abagail, gettin' herself captured by Indians sure put her at the center of the attention. Seems to me I only had one choice in the matter, and that was goin' after them savages and bringin' Abagail home.

I should have been payin' more attention to the road behind me, for it wasn't long before Will caught up to me. Like everything else he took his hand at, Will McIntyre was an excellent horseman. If there was ever a war to come, I was sure he would go off and make his pa proud. He rode like a soldier and obeyed orders like one, too, which I assumed were to bring me back to headquarters as soon as possible. I gouged Ol' Hank with my knees at the thought, but Will outrode me. He eased up aside me on his roan mare like she had wings instead of hooves. Without askin', Will reached over, grabbed Ol' Hank's reins, and yanked my horse under control. We both stopped at the same time. I didn't try and get away. It was no use.

"What in tarnation are you doin', Hallie Mae?" Will said.

I glared at him with as much anger as I could muster. My lips were sealed so tight I feared I'd never say another word in my life.

"You have to go back," Will continued. "We both do."

I shook my head no.

He squared his strong shoulders and jutted his chin like he was about to bark an order, but he didn't say anything. He seemed to think better of what he was about to do, and relented. "You can't go out there all on your own. I ain't gonna let that happen, more less be responsible for such a thing. The captain'll skin my hide if I let anything happen to you."

"Nothin' is gonna happen to me." I relented. Will's tone had changed. It was more a plea than a command. Add that to the concern on his face, and the direct look into my eyes, and he could melt any iron courage I could have forged inside myself. "I have to save Abagail. Every second those men take making plans is one more second she's closer to trouble, if that hasn't already come to her."

"Don't say such a thing."

"Any creature that'll leave a baby to fend for itself in the wilderness isn't gonna show no care to a pretty girl like Abagail. They took her for a reason, and I shudder at the thought of what that reason was."

"Don't say such a thing," Will repeated, looking over his shoulder, back toward home, back toward the rest of the men who made the decisions. "Okay," he said with reserve, "we'll go after her. Me and you. That's the way it's gonna be."

I didn't argue. How could I? "Let's go," I

said, taking the reins from Will. I urged Ol' Hank on, and he was ready to have another go at the run, especially now that he had a mare to show off for. Will was at my side in a wink, joining me in my quest to save Abagail. I hoped we weren't too late.

11

Night fell as we reached the switch. The first clouds of bitin' bugs hovered over tender bottlebrush grass waiting for a disturbance, waiting to attack or for a shift in the wind. There'd been no sign of Abagail on the Trace, but Will and I hadn't expected any. We did encounter a few travelers heading in both directions, but none of them had seen or heard anything of a girl taken by Indians. One man, a pot-and-pan salesman with a wide belly and suspicious eyes, warned us of the French, though. That brought a rise of alarm in Will, and after the salesman went on his way, Will argued that we should turn around and go home, that we were in enough trouble the way it was. I know he feared his father, I woulda, too, if I was him, but I argued back that all would be forgiven if we brought Abagail home. I rode on and Will followed. I was starting to like that, but I felt bad deep inside for the plan I had formed in my mind to keep Will from gettin' in any trouble at all.

"We should strike camp," Will called out from behind me.

I slowed Ol' Hank so Will could catch up, so we could talk while looking at each other. "Let's find Tom and Abagail's exact spot. See if we can figure out what happened."

Will looked at me like I was half-crazy, then turned his attention to the dropping sun. "We don't have much time."

"No, we don't."

We stopped in the middle of the road. No one was about. The only other living creature witness to our presence was a lone squirrel, plump and sleepy, stretched out on the branch of an oak tree like it had nothin' better to do. Songbirds chatted in the distance and the clouds of bugs hadn't found their way to us. The sky was an array of pinks and yellows, dotted with thin clouds that looked comfortable enough to sleep on. All in all, it had been an easy day of travel, considering we'd leapt off on the road on our own. I knew Will was only here because of me and I felt bad about that. I didn't twist his arm, but he was my partner, so from his point of view, I supposed, he didn't have much of a choice but to come along with me on this journey. Authorized or not. I wasn't sittin' this out because the captain was afraid of losin' me, too.

"You know they're not too far behind us, Hallie Mae." Will looked over his shoulder toward home, then back to me, his face flushed with fear and concern.

"I 'spect they'll be here anytime. Till then, I think we ought to do our best to find Abagail."

"You'd make a good captain if you weren't a girl."

I didn't even acknowledge the comment. I let it fly right by me as I nickered Ol' Hank to a trot. If Will wasn't gonna help me find the camp, I'd find it on my own.

Will caught up with me real quick, passed by me without sayin' a word, rode about ten yards and turned into the brush, following a wide deer path down a mild hill. I hoped the path was used by deer and not bear. Neither one of us had a rifle. We weren't set for bear. I had my knives and tomahawk, and so did Will. Neither of us had mentioned our lack of gunpowder or lead balls on our ride here. I suppose we didn't think we'd need it, or if we had, then that would have stopped our plan dead cold. There was no way to get a rifle from the Ranger armory without the captain's approval.

I followed Will, who'd come to a stop in a

wide spot in the path. It was an often-used camp, the ground marred black by more fires than I could count. The grass was tamped down, stunted in its growth, and there was even some firewood left behind for our use. A narrower path led farther down the hill where a healthy creek ran, populated by the snowmelt and spring rains. Everything was luscious, green, and lonesome for as far as I could see.

Will jumped off his horse and started to strike camp right away by stringing a stay line for the horses. I followed suit, setting to work on building a fire. I'd eyed that plump squirrel with moist and hungry lips and I would have had him for dinner had there been a rifle on the ride. But there wasn't, which meant we'd have to scrounge for food another way. It wasn't long before the pinks and yellows turned black and the only light around us glowed orange from the fire. Will had been able to fetch some crawdads from the creek, and I'd boiled some tender young nettles and mushrooms for a soup in our tins that'd been packed on the horses, ready for duty. At least we had that. We supped in silence, keen to every sound we heard coming from the Trace. We were off it a bit, but easy to find for any riders searching us out. So far there hadn't been any visitors and I was glad of that. I wasn't ready to be dragged home for a tongue-lashin' and possible dismissal from the Rangers.

"I didn't see no sign of Abagail's presence," Will said, breaking the long silence between us. "No shred of clothes, nothin'."

"I saw broken branches, but that could have come from anybody. The light was dim. We'll have a better look in the mornin'." Somewhere deep in my mind I heard an admonishment from Pa about fibbin', but I ushered it away by focusing on Will's sweet face.

"I'll take watch after we finish eating. You can sleep all night and get some rest."

"Not all night. You won't be worth a hoot tomorrow if you don't get no shut eye," I said, bein' as stern as I could. Call me Captain Hallie Mae Edson. "I'll take the first watch, then I'll wake you up halfway through the night. Fair is fair. That's what we done on our first ride out, this here isn't no different the way I see it. This is a mission. Maybe more important than any we may ride." I made sure my voice was hard and unwavering as I held my right hand behind my back with my fingers crossed.

"Have you ever lost an argument in your life?" Will stood up with a humph, the sweet look all gone from his face, walked over to his horse and unstrapped his bedroll. He was mad as a bee-stung mule from the sound of his stomps, but his question was a question I didn't have to answer and I wasn't going to. I could see I'd advanced my plan and I didn't want to ruin it.

Will made his way around me opposite the fire, unrolled his bedding, and got himself comfortable with some snorts and pulls. I almost giggled at him, but I wasn't a giggling kind of girl, or I tried not to be, so I held my breath.

"You promise to wake me up?" he said.

"Yes." I crossed my fingers tighter.

"All right then." He rolled over with his backside to the fire.

"Don't let the bedbugs bite," I said, then watched and waited until I knew he was deep asleep. When he gave a solid row of snores, I armed myself with my knives, secured my tomahawk, then made way down the path to the creek as silent as a weasel stealing into a henhouse.

I pulled out a piece of material I'd found trapped low in a thicket of blackberries and studied it by the light of the moon. I couldn't say for sure that the shred belonged to Abagail, but I was taking a bet that it was. When Will woke up to find me gone, facing a crowd of Rangers and his father, all he would have to say is that he came after me, didn't want to leave me out in the wilderness alone, and he'd be free of trouble. Me, on the other hand, I had to find Abagail, if she were still alive, and whisk her away from the savages that took her with my scalp still intact.

12

It helped that the moon was almost full. I could see a good ways in front of my feet to follow all the game that had gone before me. I feared steppin' into a groundhog hole, trippin' over a branch or some other obstruction I couldn't see, or stumblin' across one of them night cats that I'd heard howl on occasion, out on the hunt for fresh meat. Every creature around had young mouths to feed, and I knew I was as much prey as I was a predator travelin' at night like I was. I lacked any good advantage to survive.

I wasn't huntin' for no food this time out. I was huntin' for a girl that I hoped still breathed. Each step took me farther away from Will, from the safety of my scream callin' him to rescue me. I was alone, on my own, and that was the way I wanted it. I had been out of earshot before, but never this far from home, never this deep into the night, and never when there was the threat of Indians at hand. Pa kept us close when word of a raiding party spread through Cuzco. Now I wanted more than a sign of their presence. I hoped I wasn't being too reckless.

The air was cool and free of biters and bloodsuckers at the moment. Young nettle scratched against my ankles, but it wasn't near as itchy as it would be when the plant was waist high and full of needles that stuck under your skin. I tried to be as quiet as I could, but I didn't have the stalking skills of no redskin. I've always envied them Indians from afar, and hoped I had the fortitude and courage I would need if I found them. I would need some luck, too. A lot of luck if I was to be honest with myself.

I walked a good five miles without coming across anything that lived. Darkness ticked darker and the moon headed for the horizon like a sleepy yellow face achin' to lay its head to the pillow. I hoped Will was still comfortable in his dreamland, but I pushed away any worry beyond that. I traversed creeks, then edged a swamp thick with cedar trees that looked like giant skeletons with their thick, shaggy arms draped with moss; remnants of clothes from a former life flittering in the breeze. The shadows looked like they was made of nightmares. No game without fins or flippers could skim across the swamp's black water. I didn't know how deep it was and I sure as heck wasn't gonna find out. The last thing I wanted to do was wake a sleepin' snake. I trusted the trail and followed it deep into the ways of tall trees and more scratchy weeds, away from the swamp, farther south, if I judged correctly by the twinklin' stars over my head. It was there that I caught the first whiff of wood smoke.

I stopped to gather myself and to make sure I was really smelling what I thought I was. There was a bundle of smells in the woods and swamps in the springtime. Rot and moisture, mixed with standing water, could confuse a nose sometimes. I had broken into a small sweat, not only from the effort of walking but from the recognition that I didn't know where I was. Biters appeared out of nowhere, drawn to the nectar that only they could smell, and fed on my fear.

I was lost as a blind newborn pup inches off the teat. At the moment, my plan to rescue Abagail was startin' to seem like a fool's errand. Me and my big pants, tryin' to be somethin' I wasn't: As brave and strong as any danged boy is what I was tryin' to be. Maybe Pa was right, maybe I was just a girl. I almost worked myself up to a cry, but I warded that off with the stomp of my foot. Then I heard Pa say something else, call me young miss in my memory. He always said girls didn't have to be no rugs in this world. He sure didn't treat Mother like she was property like most men did their wives. Pa and Mother were partners. He was heartbroken is all, but in the end, he had believed in me, set me on the path to become a Ranger because I had wanted it so bad. Cryin' like a baby lost in the woods wasn't goin' to get me nothin' or nowhere. I guess doubt and fear was expected, normal, but I knew I had to get ahold of my courage. There wasn't no time to feel sorry for myself. I'd come this far. I had to find out if the smell of smoke would lead me to Abagail.

I stood tall and drew in a few deep breaths to calm myself. I couldn't see the glow of any fire, which was a no surprise. Indians were masters at hiding their presence. I was sure the smell was woodsmoke, though, and I had no choice but to follow it if I could. It was the first sign of human life I'd come across since leavin' Will to his dreams.

A slight breeze pushed out of the southwest and the smoke was riding on that. I turned and pushed back to the edge of the swamp with my short knife in my hand, ready for anything to jump out and try to take me down. Each step was as quiet as I could make it, and I tried extra hard not to snap any twigs or weeds that blocked my way. It would have been easier if Will was with me, but then he wouldn't have had no excuse to offer the captain if we came up empty-handed.

The farther I went, the more I was sure that the smoke was from a burning fire, albeit a small one. I moved like a wary snail, but before I knew it, I had gone a long way. When I looked over my shoulder, to the east, a thin line of light had nibbled out some of the darkness. Morning was coming. Daylight would give me away soon. I had to hurry.

A hint of voices drew my attention and darn near stopped me from breathin'. I had to strain to make sure I was hearin' what I thought I did. I had expected Indian gibberish, but what I heard was a language I'd heard before. It was French.

Before the Indiana Territory was carved out of the Northwest Territory, the land I walked on was controlled by France. But that had changed, especially since a man called Napoleon took over that country in somethin' Pa had called a coup. The French still had a relationship with the Algonquin and other Indian tribes in the area. I heard tell them Indians was cozying up to the British and French as a way to annoy Governor Harrison, who it seemed to me had his hands full enough with all the travelers comin' into the territory, along with Tecumseh and his brother stirrin' up all the other Indian tribes into what looked like a war on the horizon; the troubles were more than a nibble. The French, as Pa said, were troublemakers and not to be trusted. I hoped they was nothin' more than wayward travelers and didn't have anything to do with Abagail's disappearance. Regardless, I had no choice but to sneak up and take a look. One good thing, I was sure bein' sneaky would be easier against the French than it would be a camp of Indians.

I followed the smoke smell and the voices, which were low as whispers, but carried on the breeze like the first morning call of the robins. Every creature stirrin' could hear life and movement if they was awake. Even though I hadn't had any sleep, the presence of people in the darkness jolted my eyes wide open. It was like a shot of lightning had gone through my entire body. I had one other desire propelling me forward, and it was the hope that the French would be more considerate with a young girl like Abagail than the Indians would be.

I skittered from one tree to the next, stepping easy so I wouldn't leave no sign of movement in the flowers and weeds. I hid behind an old oak tree, then moved on to a stand of hickories as the voices grew louder, closer. I didn't understand a word of what was bein' said, but I could tell it was easy talk between men, most likely the change of watch, drinkin' a chicory coffee, exhangin' boredom from one to another. There was an odd smell to the smoke and I figured that was it, mornin' doin's, breakfast and such bein' readied for the day.

I got close enough to see the glow of the fire, a flicker climbing up the side of a tree. I was glad I was thin, hiding like I was behind one oak and then the next. I stopped when I could see the shadows moving. I counted three men and could make out two lean-tos made when they'd pitched camp. The lean-tos were covered with branches full of tender leaves to keep the night air and any possible rain away from those that slept.

More birds started to sing as the dawn light grew brighter. I wasn't going to be able to count on darkness to hide me much longer.

I wanted to get closer so I could see if there was anyone else in the camp, to see if Abagail was somewhere I couldn't get a look at. But I knew every movement I made could be my undoing, could alert the French that I was close by. Even if the Indians hadn't taken Abagail, I could end up in as much trouble if I was taken by the French. Then Will and the rest of the Rangers would have two girls to rescue, not one. That would be the end to my adventures once and for all. I would be stuck dippin' candles with Pa for the rest of my life — if I was lucky enough to survive at all. For all I knew these men wouldn't think twice about killin' a Cuzco girl.

I couldn't help myself. I bounced from one tree to the next until I ended up ten feet from the camp. I was so close that I could see all of it. And to my relief and fear, I saw what I had hoped not to: Abagail Peterson sitting cross-legged inside the lean-to, her mouth gagged with a tight linen and her arms tied behind her back.

13

The three men who hovered around the fire were all that I could see beyond that. It was possible that there was another man or two on watch somewhere, or a scout out that could come back at anytime. I'd have to factor the unknown into my plan to rescue Abagail if I was as smart as I hoped I was. I knew the odds were against me, that the best thing I could do was run back to Will and get help, not try and do this myself. But the problem was I didn't know what the men intended to do to Abagail, and finding my way back to camp would take some doing. I wasn't exactly sure where I was. What I did know was that I was running out of time. If I was going to act, it had to be soon, before the sun took away all of my shadows to hide in.

I took another look at the men to size up the situation again. There was one man sitting with his back to me, while the other two sat on each side; all of them faced the low fire, watching the pot come to a boil. The lean-to Abagail was stowed in was opposite the man with his back to me. Somehow, I needed to let her know that I was here to rescue her, see if she could help me in some way or another. But doing that risked showin' myself to the French. And then what? Well, I figured I had no choice but to come up behind the man with his back to me and prepare myself to slit his throat if I had to. First, I would press the sharp knife against his skin, draw blood if I had to. I took a deep breath and asked myself a question I'd never considered until that moment: *Do you have it in you to kill a man, Hallie Mae? Do you?*

I didn't know the answer, wouldn't know until I had to face such a thing, but I couldn't let my fear of the unknown stop me. I didn't come this far to bear witness to somethin' bad happenin' to Abagail Peterson.

My first piece of luck came straight away. One of the men got up and wandered off into the woods without sayin' a word. I figured he was gonna relieve himself, but I wasn't too worried about the cause, all I knew was that now I only had two men to worry about.

Abagail's eyes followed the man, tall and limber, with a flow of dirty black sweat dipping over his collar until he was out of sight. When she turned back to face the remaining two, I peered around the trunk of the oak I was hidin' behind enough for her to get a good look at my face. Good thing she had a gag on her mouth because she let out a gasp, and her eyes brightened. As it was, the noise from her drew both men's attention for a splatter of a second. Abagail was smart enough to look to the ground as quick as she'd reacted to seein' me.

The two men, one plump, the other skinny, both dirty as pigs from trekkin' in the woods for an unknown amount of time, looked around to make sure they was still alone, then went back to starin' at the pot on the fire once they was satisfied there was no threat about. I melted into the tree the best I could, glad that I'd worn the darkest clothes I had. The sun was startin' to light the tops of the trees, sending a glittering glow of soft gold through the new leaves. It was going to be a fine day, but I needed the mornin' to take its time. It wasn't the first time in my life that I wished that I could stop the world from spinning.

Not only did I plan on holding one of the men hostage, I planned on throwing my long knife behind Abagail with the hopes that she would be able to reach it and cut through the rope that bound her hands. That was all I knew to do, other than fight to the death if it came to that.

I gripped my short knife and started my sneak out of the woods, moving as quiet and undetected as I could. I was a foot from the man with his back to me before the other man noticed my presence. But it was too late. Before he could sound the alarm, I was behind my target with my blade pressed hard against his throat. "You move an inch and you're a dead man. You," I said to his partner, "say a word, and he's dead before you can say boo." I tried to sound as mean as I could. The man with the knife at his throat swallowed hard and shivered. At least he was scared. That was a good sign.

The other man, the plump one, said, "She ain't nothin' but a girl."

"A girl that means to set her friend free no matter what it takes," I said, as I tossed the long knife behind Abagail. It landed six inches farther away than I wanted it to, but she understood my intent and scooted back to get it, grabbed it up and started to saw away the rope. "Trouble's comin' your way fast, fellas," I continued. "A whole troop of Rangers is on my tail." I hoped that wasn't a lie. I couldn't imagine Captain McIntyre sitting around waitin' on us to return once he figured out me and Will went to look for Abagail on our own.

The plump man spat and stood up. "You lie, *petite fille*. There is no one but you."

I didn't panic. I pressed hard enough against my prisoner's throat to make him squeak out a plea for me to stop. The plump man stopped where he stood, eyeing me with anger and tension growing in his face. He looked over his shoulder, toward the direction where the other man went to relieve himself, but he restrained from calling out for help. All I could think of was not to lose my weapon. No matter what, I couldn't give up my knife.

Then the plump man looked to Abagail, who was making quick business of freeing herself. He started to move for her. I told him to stop, and to my surprise, he did what I said. I guess it doesn't matter if you're just a girl as long as you got a knife to someone's throat.

I had everyone where I wanted them but time was moving slow. I needed Abagail's help. I needed her to be free. Before I could do or say anything else, things got worse. The other man walked back into camp, focused on buttoning his trousers, not paying any attention to where he was going or what was going on. He looked up and said, *"Qu'est-ce que c'est que ça?"*

I could only imagine what he said. I didn't understand French. He looked to the other lean-to, and it was then that I saw their rifles lined up inside. I yelled, "Stop!" and cut into my prisoner's throat hard enough to draw blood. The new man's attention was all on me. So was the plump man's. They looked like they were about to rush me, until I heard something whiz through the air. It was my long knife, spinning fast like a falcon chasing after a sparrow. The knife hit its target with a square-on thud: the new man's chest. He didn't even have time to scream out in fear. The blow knocked him backward into the brush.

Abagail was free and rushed straight into the lean-to after one of the rifles. I pushed away the skinny man and lunged at the plump one as he came for me. I caught him in the shoulder with my knife. I buried the blade with all of my force and we toppled to the ground in a bundle, each of us fighting for our lives. That gave Abagail time to grab up the rifle, but there was no time to load it. Instead, she used it like she was trained by the captain when it came to a situation like this. She swung the butt toward the charging plump man. She caught him upside the jaw and sent him tumbling. I was still on the ground, trying to keep hold of my knife, but that was getting harder as the skinny man was trying to wrestle with me. I punched him in the face with my free hand but that seemed to give him a taste of encouragement. He had my hand with the knife in it, prying at it with his strength, which was pretty darn considerable. He was gonna win — until I took one last run at savin' myself and kneed him as hard as I could in his boy parts, like Abagail had during her test with the Miles and round man. That won the battle, but I knew he'd come for me once he caught his breath, so I took advantage and jumped up off him. There was still a war to win.

I heard a row behind me like thunder had unleashed itself, except that it didn't make any sense 'cause it was as nice a day as you could ask for. A quick glance over my shoulder answered any question I could have and gave me the relief I'd been looking for. It was the captain, Will, Tom, and the rest of the Rangers come to save us. But they didn't need to. Me and Abagail could have takin' care of the French men all on our own.

14

A month had passed before me and Abagail was allowed to return to duty. There was a lot of meetin's in Vincennes with a lot of arguing for and against the idea of girls ridin' with the Rangers. In the end, Governor Harrison prevailed, had his way and set everything in place like it was from the start. I couldn't have been more relieved. I'd been helpin' Pa dip candles with that Hopmeyer boy, while Tom got to continue his duty. They all determined that he didn't do nothin' wrong, that it wasn't his fault that

Abagail had been captured. The French had waited until Tom was asleep before they swooped in and took her. It seemed their intention was to blame the whole thing on the Indians to get everyone all riled up. Instead, one of them ended up dead and another injured. Me and Abagail came out of the thing all right, except Abagail was a little disturbed by the killin' she'd done. Turned out she'd never even killed a squirrel, so takin' a life was new to her, no matter the reason. Still, she shook it off pretty quick, took to the attention that came her way like a pig to mud, and decided right quick that she was gonna ride with the Rangers again, too, if the captain would have her. He did, and he would for as long as she wanted to ride.

I walked into the shop to the comfortable smell of sheep tallow simmerin' in the pots. More and more folks kept floodin' into the territory and it was gonna be a long time before Pa got caught up, if ever. I was glad he had help, but I was also glad to get away on my own. Candle makin' wasn't for me.

"There you are, young miss," Pa said, stopping a stir. "I see you're dressed and ready to ride."

"I am," I said.

"You're sure about this?"

"As sure as I'm standin' here breathin' before you. There's folks out there that might see trouble if I sit back and do nothin'."

"I suppose you're right, but I wish you weren't. That's not the world we live in, is it?"

"No, sir, it's not." I turned to leave, stopped with my hand on the door, then spun around and hurried to Pa and gave him a tight hug. I'd seen death close up and it had woke me a bit about how fragile everything around me was. I wanted Pa to know I love him.

I took off before we both melted into a pool of tears. Ol' Hank was outside waitin' for me. So was Tom. It was me and him on this tour. Will was ridin' with Abagail on the next ride out. That didn't bother me much. I had other things on my mind. Boys and who liked who didn't seem so important when there was Indians and the French out in the world stirrin' up any kind of trouble they could.

"You ready to go?" Tom said.

I didn't answer. I climbed onto my horse, settled myself, kneed him enough to let him know that it was a run I wanted, then pointed his head toward the Buffalo Trace. I had the wind at my back and the future waitin' ahead of me. I couldn't have been more excited and happier to get back to doin' what it was I was put on this earth for. I was a Ranger and, at that moment, that's all I ever wanted to be.

Author's Note

The Indiana Rangers, also known as The Indiana Territorial Rangers, were a militia formed by Governor William Henry Harrison in 1807 after the Larkin family was attacked by Indians as they traveled the Buffalo Trace. Well-trained men and women made up the three divisions depicted in this story. The Rangers protected the Buffalo Trace for eight years. They were disbanded in 1815, a year before Indiana became a state, at the end of the War of 1812.

SHADOW OF THE CROW

June 11, 1933

The glass exploded out of the back window of the Chevrolet sedan like somebody had thrown a brick from the inside out. Once he saw the muzzle flash, it only took Lyle "Sonny" Wolfe half a second to realize that someone had taken a shot at him.

There was no question who was doing the shooting. It was the Barrow Gang, Bonnie and Clyde themselves, just out of the Ritz Theater in Wellington, Texas, for a night of entertainment. It was hard telling what was next with these two. Less than a year before, back in August, Clyde had killed a deputy in Stringtown, Oklahoma, launching a killing spree that had captured the nation's attention and made the pair as famous as the dead actor Rudolph Valentino.

Sonny was alone, coming off duty in the small panhandle town that had been his home for nearly as long as he could remember. He was surprised at his luck, recognizing the two of them, walking arm in arm to their car, like they didn't have a worry on their shoulders, like nobody would know, or care, who they were. Their picture was plastered across the front of the newspaper every other day. Or maybe they just didn't give a rat's ass, maybe they were lying in wait for another shoot-out, another opportunity to have their names slipping off the tongues of every man, woman, and child in Texas and beyond.

It didn't take Bonnie and Clyde long to figure out that they were being followed by a Texas Ranger — the cinco badge emblem and announcement that it was a Ranger's car was plastered across the side of the black 1932 Ford in hard-to-miss six-inch white letters.

Thankfully, they had made their way out of town before the discovery occurred to them, off on a nearly deserted dirt road, when the shooting started.

With no way to communicate with anyone back at the company headquarters about his lucky find, Sonny was on his own to bring the pair of lawless gangsters in for justice — if that was possible.

The shot from Bonnie's weapon had pierced the windshield, shattering the glass in the pattern of a bull's eye just before it exploded inward in a million little pieces.

It was a near miss. The bullet whizzed by Sonny's right ear just a couple of inches away from its intended target — his forehead. Luckily, he had tilted his head in the right direction. The wrong way would have put him directly in line with the shot, and it would have been lights out. Game over. Another notch on Bonnie and Clyde's belt. A Texas Ranger added to their growing collection of law enforcement kills.

It was a sobering thought, dying this close to the end of his career, the days ticking off until he no longer wore the badge. The word for retirement didn't exist for him, it was just time to quit — he was getting too old, and the world was changing too fast. Sonny wasn't sure what the future held for him, but up until a few minutes prior, he wasn't too concerned about living to a satisfactory old age. He just wanted to finish what he had started; being a proud Texas Ranger, and alive, to boot.

The shattering windshield sounded like a bomb had gone off directly next to Sonny's ears.

He was pelted with stinging shards of the broken glass, and it felt like he'd fallen face first into a hornet's nest. But that didn't stop him. His fingers tingled as he gripped the steering wheel. The skin above his chest felt like it was going to rip open; his heart was racing like a rabbit outrunning a hawk. He could feel blood trickling down from his brow, but his eyes were safe, not hit, not blinding him — he could still see the Chevrolet swerving in front of him, trying to get away, or to get a better shot at him, one or the other, he wasn't sure.

Nothing short of death would stop Sonny now. He could see no better way to wrap up his last days as a Ranger than bringing in Bonnie and Clyde, effectively cutting the head off the snake of the Barrow Gang. That would be a fine capper. If he could have smiled at that thought, he would have.

The older model Chevrolet that Clyde Barrow was driving was no match for Sonny's newer Ford. The '32 Model B had a flathead V-8 engine and was fast off the start with sixty-five horsepower under the hood — an amazing thought, considering Sonny had been born long before the advent of automobiles, when all of the Texas Rangers, including his own father, had rode horses across the state of Texas pursuing the worst of the worst outlaws, like King Fisher and John Wesley Hardin. As a boy, Sonny would've been incapable of imagining so much power in one vehicle. Times had changed — all too quickly, as far as Sonny was concerned.

He pushed the accelerator to the floor as far as it would go, and rolled down the window. His gun was loaded and in hand almost magically, like a magnet had drawn it to his fingers. With confidence and lack of fear he aimed his Colt .45 Government Model Automatic Pistol at the busted-out window of the Chevrolet and returned fire.

Barrow swerved the car again, fishtailing it on the gravel road, spraying the hood of Sonny's car with hundreds of pebbles; little pings and thuds that sounded like gunshots finding their target but posed no real threat.

Bonnie Parker poked the rifle out of the rear window and fired again. Her blonde hair flowed behind her, and her angelic face was twisted with demonic focus as she struggled to find her aim. Sonny had seen her face plenty of times on wanted posters and in the newspaper, but seeing her live and in person with the intent to kill him was an experience he never thought he would have.

A hot, orange flash exploded from the end of the barrel of Bonnie's gun and did not stop at one. Bonnie wasn't shooting a riot gun or a deer rifle. She meant business this time around. She was shooting a Browning Automatic Rifle, a fierce weapon that could empty a twenty-shot magazine in three seconds.

The noise was excruciating, metal piercing metal, ripping into the fenders, then shattering what remained of the windshield. Sonny could hardly take a breath or gather his wits about him. He wasn't ready to die.

The radiator exploded, sending a geyser of steam spraying upward to the heavens, clouding Sonny's vision. Bullets whizzed by his ears as he pulled the trigger of his .45, not stopping until every bullet had been fired.

He thought for certain he heard a tire explode, thought he saw a sign to his left warning that the road ahead was closed, under construction, that the bridge was out, but thoughts no longer mattered. He had been hit.

A bullet had ripped into his shoulder, sending white-hot pain screaming though his body; blood gushed out of the wound like a dam had been breached, an artery severed. Bonnie had hit her target.

Another bullet hit him, not far from the other, and Lyle "Sonny" Wolfe screamed with pain, with frustration and fear, as reality left him, and his fingers slipped from the wheel, sending the '32 Ford careening into a ditch. He felt like he had been hit twice by the largest, heaviest, hardest sledgehammer anyone could ever imagine.

The last image Sonny saw before the car rolled, and he blacked out, was Bonnie Parker laughing like a maniacal child, who had just watched the funniest movie she had ever seen at the Ritz Theater.

Bonnie Parker climbed into the front seat, grabbed Clyde Barrow around the neck, and kissed him hard on the cheek. She was unscathed. Blood raced through her veins, and she felt invincible, more than human. The bullets had passed by her like she was protected by some imaginary shield.

Barrow, a thin, dark-haired man who looked much more handsome in the newspapers than in person, laughed, then pushed Bonnie off of him. "Did you get him?" The Ranger's bullets had missed Clyde, too, but he was sweating and his face was pale, the joy of the encounter lost on him, unlike Bonnie. Gunfire turned her on. She'd be purring, demanding, wanting . . . when all Clyde was interested in at the moment was escaping, making it back to Oklahoma unscathed and alive.

Bonnie shrugged, feigned a pout at

Clyde's rejection, and ran her hands through her hair as she settled into the passenger seat. "I did. I think I really did, Clyde." She laughed, but suddenly grew serious, the joy and high of the shoot-out vanishing quickly from her face. "Clyde!" she screamed, pointing straight ahead.

There was no bridge over the river. It had washed out and was being rebuilt. Clyde was driving as fast as he could to get as far away from the Texas Ranger. He jerked the steering wheel and slammed on the brakes.

The Chevrolet slid sideways. Clyde had his foot pressed down hard on the brake, as far as the pedal would go to the floor, but he lost control of the car anyway. The rear end clipped a spindly locust tree that was just big enough to bounce the car across the road, sending it careening down a deep ravine.

They hit an oak tree as big around as a beer barrel, head-on. The impact stopped the car dead in its tracks, but it was not hard enough to seriously injure either one of them. They both bounced forward and back, hardly in a whip. Clipping the locust had slowed them down just enough from slamming too hard into the tree.

But the impact *was* hard enough to send the battery flying up from its lodging, bust-ing open the hood, spiraling through the air, toppling through the windshield, and landing directly on Bonnie Parker's thigh.

The pain was too much to bear as the boulder-like battery settled into place and toppled over, spilling acid on Bonnie Parker's leg, gobbling at her flesh like a hungry bear after a paw full of honey in a buzzing beehive.

Bonnie's scream echoed across the river and into the air, but no one heard her. No one but Clyde, and he didn't know how to help her.

June 14, 1933
The volume of the radio was turned down low, the voices distant but decipherable. "The Nazi Party was made Germany's only legal political party today. Any political opposition is punishable by law . . ." the announcer said in a droning voice.

Sonny reached over with his left arm, and was about to turn the radio off when he heard the announcer go on to say, "And in local news, the manhunt for Clyde Barrow and Bonnie Parker continues after their car was found wrecked and abandoned just outside of Wellington. They are to be considered armed and dangerous. If you see the duo or know anything of their whereabouts, contact your local police or the Texas Rangers. Bonnie Parker is reported to be injured."

Sonny took a deep breath as he struggled to turn the radio off. His right arm was bound and unmovable, and he had always been right-handed. Any coordination and strength that he had in his left hand was lacking, to say the least. He really wasn't supposed to move, but he didn't want to hear any more news, even though he was reasonably interested in hearing about Bonnie and Clyde and what had happened to them after he had been shot. It was the first time he'd heard they'd wrecked. The idea that he had something to do with that settled easy on his shoulders, but it didn't make the pain, or lack of use of his arm, go away. All he really wanted was silence at the moment, and nothing more.

He eased down onto the hospital bed and stared out of the third-floor window.

Summer had set in with a vengeance.

The windows were cracked, but there didn't look to be a breeze outside. Every tree he could see was still as a statue, leaves drooping. The sky was perfect and clear, the color of a roan mare he used to know, and the sun was a red-hot plate, beating down relentlessly on the earth, scorching everything in sight; the grass had already given up all of its green and browned out. The landscape out the window was desolate, hopeless, but familiar. Hot, uncomfortable summers were just part of the deal when you lived in Texas.

The door to the hospital room was cracked open, and a murmur of low voices found its way to Sonny's ears. He couldn't make out the words. It was like a small group was consulting three or four doors down, all whispering in soft, professional tones.

He closed his eyes and hoped for sleep to come and take him away from the reality he'd woken up to, but that wasn't to be.

The door pushed open slowly, along with Sonny's eyes at the noise. A very old Mexican man, hair as white as cotton balls, skin as brown and leathery as a hundred-year-old holster, pushed a mop and bucket into the room, trying to be as quiet as possible. He was unsuccessful in the attempt. The wheels on the mop bucket squeaked like fingers slowly scraping down a chalkboard.

The man wore a blue short-sleeved work shirt with a pack of Chesterfields poking out of the pocket. He had the largest collection of keys dangling from his belt that Sonny had ever seen.

It was tempting for Sonny to close his eyes

again and let the man do his job, but he couldn't keep himself from acknowledging the janitor's presence. "Hola," he said, his voice weak but steady, as he stared directly at the man. The patch on the Mexican's work shirt said his name was Frank, but Sonny doubted that was really the case.

Sonny had startled the old man. His shoulders jumped, then he looked up, glancing over at Sonny sheepishly, then back to the floor as he pulled the mop out of the water. "Hola," he answered. "Hablas Español?"

Sonny nodded, and tried to pull himself up. "Yes, I learned to speak Spanish a long time ago," he said, speaking fully in the Mexican's language.

The janitor smiled, relaxed a bit, then pulled up the mop, and let it drain through the ringer. "You speak very well."

"I was raised by a Mexican woman."

"Really?"

"Yes. She was with me every day until I grew up, and left home."

"What happened to your momma?"

"She died when I was born," Sonny said, looking away from the man, out the window. "What's your name?" he finally asked, pushing away his childhood the best he could.

He was sixty-two years old, and should

have been long past the sadness of losing his mother and nanny, if the woman who raised him could be called that, but Sonny thought about Ofelia Martinez everyday. She taught him everything he knew about being a decent Anglo man living in Texas.

"My name is Franco," the Mexican said.

Sonny smiled. He knew it wasn't Frank.

"And what is your name, señor?"

"Lyle. Lyle Wolfe. But everybody calls me Sonny. They have ever since I was four or five."

Franco returned the smile. "You are that Ranger that was shot by Bonnie and Clyde, aren't you? You are lucky you are not dead, señor."

"Yes, I know."

"Your arm, will it get better?"

Sonny shook his head no. "I'll be lucky to feel anything, or be able to use my hand ever again."

"Then you are done working. It is all over for you?"

"Seems that way. Times are tough all over. Another man can take my job. I've had my life, and it's been pretty good up until now."

"Yes, yes, times are very bad. This Depression seems like it will go on forever. I, too, am happy to have a job. I have hungry mouths at home who depend on me, even at my age. What about you, do you have children?"

Sonny nodded yes. "A son. He's a Ranger, too, down in Brownsville. He's married with a couple of little ones of his own." A smile crossed Sonny's face, then quickly flittered away. He hardly ever saw his grandchildren. The distance between them was too far to encourage a closeness, and that seemed just fine with his son, Jess. They never seemed to see eye to eye on anything. It had always been that way, and Sonny didn't expect it to change now.

"You are lucky then. You will have someone to help you when you go home."

Lyle didn't answer. He looked away and stared up at the ceiling. There was no use telling Franco that he'd be all alone when he left the hospital. The house was empty, a collection of dusty furniture and a clock that ticked to no one. Martha, his wife, had been dead for ten years, struck down in a single, unforeseen blow by a massive heart attack. The emptiness was his sadness to bear and no one else's.

Franco didn't broach the silence. He let it hang in the air knowingly.

Like his father, Sonny had always been tall and rangy, and he could only imagine how he must look to the Mexican; skeletal, gaunt, each breath a rattle on death's short chain. He closed his eyes then, the strength not in him to push away the memories of the past. Ofelia, Martha, Jess, the good times, and the bad.

When he opened his eyes again, it was dark in the room, and chilly. It was like he had been abandoned in a tomb, and Franco was gone, as if he had never existed at all.

August 12, 1933
Bonnie and Clyde's Chevrolet was sitting inside a barn. Three bullet holes had pierced the rear fender, and both of the tires on the driver's side were flat. Straw and dust covered the roof of the car, and a red tabby cat lay sleeping in the back seat, the coils poking up through the brown velvet material that was slowly being carted away, one mouthful at a time, by a herd of opportunistic mice . . . when the cat was away, of course.

Sonny stood back staring at the car, afternoon filtering in through the barn walls, and the August heat, stifling and humid, made him sweat just at the thought of walking the rest of the way inside.

"Been chargin' a nickel a peek," Carl Halstaad said, a dairy farmer the size of a bull himself, as he chawed a big wad of Red Man tobacco in his right cheek. "But I 'spect I won't charge you a penny since you're the man who put them bullet holes there."

"I appreciate that, Mr. Halstaad."

"Carl. You can call me, Carl, Ranger Wolfe." He spit a long stream of brown liquid from his mouth, splashing a good two feet from Sonny's boots.

Sonny nodded. "My Ranger days are behind me now."

"Ah, heck. I can see you got a bad limb, there, but once a Ranger, always a Ranger, right?"

"Well, yes, I suppose so." The doctors had wanted to amputate the arm. They feared gangrene would set in, but so far it hadn't. It just hung there useless and numb, an annoying reminder of the times when he felt whole, and young. Most days he kept busy, didn't allow himself to feel sorry for the loss or grow too angry. He just regretted not being a better shot. Killing Bonnie before she pulled the Browning on him.

He walked up slowly to the driver's door and peered inside the window. The windshield was shattered, and the battery lay on the floor in front of the passenger's seat.

"People say Bonnie's got a limp now," Halstaad said. "The acid burned her bad, but maybe not bad enough."

"Maybe not," Sonny said.

"Some folks up in Dexter, Iowa, seen them at an amusement park a couple weeks back. Bonnie was bandaged up pretty good. They was surrounded, but somehow they managed to get away again. Must be magicians, or blessed with dark skills. The one they called Buck died after surgery for a gunshot wound. And they just left him, ran from him like thieves in the night. There are no true friends to those two."

"What are you going to do with it?" Sonny asked, pulling himself from the window, ignoring the news about the Barrow Gang's whereabouts. The inside of the car smelled like cat urine, pungent and sour, mixed acid and dried blood. His stomach lurched.

"The car?" Halstaad asked.

Sonny nodded.

"I suppose I'll just hang onto it, keep gettin' my nickels from it for as long as I can. Why? You want to buy it?"

"No, I've seen all I need to." Sonny turned and pushed past Halstaad. He knew about the Dexter, Iowa, incident. He followed Bonnie and Clyde's every move on the radio and in the newspapers. He'd been practicing shooting left-handed, just in case another chance at them ever came his way.

■ ■ ■ ■

May 23, 1934

Clyde Barrow had given up on Chevrolets and now preferred Fords, particularly '32s with V-8 engines. A quick getaway meant the difference between life and death. There would be no prison for him. The Feds wanted him dead. Wanted retribution. Revenge. Bargaining was out of the question now. Now that he'd pulled the trigger and killed nine lawmen. Every breath could be his last. Nobody knew that better than Clyde.

Dawn was just beginning to break over the horizon, and the world was silent, still asleep. The first robin had yet to chirp, and the stars pulsed like little drops of mercury clinging to the solid black sky.

Clyde pulled back from peering out the window, took a long, last draw off a cigarette, and stubbed it out as quietly as he could.

Bonnie lay on the bed, nothing on but a pure-white satin slip and a lace Kestos bra. She looked blissful, like an angel sleeping on a cloud, instead of a wanted killer holed up in a dingy motel room.

Clyde bristled at the thought of Bonnie as

a killer. The picture of her with a machine gun and a cigar had been for laughs, but the world, and newspapers, took it seriously, made a legend of her meanness when none existed. As far as he could remember, Bonnie had only fired a gun three times, and that had been to save their ass every time — including that Texas Ranger who ran them off the bridge.

He hated to wake her. The road had been long, and she was getting jumpy, tense. Bonnie knew their bargaining days were over, too. They'd talked about it, come to terms with it, but both of them were only twenty-three. The doomed road ahead was certain.

They joked about getting old together, about having kids that would turn out to be better outlaws than them, but they both knew that it was all a joke, a dream, a sad longing that was never to be for either of them. Fate had conspired long before they ever met as to how things would end. That's just the way it was for the likes of them.

Clyde slid into the bed and hugged Bonnie, pulled her close, breathed in her sweet smell. He had his pants on, an undershirt, and no shoes. He'd already shaved. He was ready to go, but he couldn't restrain himself at the sight of her. He nibbled at her neck.

"Hey, baby, wake up. We need to get

across the state line before daylight." One of Clyde's survival techniques had been to ride the state line wherever he went, crossing over at will, dashing out of jurisdiction at the last second, leaving his pursuers with no law to hang onto.

Bonnie stirred, stretched her arms, then flittered open her eyes, and smiled. "I was havin' a real nice dream, Clyde."

"That's good, baby." He propped himself up on his elbow.

"Was I in it?"

"Always." She reached up and kissed him softly, then pulled away. "What's wrong?"

"Nothing."

"You're lyin'."

"Just got a bad feeling that's all."

"You've had those before." There was concern in Bonnie's voice, like she didn't believe what she was saying.

"You're right."

Clyde kissed Bonnie again, deeply, more passionately, the thought of restraining himself, and getting across the state line before daylight, vanishing quickly in a wash of desire and need that he couldn't and didn't want to control. Their hands became a tangle of knowledgeable moves, each one to the delight of the other, and they made love with the same force and enthusiasm as the day they had met.

The Ford was loaded down with two sawed-off shotguns, two machine guns, ten automatic pistols, and fifteen hundred rounds of ammunition. The sun was slowly rising into the perfect blue sky, and the fragrant smell of spring was in the air as Bonnie and Clyde crossed over into Louisiana. They were ready for anything that came their way.

It was a quiet road, little traffic. It was a little after nine o'clock in the morning, and Clyde was in a hurry, trying to outrun the bad feeling he'd had hours before. Bonnie sat next to him, and he rubbed her bad leg nervously.

"Once we get to Methvin's house, we need to lay low," Clyde said. "Take some time off the road. Have a real life for a month or two, give the newspapers something else to yak about. We'll sleep till noon and eat fried chicken for breakfast if we want. That sound good, baby?"

"Sounds dreamy to me," Bonnie whispered, snuggling up to Clyde as close as she could.

The road lay out flat in front of them, plain and open, trees and shrubs thick on both sides.

At first Bonnie thought she heard a thunderclap, but the sky was clear. It only took a breath, a second, to realize that it had been a gunshot she'd heard.

The driver's side window shattered, and the bullet smacked Clyde's head so hard it nearly tore it clean off. He didn't even have time to scream, to yell out in pain. The shot killed him instantly. Blood splattered everywhere, raining down on Bonnie as the Ford careened toward a ditch.

Bonnie did have time to scream, time to try and reach for a gun, but that's all the time she had.

They had been ambushed, and a storm of steel-piercing bullets exploded into the Ford relentlessly. Before it was all said and done, Bonnie's and Clyde's bodies were so riddled with holes that the mortician couldn't even fill them with embalming fluid.

May 29, 1934
Sonny watched a car come up the road, leaving a trail of dust behind it a mile long. It was a fine spring day, and he had been sitting on the front porch, relaxing, drinking a cup of coffee and reading the newspaper.

He stood up when he recognized the car, surprised, since he wasn't expecting a visit.

The car, a year-old Plymouth, was covered with dust and belonged to Sonny's only son,

Jess. He came to a quick stop a few feet from the house.

"What're you doing up this way?" Sonny said, ambling down the steps, steadying himself the best he could. His balance was never going to be the same since they'd cut off his arm. Gangrene *had* set in, like the doctors feared. He was glad to be without the pain — except sometimes in the night, the pain was still there, like his arm was attached, and nothing had ever happened to it. He woke up screaming then, but there was no one there to hear him.

"Come to see how you're gettin' along, that's all, Pa," Jess said. He was alone, dressed for work, wearing a white Stetson and the Texas Ranger cinco badge.

"You expect me to believe that?"

Jess stuck out his right hand for a shake, and Sonny stared at it, then offered his left hand, and shook it weakly.

"You heard about Bonnie and Clyde," Jess said, heading to an empty chair next to the one Sonny had been sitting in.

Jess favored his mother, was a little shorter and rounder than most Wolfes, but there was no mistaking his heritage; his facial profile was the spitting image of Sonny's, and of Sonny's father, Josiah.

Sonny nodded. "I heard."

"Frank Hamer told me to send you his regards."

"Were you there?" Sonny sat down, steadying himself as he did.

"No, I wish I would've been."

"It was some shoot-out."

"There were six of them that ambushed 'em," Jess said. "Each one of them had a shotgun, automatic rifle, and pistols. Hamer put his manhunter skills to use, and since Clyde was such a creature of habit, always skirtin' the state line, it was an easy task in the end. They caught them unawares."

"They'll just be more."

"What?"

"Somebody else'll take their place."

"What makes you say that?"

"Just the way it is."

Jess stared at Sonny, started to say something, then restrained himself. Instead, he dug into his pants pocket and offered something to Sonny.

Sonny held out his hand, and Jess dropped a shell casing into it. "A souvenir."

"From the shooting?"

"Hamer thought you'd like to have it. He knows you would've like to have been there, taken a shot. He did it for you as much as the rest of the fellas they killed."

Sonny handed the casing back to Jess.

"You take it. I've got enough to remember. This is just the end of my life. It's not my whole life. Those two didn't take that from me. The bad ones never can, no matter how hard they try."

"You sure?"

"Sure as it's daytime. You want a glass of lemonade, or do you have to get back to work?"

"No, I can sit here with you for a while."

"Good."

Sonny stood up and walked into the house, a smile on his face, glad to have a moment with his son, glad that time could stop for an hour or two, glad that the past was gone and the future didn't exist.

ACKNOWLEDGEMENTS

"A Cow Hunter's Lament" is an original story

"Rattlesnakes and Skunks" appeared in *Out West,* issue #1, June 2006

"By Way of Angel Mountain" appeared in *Christmas Campfire Companion,* Port Yonder Press, 2011

"The Treasure Box" appeared in *Cactus Country 2,* High Hill Press, 2011

"Silent Hill" originally appeared in *Ghost Towns,* Kensington, 2010

"Lost Mountain Pass" appeared in *The Traditional West,* Western Fictioneers, 2012

"The Longest Night" appeared in *Six-Guns and Slay Bells,* Western Fictioneers, 2012

"The Harrows" appeared in *The Spoilt Quilt,* Five Star, 2019

"The Prairie Fire" appeared in *The Trading*

Post, Five Star, 2018

"The Buffalo Trace" appeared in *Fire Mountain,* Five Star, 2021

"Shadow of the Crow" appeared in *Beat to a Pulp, Round 2,* 2012

ABOUT THE AUTHOR

Larry D. Sweazy is a multiple-award-winning author of nineteen western and mystery novels and over one hundred nonfiction articles and short stories. He lives in Indiana with his wife, Rose, where he is hard at work on his next story. More information can be found at www.larrydsweazy.com.

The employees of Thorndike Press hope you have enjoyed this Large Print book. All our Thorndike Large Print titles are designed for easy reading, and all our books are made to last. Other Thorndike Press Large Print books are available at your library, through selected bookstores, or directly from us.

For information about titles, please call:
 (800) 223-1244

or visit our website at:
 gale.com/thorndike